Dedicated to my husband, Ralph. My biggest fan, supporter, and soulmate.

HEAVE HO

JANUARY 1951, TRIESTE, ITALY

*N*orth Korea's invasion of South Korea in June of 1950 found the United States military engaged in warfare once more.

Crossing the Atlantic Ocean on military transport was uncomfortable for the masses of soldiers shipping off to parts unknown. However, this particular journey, taking place in January, was brutal. There was no VIP treatment for Army grunts, stacked and racked in the bowels of the boat.

Cramped in a vessel carrying hundreds of Army recruits headed east, draftee Eddy Kepler, high school athlete, svelte and chiseled from basic training, swung back and forth in his sickbay hammock. The boat pitched, causing Eddy to grab his bucket. He wretched, gagged, passed gas, choked, then coughed. His stomach gave nothing but acrid bile.

"Damn, Kepler. I don't know what's worse—the boat rocking, or the noise and stench you create."

Eddy moaned, rolling over onto his side. His trousers slid down off his hips. Seventeen days in transit, with the last ten spewing his guts all over the deck, did nothing to cheer his mood or maintain his physique. He was even too queasy about going up top for the magnificent view when passing through the Straights of Gibraltar.

Eddy pulled up his pants, mumbling, "When do we dock?"

"Tomorrow."

He dozed. The pitching lessened as the ship turned north, out of the Mediterranean and into the Adriatic.

He awoke to someone shaking him. "Come on, Kepler, get up. *Jaysus*, you smell."

"Huh?" Eddy instinctively reached for his bucket. "Where am I?"

"Docked. Now get your ass off of the ship. It's going to take weeks to clean up after you."

He managed to sit up. Slipping out of the hammock, Eddy's knees buckled; he grabbed hold of his bed for support.

"I'm pretty weak, doc."

"Yeah, yeah. Get off my boat, Kepler," the medic grumbled, continuing his rounds.

Unsteadily, Eddy dragged his duffel down the gangplank, running straight into a burly sergeant. As their bodies bumped, Eddy vomited clear liquid; it landed directly between the Sergeant's eyes.

"Private, Christ Almighty!" Sergeant Hill barked. "Was that on purpose?" Hill wiped his face with his handkerchief. "What's your name, Private?"

Eddy latched onto the sergeant's shoulders, keeping himself upright, his fingers digging deep.

"Get off me, you buffoon! Think you're a funny guy, do you?"

Sergeant Hill pushed. Eddy tumbled backward, landing on his butt, his trousers down around his knees.

"MPs! Get this clown out of my face."

Eddy managed, feebly, to get to his feet before the MPs

arrived. After stumbling over to a waiting fleet of jeeps, he tossed his bag into the first vehicle and collapsed into the seat beside it.

"Who the hell do you think you are, Private?" questioned a surly red-headed corporal behind the wheel. "This vehicle is for officers only! Noncoms queue over there for truck transport."

The driver pointed to a convoy of trucks, then looked at Eddy's green face, sunken eyes circled with black rings, and pants around his ankles.

The driver chuckled softly. "Okay, buddy. Let's get you over to sickbay, straight away."

Unable to speak, Eddy groaned, closing his eyes and trying not to puke as the jeep drove off.

"Doc, I got a ripe one just off the boat," yelled the driver.

Two corpsmen wheeling a gurney lifted the dry-heaving private out of the jeep.

"Take it easy, fellow. I'll be back around to collect you in a couple hours when your head stops floating," Corporal Walter Stuart said, then laughed as he drove away to pick up his next passengers.

∞ ∞ ∞

Later that evening, Eddy began to arouse. "Where am I?" A pain shot through his hand as he reached to scratch his itching nose. "Ouch," he said. The movement tugged at the IV line dripping into his arm. "What the hell?" His pupils adjusted to the overhead lights.

A voice from the opposite side of his bed answered. "Welcome back, Private Kepler. Looks like you had quite the ride getting here. Your records indicate that you lost twenty pounds. No wonder you came in with just your skivvies."

Eddy twisted his head to see a red-headed corporal sitting

in a chair beside his bed reading a medical chart. "Came in where?" Eddy searched the room to remember but found nothing familiar.

"Trieste, Italy. You're off the boat, in sickbay. They gave you several pints of liquids—you were severely dehydrated. You should perk up now," the man replied.

Eddy looked at the man, cocked his head, and asked, "Do I know you? You look familiar."

The redhead burst into laughter, exposing the gap between his front teeth. "I'm the one who rescued you at the dock. You tumbled into my jeep."

"Oh yeah, sure." Eddy's blank face feigned recognition.

"Private, I think we may end up friends. They're keeping you overnight. I've already reported it to your commanding officer—who you happened to barf on. I'll be back tomorrow afternoon to pick you up and take you to your barracks." Turning to leave, he added, "Oh—by the way, I'm Corporal Walter Stuart. Call me Wally.

THE PARTNERSHIP

*T*hanks to Josip Tito's Yugoslavian interest in Trieste, Eddy found himself in a subtropical paradise instead of Korea. A continuous gentle breeze from the Adriatic and a moderate climate proved therapeutic. Two weeks was all it took for him to recover from his journey. The prescription of three generous portions of un-tasty food and daily exercise enabled Eddy's trousers to remain at his waistline before long. Sergeant Hill refused to forgive their initial introduction, so consequently, Eddy pulled extra kitchen duty. This was not much of a punishment—it was only really a source of more calories.

Wally actively educated the greenhorn to the *mostly legal* ropes of military life and the lay of the land: a beautiful port city in the throes of a tug-of-war between Italy and Yugoslavia. While spending off-duty time at the docks, Eddy became a regular visitor to the shipping merchants. Wheeling, dealing, and the fresh salt air mixed with jasmine and fish became the *dish du jour*.

"Cappy, got any whiskey to trade for American cigarettes?" Eddy asked one of his newly befriended small boat captains.

"Private Eduardo, *ciao. Si.* Today I have a special on Scottish single malts. Interested?"

"How many cartons for one bottle?" Eddy checked the inventory in his pouch.

"Four cartons, I give you one bottle."

Shaking his head, Eddy bargained. "Cappy, greedy today! Four cartons for two bottles. Take it or leave it."

The deal was made. Eddy stashed the bottles of booze, then moseyed on to the next boat and the next deal.

Wally, a member of the motor pool, called from the waiting jeep. "Eddy, you done yet? I need to head back to base. I'm driving a big wig around this afternoon."

Lumbering up the slope, Eddy lugged a full bag of treasures.

"What did you manage to buy today?"

Eddy surveyed his tote. "Today was a good day, my friend. Two-fifths of Scotch, a bottle of French perfume, three pairs of ladies' stockings, and a radio transformer."

Wally rubbed his chin. "Kepler, already the go-to guy." He hesitated, then added, "What do you say about forming a little enterprise, you and me? Stuart/Kepler Acquisitions!"

Both men chuckled.

"No, man," Wally insisted, "I'm serious. You make the contacts and deals; I transport and store the product. We split any money fifty-fifty."

Eddy grinned at his new friend. "Sounds good to me, Wally. I can use the extra spending money. I send Harriett half my check."

Wally shook his head. "Ah, no money now. We keep all profits for when we rotate home, make ourselves a little nest egg. Maybe start a business back in the states?"

"Seriously?" Eddy scoffed. "I'll never be able to save the cash."

"Yeah, I know, man; your fun comes out of your paycheck. You let me take care of the saving and investing, okay?" Wally stared into Eddy's eyes. "I promise, you'll have a nice stash to take home to that pretty little bride of yours."

∞ ∞ ∞

The pact made, Eddy and Wally spent most of their daylight free time at the docks. Eddy quickly made friends with everyone—except Sergeant Hill—by flaunting his natural charm, endearing smile, and sparkling eyes. His demeanor was that of an impish child on the verge of misbehaving who required creative admiration. On evenings off, the pair roamed the Barcola, sightseeing Italian female physiques and drinking at a local bar.

"Hey Eddy, hot news," Wally said as he sat down at mess for dinner. "I overheard the supply sergeant mention that Corporal Krouse is rotating home; he needs a new assistant. Why don't you try for the job? Get away from Hill."

"How the hell am I supposed to get a cake job like that?" Eddy questioned. "I'm low man on the rope."

"You're clever. Be creative."

Wally stuffed a forkful of mashed potatoes into his mouth, allowing Eddy to chew his meat and consider his suggestion to the din of male voices and clinking tin.

∞ ∞ ∞

Instead of trading at the docks the next day, Eddy hung around outside the supply office, listening. From inside the open window, he overheard Sarge talking to one of the base commanders.

"Sir, one day is not enough notice to get a bottle of Midnight in Paris. I need at least three days, but I promise you'll have it."

Eddy couldn't make out the conversation on the other end of the receiver, but he could recognize that the voice increased a decibel or two in volume, followed by a stammering Sarge.

"Yes, Sir—I'll do my best, Sir. I understand. Tonight."

Searching through his bag, Eddy found the precious perfume. He knocked on the door.

Sarge barked, "What?"

Eddy poked his head inside. "Sarge, may I come in?"

The supply sergeant was sitting in his chair with his head buried in his hands that rested on his desk. A stack of papers to the side fluttered from the pulsing window fan.

"What do you want, Private? I'm busy," Sarge moaned.

Eddy pushed open the door and entered the modest space, which was crowded with filing cabinets, two desks, a field radio, and a phone. Eddy reached into his bag as he approached his superior. After pulling out the bottle of Midnight in Paris, he waved it under Sarge's nose.

"Ah, sorry. I overheard. Will this help?"

Sarge scarfed the bottle from Eddy's hand. "How the hell? Private, I should be mad that you eavesdropped, but you may have saved my career. What's the catch?"

Sarge opened and closed his desk drawer, hiding the perfume.

Grinning, Eddy offered, "It's yours, free of charge." He paused. "Let's say…free of *money*. The only thing it'll cost you is Corporal Mason's job. I hear you need a new assistant."

Sarge wrapped his tongue around the corner of his mouth. "How'd you hear that?"

"I'm resourceful." Eddy patted his satchel.

Scratching his head, Sarge asked, "What's your name,

Private? And who's your commanding officer? Let me see how resourceful you are."

Eddy opened the bag for Sarge to inspect. "Sergeant Hill. I'm Eddy Kepler. Echo company."

Sarge peaked at the contents before scribbling both names on a notepad, then extended his hand. "Leave it to me, Private Kepler; I'll bring you in to shadow Krouse."

The men shook on it.

∞ ∞ ∞

Eddy reported for duty, glad to be free of Sergeant Hill's anger and the extra kitchen duty. By watching Corporal Krouse closely, it didn't take long for Eddy to catch on.

Three days on the new job, Sarge called out, "Kepler, hand me the file on available supplies. I need to know how many blankets were issued last week."

Passing the folder to Sarge, Eddy answered, "Twenty-seven, Sarge. Fifteen to Alpha and twelve to Delta. We have one hundred thirty-seven in reserve. Need anything else?"

Sarge's mouth dropped. "You answered without looking. You know that off the top of your head?"

"Sure, Sarge. I know most of what goes in and out—officially and unofficially," said Eddy with a laugh.

"Damn, Kepler!" Sarge looked at Corporal Krouse. "So Krouse, why didn't you answer?"

The corporal grumbled, "I'm not a freaking machine. Geez, if you want me to *memorize* everything, I'll be happy to turn things over to him."

Sarge sneered, exposing clenched teeth. "Corporal Krouse, I'm happy to replace you with Private Kepler."

Eddy's reputation grew; soon, the entire base referred to him as the "Go-to Guy" for Army issuance and otherwise. Expanding his extracurricular enterprise, Eddy began supplying dates. As in Campbellsville, Eddy needed to send no invitations for a bevy of beauties to begin following the blond-haired, muscular man.

On his last day on base, Krouse approached Eddy. "Kepler, think you can get me a going-home date?"

Biting his lip, Eddy bobbed his head up and down. "What's your pleasure? You like butts, boobs, tall, short, skinny, plump? Blondes are hard to find, but I can get lots of dark-haired lookers."

"Geez, Kepler, you keep a harem?" Krouse thought for a moment. "Slightly plump, short."

"No harem, and no pimp, either. You pay me ten bucks to find you a date. The girls go out willingly for a good meal, some wine, and some dancing. That's where it ends. Anything else is strictly between the two of you—and I don't want to know, because I usually share my personal stash of females with you guys." Eddy flashed a Kepler grin.

Krouse glared at the private. "But you're married!"

"Don't be judgmental. They're only to have something pretty hanging on my arm or for a quick fix. All men need relief, don't they? I'm faithful to my little Harriett."

"Kepler, you're a real piece of work. Here are ten bucks; I'll see you back in the States."

Eddy stashed the money in his pocket. "I doubt it, but safe journey."

SNOW DAY

JANUARY 1951, CAMPBELLSVILLE, PENNSYLVANIA

*T*he sun had not risen when Harriett Bailey Kepler buttoned her coat and slipped into her boots. The winter of 1950 dropped two feet of snow on the small town of Campbellsville, Pennsylvania. Wrapping her wool scarf tightly around her neck, she readied herself to trudge into the cold for the walk to the bus stop. The usual forty-minute ride to Madison took well over an hour in this weather, and Harriett, head of the secretarial pool for Dugan and Company, wanted to arrive on time.

Her father, Tobias "Tabs" Bailey, entered the kitchen of the spacious home, ruffled his thick mop of brown hair, then sleepily stoked the fire in the coal cooking stove as Harriett called goodbye.

"Have a good day," she said. "I have a late class tonight, so don't hold supper. Love you, Papa."

Walking the four blocks down Maple Street to the bus stop proved to be a challenge. Harriett slipped and slid on packed snow and ice through the blowing wind. She happily climbed aboard the half-empty vehicle, found a seat to herself, opened her notebook, and began studying. Practical

Harriett completed the requirements for an associate degree immediately after high school graduation in 1947. Dugan and Co., her employer, supplemented her college education funding, helping her work toward a bachelor's in business and finance while maintaining full-time employment. With perseverance, Harriett would graduate in December 1952.

After exiting the elevator on the third floor, Harriett peeled off her outer layer.

"Good morning Mrs. Kepler," said Kimberly Coil, the newest member of the secretarial pool.

Harriett jumped. "Kimberly, goodness you're here early."

Hanging her coat in the closet, Harriett, lead secretary, sat at her desk and reviewed today's agenda.

"I wasn't sure of how quickly the bus would travel, so I left early. How was your holiday, Mrs. Kepler?" Kimberly asked.

"Thank you for your diligence. I had a quiet New Year's Eve. I'm a homebody until my husband returns from the war. But Christmas was spent with family. The children make it special. I hope you had a pleasant respite."

"Yes, Ma'am, thank you. I'll not bother you further. Have a good day."

Harriett's phone began ringing earlier than usual, resulting in five of the sixteen girls she supervised calling off sick. The rest of the morning was spent prioritizing requests and work requirements of the secretarial pool, shuffling and reshuffling as the morning progressed.

Harriett, Caroline, Kathryn, and Mary, her executive secretary friends from the fifth floor, met in the cafeteria at lunch.

Kathryn White, secretary for Thomas Roland, company CFO and head of personnel, chuckled and munched on freshly roasted cashews as a frazzled Harriett joined them twenty minutes late.

"Tough day?"

The tall, slightly rounded woman looked like a giant compared to petite Harriett. Kathryn's blunt-cut, shoulder-length, straight black hair appeared sophisticated next to Harriett's wavy brown, semi-bouncing locks. She was Harriett's best friend.

Harriett sat down, arms hanging behind her chair as she slid in her seat. "Goodness, I am five girls short. I don't know if it's the weather or too much holiday. We're *hopping* down there." Harriet grabbed a handful of nuts. "Gosh, these are good. I'm starving."

Middle-aged Caroline Smythe, who worked for the COO, added, "I heard one of the young whippersnappers complain that he had to wait until tomorrow to have a letter dictated."

Harriett sighed. "Oh, I know. He wants a memo taken regarding Easter. Good grief, Easter can wait until January third! Shall we change the subject? How was your holiday?"

Mary Payne, the administrator to the President and CEO, Mr. Dugan, answered first. "We had the children over. I wish they would start giving me grandchildren. How about you, Harriett?"

"Goodness, it was a zoo. Alice and Teddy hosted. She's five months pregnant and doesn't want to be stuck hosting next year with an infant. Kids everywhere. Darrel and Esther's four are getting big. Toby's already fourteen, and little Violet is three. I can't believe how quickly they grow. June's Susie is seven."

"Did your mother behave herself?" asked Kathryn. The four women snickered.

"Olive, *Mother Dear*, was as malcontented as ever. As expected, she stayed at home with no surprise appearance, but I convinced Papa to join us. I spent New Year's Eve studying alone in my bedroom. I can't wait to be able to put a down payment on a place. I need to get out of her house.

Eddy sent me a little extra last month; I hope that's a sign of things to come—and that he's behaving himself."

Lunch and conversation ended too quickly, sending Harriett back up to the madhouse of egocentric junior executives wanting priority service. It was eleven in the evening when Harriett finished class and her bus stopped in Campbellsville.

Tabs waited for her in the kitchen. "Hi Janie, I waited up. Wanted to be certain you made it home safely."

Kissing her father's face, Harriett said, "Papa, you are so sweet, thank you. What a day. I'm afraid I'm exhausted; I'm going straight to bed."

"Sweet dreams, my darling Harriett Jane."

∞ ∞ ∞

Blessed with an entire staff the next day, Harriett managed the completion of all work requests. Her phone rang at four o'clock. She smiled at her empty 'in box' before answering.

"Good afternoon. Harriett Bailey Kepler, lead secretary speaking."

"Harriett, it's me, Kathryn. Mr. Roland would like to speak to you. Can you come up?"

"Sure, what's up?" Scratching her head, she pondered Kathryn's secrecy. Nothing out of the ordinary was mentioned at lunchtime.

"Can't say, but he was smiling. See you in a minute." Kathryn clicked off.

Grabbing a steno pad and pen, Harriett raced up the two flights of stairs, foregoing the elevator for physical exercise.

"Go in, Mrs. Kepler. Mr. Roland is expecting you," Kathryn said, smiling.

Harriett stuck out her tongue at Kathryn, making a face

before knocking on Roland's door. She entered after hearing, "Come in, please."

"Good afternoon, Mr. Roland. How may I help you today?"

Harriett's perfect posture stretched her torso so she stood a total of five feet tall, across from the six-foot-five CFO.

"Please have a seat, Mrs. Kepler. I hope your holidays were enjoyable."

Harriett smiled politely. "Yes, sir. Is there something you need, sir?"

Thomas Roland chuckled. "Always the professional. Yes, Mrs. Kepler. I need you to consider becoming the General Manager, Operations Department."

Harriett gasped. "General Manager of Operations? Goodness, what does that position entail?"

"I heard about yesterday—"

"I am so sorry, sir. We are completely caught up today," Harriett apologized.

"You spoke too soon. It's how you handled the staffing shortage, prioritizing all vital work and ensuring it was accomplished first, that convinced me I had the right candidate." Mr. Roland pulled a file folder from a drawer. "Here is a formal proposal, salary and such, with a list of responsibilities. Take a few days, read it, think about it—but as head of personnel, I am confident you are capable of both school and a junior management position."

Roland handed the packet to a dumbfounded Harriett.

Harriett sat a moment stunned, then stood. "Thank you, sir. I shall consider this seriously."

"I expect nothing less of you, Mrs. Kepler. I also expect even bigger things when your education is complete."

Harriett left the office to find Kathryn waiting for her. "Harriett, over here where it's private." They walked down the carpeted hall, away from Mr. Roland's door. "Well, are you taking it?"

Flicking Kathryn's shoulder, Harriett asked, "How long have you known?"

"Oh, let's see, mid-December?" Kathryn giggled then patted Harriett on the back. "You deserve this. I don't know of anyone who works harder or is smarter than you."

Exhaling, Harriett shook her head. "I'll think about it, but perhaps I'm taking on too much. I'll have to consider what's in here." She held up the packet.

"Oh dear friend, prepare yourself to be surprised."

4

STEPPING FORWARD

*H*arriett sat on her yellow flowered bedspread and stared at the matching drapes. The file folder lay open on the bed beside her.

"Amazing!" she said to herself, while thinking *I need to speak to Papa about this. He's a foreman; he'll understand.*

After several minutes of gazing into space, she picked up the sheet outlining the offered compensation package and headed downstairs.

Tabs entered the kitchen after shoveling the sidewalk around the house. Blessed with more snow, Campbellsville looked like a winter wonderland.

Harriett had tea waiting for her father. "Papa, do you have a few minutes to talk?"

Tabs hung his outerwear on the hook behind the door. "Sure, Janie, what's on your mind?"

The two sat around the white-painted, square kitchen table. Harriett grabbed two cookies each from the jar sitting on the Hoosier. She opened her folder, then handed Tabs the detail page.

"Janie, what are you showing me? That's an impressive number."

"Papa, I've been offered a promotion. That's my new salary."

Tabs whistled. "I'm proud of you, sweetie."

Harriett wrung her hands together. "I don't know if I'm going to take it." She dipped her cookie into her tea. "Papa, you're management. Am I biting off too much? With school, and all?"

Smiling at his youngest daughter, Tabs said, "Janie, you're as smart as your mother; I'm confident you'll handle the job with ease. My only concern is that you complete your degree."

She nodded, beginning to smile. "Papa, if I take this job, I'll have enough money for a down payment on a house in a *year*. I love being close to you, but I'll be twenty-one; I need to get away from Mother's caustic behavior, especially since I seem to antagonize her more than Esther, June, Albert, or Alice."

"Janie, with your schedule, you rarely see Olive as it is." Tabs poured them each more tea. "Don't take this job to escape; take this promotion because you are a confident, strong, brilliant, capable young woman. Escaping is a *bonus* of the position."

Tabs stood, walked behind his daughter's chair, leaned down, and kissed her cheek. "You impress me daily. Continue to strive for great things, and they'll be yours. Your mother dreamed big, talked a good game, but when it came to action, she was confused, never had a clear pathway. She never had anyone backing her. I tried to support her, but she was her own worst enemy in the end. You, my dear, see your life's direction, unobstructed."

Harriett hugged Tabs. "Papa, thank you. I love you so much. I knew I'd feel better after talking to you. Now, if you'll excuse me, I need to write to tell Eddy my exciting news."

∞ ∞ ∞

Back on her bed, Harriett began writing.

Dearest Eddy,

Gosh, I miss you terribly. I hope your journey to Italy was uneventful. It has been snowing here for six weeks. We literally have three feet of snow on the ground, with no break in sight.

I have some exciting news; I've been offered a promotion to General Manager of Operations. I'll report to Mr. Vincent, our COO. But Eddy darling, I get a big, I mean BIG raise, my own private secretary, and a small office.

What do you think, should I take it? I know they'll want my decision before you have time to answer, but I want you to feel that you have a say in all aspects of our life. We are partners, two against the world.

I'm pretty sure I'll take the job. I'll we'll be able to put a down payment on our own place next year. Think of it, our own home, away from Mother!

Enough about me, how are you adjusting to life abroad? Is it wonderful? Maybe someday we can both travel back to Italy for a special vacation? I'd love to see where they sent you since you're not in horrible Korea.

I love you and miss you, dear husband. Please write when you have time.

I give you my love and my life,
Harriett

Harriett applied lipstick, kissed the letter, spritzed it with perfume, and placed it in an envelope to be mailed in the morning. She crawled under her blankets and dreamed of Eddy, king of their castle.

∞ ∞ ∞

The next day at work, Harriett scheduled an appointment with Thomas Roland. She accepted the promotion, and he scheduled her to start next week. In the meantime, she was to select her new secretary and recommend a candidate as her replacement.

Roland assembled key personnel to announce Harriett as General Manager of Operations, a new position. Mr. Vincent and Mr. Dugan eagerly welcomed her as the first female manager and junior executive in the sixty-year history of Dugan and Co.

Her male peers were less receptive. Some thought her incapable. Others, knowing her abilities, were fearing their chance of advancement.

"The old man's gone mad, a woman manager!"

"Not Harriett Bailey Kepler, damn, I'll never be promoted."

"Shit, she'll keep us all on a tight leash."

"There goes my two-hour lunch break!"

Harriett scheduled interviews with five interested secretarial candidates. Dugan and Co.'s policy of promoting within required evaluation of all interested internal candidates before opening the position to outsiders. Using the executive conference room, the senior ranking girl from the secretarial pool sat across the oval mahogany table, waiting for Harriett to begin.

Harriett tapped a stack of papers on the table to straighten their edges, then looked directly at the girl. "Miss Francesco, thank you for your interest. Today, I'll ask you a series of questions, you'll have the opportunity to question me, and the session will end with a follow-up appointment early tomorrow morning. I shall give you assignments to take home—study them and carefully consider your answers. You'll outline your responses, which we'll discuss tomorrow. Any questions before we begin?"

Amelia Francesco's mouth dropped. "I'm getting homework?"

"Yes, you are."

Amelia stood. "I don't do any work off the clock, and I'm not doing homework for a stupid interview."

Harriett frowned, wrote several notes in her steno pad then spoke. "Thank you for your time, Miss Francesco. You may go."

Amelia stared at Harriett. "That's it? You're not going to interview me?"

Harriett met Amelia's gaze. "No, I'm not. The assignment is part of the interview process. If you are unwilling to complete it, I shall not waste my time any further. You're not qualified. Please send in Miss Coil when you leave."

Amelia stood. Stomping her feet, she noisily left the conference room, slamming the door on her exit. "Kim, you're next. Good luck with that bitch!"

Thinking otherwise of Harriett Kepler, a bewildered Kimberly Coil sheepishly entered the conference room. "Hello, Mrs. Kepler. Thank you for seeing me, considering I'm your newest staff member."

Her first visit to the executive floor, Kimberly memorized the large windows, corner plants, built-in bookcases, and glimmering waxed woodwork that adorned the space until invited to sit.

Harriett began writing. "You're welcome, Miss Coil. Please have a seat. Today, I'll ask you a series of questions, you'll have the opportunity to question me, and the session will end with a follow-up appointment early tomorrow morning. I shall give you assignments to take home—study them and carefully consider your answers. You'll outline your responses, which we'll discuss tomorrow. Any questions before we begin?"

"No questions, Mrs. Kepler."

Harriett smiled. "Excellent. You've been with Dugan and Co. for five months. Where did you work prior?"

Kimberly dried her sweating hand on her skirt. She had emulated the modest professional dress of her superior. "I was with an attorney's office for four months."

Harriett tilted her head. "Only four months. Why did you leave?"

"Well, that's personal..." She paused to think. "But I trust you, Mrs. Kepler, to be discreet. One of the young law clerks made an aggressive pass at me. When I complained to my boss, he laughed and said I should get used to it, as a 'pretty thing.' So, I resigned."

Harriett bit her lip. "I see. Has anyone made a pass at you here?"

Kimberly laughed. "No, Ma'am. There are too many girls here *willing* to wear tight sweaters and skirts. The men don't need to bother with the likes of me."

Considering her words carefully, Harriett said, "Never hesitate to tell me if you feel threatened in any way. That behavior is unacceptable, no matter how high the position. Do you understand?"

Blushing, Kimberly said, "Yes, Mrs. Kepler. Thank you."

"Let's continue. Please consider carefully your answers to the overnight assignment, and do not discuss your answers with anyone else. First question: How do you file, and why do you consider it the best method? Relate your answer to the general manager of multiple departments within one company. Second question: please list attributes of a good employee. I want this to be about more than just typing and dictation skill level."

Harriett went over the questions for several minutes as Kimberly answered and jotted down notes.

Concluding, Harriett asked, "Are you clear on your assignment?"

"Yes, Ma'am. No problem. Shall I schedule tomorrow's meeting?" Kimberly finished writing her note, then looked up to see a smiling Harriett.

"Thank you, Miss Coil, but tomorrow's schedule is completed. See you here at nine am."

"Thank you again, Mrs. Kepler, for this opportunity. I'll be here at nine, sharp."

Harriett's third interviewee, Megan Edwards, arrived soon afterward. Harriett scanned the platinum blonde girl, who was chewing gum and wearing a red, form-fitting mohair sweater, bright red lipstick, stiletto heels, and a skirt so tight it inhibited leg movement.

Harriett commented, "Miss Edwards, is this a new look for you? I don't recall—your hair being so—light."

"Oh yes, Mrs. Kepler. My cousin from New Jersey said that I need to vamp my looks if I want this job. I bleached my hair myself. Like it?" Megan Edwards fluffed her curls for Harriett's benefit.

Harriett avoided commenting on the hair. "You usually wear blouses, don't you?" Harriett failed to recall Megan in outlandish clothing. She couldn't picture her in anything other than slim pencil skirts.

Megan stood, running her hands down the sides of her torso; she said, "My cousin said that I should display my body."

"Oh, did she? Miss Edwards, thank you for coming today." Harriett extended her hand, trying not to grin.

Megan returned her hand bent at the wrist, palm down.

"My pleasure, I'm sure."

Harriett caught herself mid smirk. "Miss Edwards, I intend to shake your hand, not to kiss it."

Megan cracked her gum, giggling. "Silly me. Call me Meg. All the boys do, I'm sure."

"Miss Edwards, please have a seat." Harriett motioned to a chair across the table.

Megan sat down, crossing her legs, the skirt slid up over her knees. Harriett tried not to notice, but her eyes immediately drew to the exposed long legs, despite the table. She was sure every man in the company was privileged to the same extended view. Megan cracked her gum, twirled her hair, and giggled nervously as Harriett wrote a note on her steno tablet.

Annoyed with the loud lip-smacking, Harriett asked, "Do you always chew gum?"

"Oh yes, Mrs. Kepler, it helps me think." The gum popped as she stuck out her chest and twisted her bra.

Forgetting to ask if the gum irritated others, Harriett withheld a gasp. "Miss Edwards, what are you doing?"

"Fixing *the girls*." She laughed. "Need to have them facing forward."

Wiggling, Megan settled back into her chair as her skirt slid even higher, exposing the top of her stocking.

"Okay then, I'm ready. I'm all yours."

Assuming this to be a typical entry routine, Harriett made a note to monitor for inappropriate behavior from Megan.

Harriett asked the standard questions to complete the interview, including the assignment. She dismissed the lip-smacking Megan Edwards, who wiggled out of the room.

Harriett summoned the next interviewee, Jean Ashcom, the fastest typist in the secretarial pool, and motioned for her to sit across the table. Before Harriett could speak, Jean said, "You know I'm the best typist at the company. That includes being faster than you, Kathryn White, Mary Payne, or Caroline Smythe."

"Yes, Miss Ashcom, I am your boss and aware of your speed. I am also aware of your *mistakes*, thank you. Shall we begin?" Harriett snatched her pen from the table.

Jean scoffed. "Well, if that's the attitude you're going to take!"

"Meaning what? I'm unclear what you are implying." Harriett folded her hands on top of the table then made eye contact with Jean.

"Well, I mean if you have a closed mind—"

"Stop there. My mind is not closed. I haven't even begun this interview. You stated a half-truth, which I corrected. Quickness means nothing without accuracy. Now, I'll ask again, shall we begin?"

"Start." Jean ticked her tongue, crossed her arms in front of her, and waited for Harriett's questions.

Harriett completed the interview, then sent Jean on her way with a time to report the following day.

Harriett opted for a quick trip to the restroom before her last and final interview of the day. Pamela McKay sat waiting outside the conference room.

"Miss McKay, I'll only be a moment. Please go in and take a seat." Harriett hurried down the hallway to the executive females' washroom.

Pamela sauntered into the room, surveying the large table surrounded by generously-sized armchairs. Glancing at the stack of file folders, she looked over her shoulder to see if anyone was watching. All clear. She flipped open the top file to spy the name Jean Ashcom. *Well, I have some competition,* she thought. The sound of heels on a wooden floor echoing down the hallway interrupted her before she could open the second folder.

Harriett entered the room as Pamela backed away and

into a seat.

"Ah, thank you, Miss McKay. Shall we begin?" As Harriett reached for her steno pad, she noticed that the stack of papers was slightly askew. Her habit of straightening paper edges verged on obsession. Harriett reiterated the process once again before beginning.

"Miss McKay, please tell me why you are interested in the position of head secretary." Harriett scrutinized the woman across the table.

Pamela cleared her throat. "No offense, Mrs. Kepler, but you were promoted out of turn. The job is rightfully mine."

"Oh. Why is that?" Harriett cocked her head to the side before scratching a note on the steno pad.

"I was next in line after Miss Jones. You remember the old woman you replaced as lead secretary." Pamela set her jaw before continuing. "She was verging on senility, but old man Dugan kept her on for sentimental sake. I ran the secretarial pool, not Jones." Her hand flew to her hips.

"I see. I don't remember getting assignments from anyone other than Miss Jones. Did she divide the staff with you?"

Pamela coughed. "I told that old biddy what to do! She was incapable of organizing the workload."

"I'm happy to hear you feel highly about your organizational skills. That leads directly into your assignment. I want you to outline a filing system for the company general manager. How would you go about organizing multiple departments?"

"Oh. Interesting!" Pamela fidgeted in her seat. "I see what you're doing. You want me to do your work for you. I do this as homework, and you take the credit. Sounds too much like ghosts of jobs past."

"I appreciate you paraphrasing Dickens, but I assure you it is not like that at all. I already have my new position outlined and organized. Miss McKay, I'll be working closely with all department heads, including the lead secretary. I need to ensure that my replacement has similar strengths and strategies to my own."

"Rationalize as you wish."

Harriett's eyes widened. "Miss McKay, are you interested in the lead or not?"

"Of course, I want the job. I wanted it before you got it." Pamela puckered her lips, scrunching her nose.

"Then perhaps you should approach this with an air of cooperation?" Harriett automatically tapped the edges of her folders on the table. With an upward glance, she continued. "Miss McKay, do you understand your assignment? If not, please ask now."

"I got it, Harriett. You only need to tell me once." Pamela stood, turning her back on Harriett. "I'll see you tomorrow?" she called over her shoulder as she walked out the door.

∞ ∞ ∞

Today, Harriett was thankful for the snow. Madison College, Campbellsville schools, and Madison schools closed due to weather. Before leaving the office, Kathryn called again.

"Harriett, do you still keep an overnight bag in your desk?"

Pulling out the drawer to be sure, Harriett answered, "Yes, why do you ask?"

"Why don't you stay with me tonight? That way you don't have to worry about the bus on these roads. It'll be fun, don't you think?"

Harriett thought for a minute. "I'll need to contact Father at the factory, but I've never been to a sleepover. Sounds like fun."

Harriett dialed the Campbellsville Spring Factory, left a

message for her father with the receptionist, and planned an adventure.

∞ ∞ ∞

That evening, Kathryn and Harriett made tuna salad for dinner. "I'm not much for cooking," confessed Kathryn as she sliced a stalk of celery.

"Goodness, neither am I. I suppose once I get my own place, I need to learn to feed my husband." Harriett chuckled; ripping open a bag of potato chips, she poured some onto her plate.

"You know what they say; a way to a man's heart is through his stomach."

"Not my Eddy. Before me, all you needed was to wear a skirt." Harriett frowned, thinking of the Eddy Kepler of old. "I'm not sure why he chose me, but too late now. I am so in love with him; he's not getting rid of me. Never!" Harriett pulled Eddy's latest picture, in uniform, from her wallet. "Isn't he a handsome soldier?"

Taking the photo, Kathryn examined closely his chiseled jawline, broad, muscular arms and shoulders, soft wavy hair. "You're right. He is a good-looking man. The two of you are going to make beautiful, brilliant babies." The girls giggled. "Oh, I forgot, I have bottles of Coca-Cola. Want one?"

"Kathryn, this is a real treat, especially after my day." The girls moved to the small kitchen table, each taking one of the two chairs, and began eating supper. "I'm at a loss recommending someone to replace me. I need to expand my candidate list," Harriett said as she crunched a chip. She wiped her hands on a paper napkin, pulled out her steno pad, and began reviewing her notes from the morning.

"Eat first. You'll figure it out, I'm positive!" Kathryn popped the caps off the bottles. Handing one to Harriett, she said, "Put away your work. Tonight, we're giving each other manicures!"

∞ ∞ ∞

Follow-up interviews presented no surprises. Meeting with each girl individually, she listened to their answers or completed outlines, and confirmed her initial assumption of each candidate. Megan Edwards, chewing gum, wiggled in, tugged at her sweater, sat down, and began.

"I file alphabetically."

"Alphabetically by what? The project name, the subject matter, the department, or something else?" asked Harriett.

"Oh, just alphabetically," she said as she chomped her gum.

Harriett thanked her, "Miss Edwards, please discard your gum before you go back to the secretarial pool."

Megan's eyes narrowed. She removed her gum and stuck it onto the bottom of the pristinely polished conference table.

"I'll be dumb without my gum!" she said, shaking her head in protest as she wiggled past Harriett and out the door.

Harriett waited for Megan to exit, turned her head, and broke out laughing. She reached under the table, wrapped the gum in a piece of paper, and tossed it into the trash.

Jean Ashcom was up next. When asked her description of a good employee, she answered, "Someone that can type seventy-five words per minute."

Harriett tried not to roll her eyes. "What about floor workers or junior executives?"

Jean crossed her arms. "I don't care about them."

Pamela McKay went next.

"Miss McKay, thank you for taking the time to work on this assignment. What have you prepared?"

Pamela remained standing. "Harriett."

"I don't mean to interrupt," Harriett blurted out. "But it is 'Mrs. Kepler.' The company rule has always been professional on the work floor, Miss McKay. Perhaps since you are older than me, you feel you have the right to address me by my given name?" Harriett waited for a response.

Pamela clenched her teeth. After waiting several moments, she replied, "Yes, Harriett. Not only am I older, but I am also better than you. I am *not* telling you how to function in this new position. You need to do that on your own."

"You disappoint me, Miss McKay. Please have a seat for what I have to say next." Harriett waited for Pamela to stop squirming in the chair before she continued. "I had big hopes for you. You were my replacement frontrunner, at least up until now." Harriett let out a deep sigh. "I recognize that you are talented, but Miss McKay, you mistakenly credit yourself. Miss Jones remained in total control of the secretarial pool until the very end. She was and is a capable woman, despite her advanced age. I'll give you one more chance; what is a good employee?"

"*I* am a good employee, Harriett." She pointed to her chest. "I am a born leader."

"I see. Thank you for your time. I'll let you know my decision. Please send in Miss Coil."

Harriett walked to the door and opened it, motioning for Pamela to leave. *There goes my number one candidate*, she thought. *It's all up to Kimberly Coil now, or I'm looking elsewhere.*

Kimberly Coil did not disappoint. She entered the conference room, presented Harriett with a personal copy of her proposals, and began.

"I have five different lists of employee criteria, depending on their work area, that I think should be considered for evaluations. Each is about a page long."

Harriett followed along as Kimberly outlined her lists.

Kimberly turned to her filing system recap page. "You see, Mrs. Kepler, a separate file for each department is necessary. In fact, you may want to dedicate an entire drawer to each of the different departments, at least separated by their broader scope of function."

Harriett pondered Kimberly's suggestion. *A distinct drawer is an excellent idea*, she thought to herself.

Kimberly stood to leave. Harriett shook her hand. "Thank you, Miss Coil. You'll have my answer tomorrow."

Harriett watched as Kimberly Coil walked past the elevator call button to the stairwell, opened the door, and descended two flights. Harriett grinned at the similarity.

She stopped at Kathryn's desk before retrieving her paperwork. "Does Mr. Roland have time to see me today?"

"Silly girl, I already have you on his schedule, two o'clock. Well?" Kathryn grinned at her friend, then picked up her hand. "How's the polish holding up?"

Sighing, Harriett leaned closer to Kathryn. "I really want Kimberly Coil to be my secretary, but she is more than capable of being my replacement as the lead. I'm not sure if the other girls will accept her, though. I'll talk it over with Mr. Roland."

∞ ∞ ∞

Harriett was waiting at Kathryn's desk to be summoned into Roland's office at two o'clock sharp. "Have a seat, please. Have you had time for adequate deliberation?"

Harriett handed Roland five files containing a typed overview of each interview for his personnel records. "As you can see, Miss Francesco is unsuitable. Then there is the simple-minded, gum-chewing Miss Edwards. Miss Ashcom thinks too highly of herself and no other positions. I'm disappointed in Miss McKay. She was my candidate of choice, but she's too uncooperative; to be either in charge or a team player. That leaves Miss Coil, who is perfect."

Roland cocked his head and smiled. "Perfect for which position."

"Ah, therein lies the problem." Harriett returned the smile and exhaled. "She is perfect for either position—more than capable of replacing me. However, I fear the other girls will be less kind to her than me. She's only been our employee for five months. On the other hand, she is also perfect as my secretary—perhaps overqualified."

Roland folded his hands on his desk. "Consider this. Do you think her capable of someday being General Manager of Operations?"

"Are you getting rid of me so soon?" She maintained her smile while trying to disguise her concern.

Roland laughed out loud. "No need for anxiety. Think five, perhaps ten-year plan."

"Well, yes, but what about all the men in this company that feel entitled?'

His laughter continued. "Mrs. Kepler, you just nailed my problem: their entitlement. Of course, she will need to prove herself in time, just like you have done. However, I no longer want a man to feel the job is theirs just because of their gender. Hiring you, Harriett Bailey Kepler, was the best thing for Dugan and Co. You shake things up!"

Harriett blushed. "I'm flattered, Mr. Roland, although I think you exaggerate."

"Mrs. Kepler, take Miss Coil as your assistant—meaning lead secretary *and* personal assistant, to help you any way you see fit. Teach her the ropes, and we'll keep all the male employees on their toes. Everyone wins." He reached across the desk. Extending his hand, he said, "Do we have a deal?"

Harriett grasped firmly and shook. "Yes, sir, we have a deal. Here's to female opportunity and company motivation."

5

THUNDERBOLT

FEBRUARY 1951, TRIESTE, ITALY

*E*ddy and Wally, on their usual rounds, cruised the Piazza Grande and the Piazza della Borsa looking for girls. A fresh saltwater breeze cooled the evening.

As they turned the corner to enter the Piazza Grande, Eddy called out, "Stop Wally!"

Eddy spotted Sergeant Hill speaking with a group of young women. One reached out, slapping his face so violently Eddy heard the crack. Hill jumped backward, exposing a beautiful young girl. Eddy gasped at the sight of her.

Wally's bush of red hair looked in the direction of Eddy's gawk.

"Oh no, you don't!" Wally punched Eddy's arm. "That's The Untouchable. Besides, she's just a kid. That stuff will land you in jail! Looks like Sergeant Hill just struck out, literally, which makes it even more reason to stay away. Hill already has it in for you."

Eddy was mesmerized. Never had a girl taken his breath away—that is, until now. "She looks like an angel," Eddy mumbled.

"No way, Eddy, we're moving on. Sully told me about a new bar down the street from the Torre. That's where we're headed tonight."

Wally looked at his friend, who had not moved. Eddy was enchanted with the silky, long black hair and sparkling smile of the petite, voluptuous teen.

"Cool it, old man, you're scaring me."

Eddy managed to murmur, "What's her name?"

"Eddy, I'm telling you, she's off-limits. Everyone on base knows Rosa is untouchable. Besides having a protective father, she's refused any and every invitation."

Eddy, struck by a thunderbolt of love at first sight, continued gaping, open-mouthed. Wally's warning morphed into a threat. He grabbed Eddy's shirt sleeve then raised his voice.

"Be smart, man. You're married. Think of that cute little wife of yours back in the States. Christ's sake, Eddy, snap out of it."

Eddy jumped out of the jeep. Walking toward the group of girls, he smoothed his curls and replaced his hat.

Turning, he called to Wally. "I'll catch up with you later." Calmly, he approached the exquisite, bewitching girl. "Hi, I'm Eddy Kepler; care to walk with me?"

He smiled a beguiling, charming smile, the infamous Kepler grin.

Both Sergeant Hill and Wally watched the exchange, chins dropping, mouths hanging open as Rosa linked arms with Eddy and said, *"Ciao,* I'm Rosa. *Si,* we walk."

Hill felt the blood rush to his face. Seething, he grumbled, "Kepler, you're dead meat."

"Kepler, You're a fool. This will only bring you trouble," Wally warned so softly that no one heard.

The couple strolled arm in arm past city hall, the Palazzo del Municipio. Eddy grinned, a glowing Rosa by his side. She was wearing an embroidered, green-and-yellow silk shift that gently draped from her shoulders, falling to her curvy hips. As she walked, the movement of the silk accentuated her body. Loosely braided hair, secured with a green silk ribbon to match her emerald-green eyes, exposed a long, graceful neck garnished with a stunning string of matching, six-millimeter, cultured pearls. Red toenails peeked through the front of a green, stacked-heel shoe. She looked more adult than child. Every GI they passed stopped to stare at the couple: Rosa the Untouchable, on the arm of Eddy the Go-to Guy.

Wally waited for them to turn the corner toward the Barcola before driving off. He noticed Sergeant Hill, hands on hips, watching the couple walk away. Wally headed to Sully's new haunt, parked, and found a seat with his friends at the bar.

"Hey, Sully," Wally greeted.

"Where's Kepler? I thought he was coming tonight. I have a new boat captain for him to meet."

Wally frowned as he motioned the waitress. "Not happening tonight. Eddy's—predisposed."

Jake Patterson, rushing into the bar, interrupted Wally. "Holy shit! You'll never believe what I just saw. Rosa the Untouchable on the arm of the Go-to Guy."

Straightening his back, Sully asked, "That right?" Shaking his head, Sully continued. "Is Kepler actually that stupid? To cross her father *and* Sergeant Hill?"

"I'm afraid so. The boy's got balls, I can tell you that much." Air whistled through his diastema as Wally sucked a deep breath. He motioned for the barkeep and ordered another beer.

"He is a cocky son of a bitch. I'd advise him to be careful, but his likes won't listen to me." Sully spit as he spoke.

Wally gulped his beer. "Yeah, and the bastard has a sweet

wife back home, too. Seen her picture. She's a cute little thing; according to Eddy, she's smart as a whip."

Laughing, Sully spouted. "Can't be that smart if she married Kepler!"

∞ ∞ ∞

Eddy and Rosa sat on the stone wall, watching the shimmering moonlight on the harbor. Boats, large and small, bobbed up and down with the gentle pulse of the tide, their reflection glistening on the water in the soft moonlight.

Eddy reached for Rosa, who placed her hand into his. He ventured to converse. Pointing to an ancient building silhouetted in the night sky, he asked, "Rosa, what is that over there?"

"Miramare Castle. It's a royal palace of the Hapsburgs." Blushing, Rosa added details, proud of her local knowledge. Her legs swung back and forth like a shy schoolgirl.

"Royal, huh? Then I'll be sure to take you there." Eddy moved closer to Rosa. "Gosh, it sure is pretty here."

"*Si.* I love the water. I swim every day." Rosa's eyelashes fluttered on Eddy's cheek as she spoke.

Eddy straightened, then pulled away. "Swim? Here in this water?"

"No, silly GI. I swim in my grotto. What do you call it— pool?" The girl chuckled at the thought of swimming with all the boat traffic and diesel fuel. "This water here," she said, pointing to the harbor, "Too many people. Father would never allow it."

Regaining closeness, Eddy and Rosa fell into an easy, comfortable conversation, enjoying each other's company. The evening passed too quickly. Watching the moon rise higher in the night sky, knowing he needed to be back on base, Eddy caressed her hand. He raised her hand to his mouth, then delicately kissed the top. Rosa blushed again but smiled. An unfamiliar feminine quiver in her breast moved through her torso and down her legs. Finding no resistance, Eddy snuggled tighter to Rosa, their noses close to touching. Leaning in, he cupped her face, gently pulled her close, and this time, tenderly kissed her lips.

Rosa gulped. "Oh my," she gasped for air. "That was like being kissed by an angel's feather." Her green eyes dreamily met Eddy's.

Eddy laughed. "I've never made out with a feather. I wouldn't know."

Rosa cocked her head. "Made out?"

"Necking—hugging and kissing," Eddy fumbled, trying to translate.

Rosa wistfully gazed at the GI sitting beside her. "Hmm. It was a feather's kiss."

Eddy nuzzled her neck. "Then I have a whole pillow full of kisses for you." He kissed her again.

6

MR. MAGISTRATO

*T*he next morning, Eddy was busy at his desk working when a man barged into the office. Looking up, he greeted the Italian civilian.

"May I help you, sir? You really should not be here. This is for Army personnel only."

"Arrest this man!" the Italian screamed at two MPs waiting outside the door.

Eddy stood. Placing his hands on the desk, he yelled, "Now, wait just a minute. First off, you are not supposed to be in this office. Secondly, you have no authority over military police. Just who the hell do you think you are!" Eddy balled his fingers, slamming a fist on the desk.

"I am Magistrato Giovanni Romano. As magistrate of Trieste, the army permits me access to anyplace on this base. The better question is, who do you think *you* are?"

Romano's face was colored beet red. The veins in his neck bulged, pulsing in and out. Eddy's defensive mode kicked in. He stuck out his chest, walking over to Romano; he towered over the shorter Italian.

With one hand on his hip and the other poking Romano

in the chest, Eddy spouted, "Get out of my office now. I don't know what is bugging you, mister, but I suggest you back down and leave—"

"Are you threatening me, Private?" Romano splattered Eddy's face with saliva.

"Damn right, I'm threatening you." Eddy moved forward, herding Romano toward the door.

Romano spread both arms out; grabbing the threshold, he stopped. "That's enough, Private. MPs, arrest this man immediately!"

The two MPs looked at each other questioningly, pausing long enough for the supply sergeant to notice the commotion in the doorway.

Sarge approached the MPs. "Easy, boys. No one is arresting anybody. You understand?" Looking past Romano to his underling, he asked, "Kepler, what the hell is going on here?"

"Good question, Sarge. This man barged in here trying to arrest me. He has no authority, as far as I can see. I don't even know what his beef is."

Romano turned to face Sarge. "My 'beef,' as you call it, is that this private molested my daughter last night. I want him arrested!"

"What?" Both Eddy and Sarge screamed in unison.

"This right, son? You mistreat his daughter?" Sarge scolded Eddy as if he were his child.

"No, Sarge. I abused no one." Eddy's face color matched Romano's.

Shaking his head, Romano disputed Eddy's claim. "Not true. My men saw you kissing her at the Barcola."

Eddy stared at Romano. Stammering, he asked, "You're Rosa's father?"

Romano flung his finger furiously in Eddy's face. "You see? He admits it. Arrest him."

S. LEE FISHER

"Woah! I never had my way with her. We kissed, that's all."

Romano pointed to Eddy's ring finger. "You're an old man compared to my little Rosa, and you're married. How dare you lead on an innocent with your tall American good looks, muscles, and wavy hair. Of course, it's hard for her to resist the looks of a movie star! You take unfair advantage."

"Mr. Romano, is it? I did not take advantage of Rosa. I kissed her, and she kissed me back, end of story." Eddy made the sign of a cross over his heart.

"Yes, it is the end of the story. Rosa is forbidden to see you again, even for what you call a harmless stroll. Do you hear me, Private? If I see you with my daughter, I'll act off base. And you can consider this a bonafide threat!"

Romano spun on his hill, donned his bowler hat, and stormed away.

Dumbfounded, Eddy gaped at Sarge. "Wow, that's one mad dad."

Heaving a heavy sigh, Sarge said, "Don't joke about Giovanni Romano, Private. He's a powerful man who is used to getting his way. I recommend you forget about this little girl and concentrate on your work—and your wife. Self-relief is less satisfying, but a hell of a lot safer!"

∞ ∞ ∞

Sarge issued Eddy extra duty that evening, a feeble attempt to keep him out of trouble. Before lights out, Eddy met Wally outside his barracks.

"I need a favor, Buddy," asked Eddy.

Wally shook his head while kicking gravel with his boot. "I'm not helping you if it has anything to do with a black-haired magistrate's daughter. And you'd be smart just to forget you ever saw that vixen. The whole base is talking about your confrontation with Romano."

Wally tossed Eddy a cigarette as a peace offering.

Eddy lit it from the one in Wally's mouth before speaking.

"Look man, her father has his goons out watching for me. I need you to give her a note, that's all. Just hand her a piece of paper, nothing else. I'll break it off," Eddy said, blowing smoke in Wally's face as he exhaled.

"You really gonna break it off, or are you playing me for a fool?" Wally flicked the lit cigarette out of Eddy's lips.

"Hey, I was still smoking."

"That's what I'm afraid of. Here." Picking up the fallen butt, Wally took a drag to ensure it was burning before handing it back to Eddy. "Just this once. Eddy, you push the limits, don't you?"

Flashing the Kepler grin, Eddy winked. "What's the fun in life if you don't take it for a ride?"

∞ ∞ ∞

The next evening, Wally drove to the Piazza Grande, praying silently not to find Rosa Romano. To his dismay, she was there, surrounded by other girls. As the jeep approached, the circle parted, giving Wally access. He tramped on the clutch, throwing the gear into neutral, and called out above the sputtering engine.

"Miss Romano, I have a note for you. Please. Here." Wally thrust his hand with the note out the open window.

Rosa walked to the jeep. Reaching forward, she snatched the note, then slapped Wally sharply across the face.

"What the—?"

"My father has spies all around the city. Thank you, my friend." Before turning, she slapped Wally a second time.

41

Giggling with her girlfriends, they walked away, leaving Wally
to rub his cheek.

∞ ∞ ∞

Back on base, Eddy waited outside his office for Wally's
return.

"Did you give it to her?" he yelled, pacing back and forth
as the jeep screeched to a halt.

"I should give it to you! First off, she slapped me—twice!
Second off, you lied, you son-of-a-bitch." Jumping out of the
vehicle, Wally lunged at Eddy's collar.

"You read my note?" Eddy clenched and raised both fists,
ready to fight.

"Damn right, I read it. I only gave it to her because we are
friends, but I don't want to be part of it, Kepler; I swear I
don't. Arranging a signal code of how and where to meet."

Wally pushed Eddy in the chest, forcing him to take a step
backward.

"Come on, partner. I thought we were a team." Eddy
flashed a smile.

"We are business partners, that's all." Wally grimaced.
"And I should dissolve that, too, before I'm in too deep with
you. I don't know what that little filly back home sees in
you."

"She sees *potential*, my friend, just like you!"

Eddy wrapped his arm around Wally's shoulder, swatted
him on the backside, and sent him into the barracks, shaking
his head.

7

TWO OF THEM

MARCH 1951, CAMPBELLSVILLE

*H*arriett met her two oldest sisters, Esther Cline and June Ralston, at Esther's house on Pine Street, the business street of Campbellsville. Eleven years older than Harriett, Esther was more of a mother figure than a sister. Esther was the one who shared the facts of life with Harriett, not their mother. Tonight's topic of discussion was the planning of a baby shower for Alice Jenson, the other Bailey daughter. Their only brother, Albert, was Alice's pseudo-twin—they were so close in age that they spent their entire childhood together. Despite the objection, Albert was banned from today's organizational meeting. However, the siblings did appease him with the promise of an invitation and permission to share the costs.

Harriett took dictation as June and Esther talked.

"How many guests are we expecting?" June asked as she bit into a piece of fried chicken.

"Most likely somewhere between forty and fifty," Esther responded before wiping her mouth with a napkin. "It's why we're renting the Campbellsville Social Hall."

Harriett coughed. "Where are you finding fifty people to invite?"

"Sister, you forget the Lupinettis consider Alice their daughter. I've already spoken to them, and they all want to come. Then there are the ladies from DAR; many are our relatives, so that's two birds."

Alice's first husband, Tony "Lupi" Lupinetti, the town grocer's son, was killed in World War Two at the battle of the Bulge. The Lupinettis welcomed Alice's new husband, Teddy Jenson, town pharmacist, with open arms.

Harriett scanned her notes. "Is someone making favors?"

Esther immediately responded. "Heddy wants to oversee table favors. Toby, Lloly, and Susie will help. I'm sure Violet will contribute her four-year-old skills, somehow. Those children love their Aunt Alice."

June nodded in agreement. "They *should* love her; she cared for them while we worked during the war. She's going to be a wonderful mother."

Esther reached into a brown paper sack. Pulling out five packages of invitations, she divided them into three stacks. "If I give you each a list of names, will you help address? Aren't they darling?"

The women inspected the imprinted note cards displaying a stork carrying two babies wrapped in blankets, one blue, one pink. The caption read "Girl or Boy?" with date, time, and place printed below.

Harriett grabbed the entire stack and tucked them into her tote bag. "I'll do all of them. I'm not cooking—"

"—thank goodness!" June interjected. The three laughed.

"Since I'm sparing you my signature egg salad sandwiches, and the two of you are doing all the food preparation, I got these."

Esther walked to the buffet. "Mrs. Lupinetti is also cooking. She insists. Where did I put that bag? I need to get it to Albert."

June pointed to the floor. "There. Esther, you and I can coordinate with Mrs. Lupinetti on the menu. Albert's adamant he's decorating. Harriett, here is the guest list. I think we're done, if you need to head home." June paused. Biting her lower lip, she asked, "Will you talk to Mother about attending? She doesn't need to do a thing, just buy a new dress and show up."

Harriett sighed. "Of course she'll buy a new dress, whether she comes or not. That's a given. But why me? You know she resents me."

"Yes, Sister dear, but you live with her." Esther smiled unconvincingly.

"A fact I hope to change soon!"

June took both of Harriett's hands. "Please, talk to her. Mrs. Jenson is driving in from Pittsburgh, even though she is having a posh shower for Alice at their country club. Mother should attend."

Harriett shook her head. "Yes, Mother should be there, but when does Mother conform to decorum?" She let out a long exhale. "But I'll try! And I'll take my leave before you ask me to do anything else with Mother!"

"Thanks, sweetie!"

"You're a good little sister."

"Yeah, yeah, whatever you say!" Harriett kissed her sisters, packed her canvas bag, and headed home, smiling as she walked.

∞ ∞ ∞

That evening after dinner, Harriett knocked on the back parlor door. Olive sat alone in her sanctuary, reading a book.

Looking up at the interruption, she quipped, "Make whatever you want fast!"

Rolling her eyes, Harriett greeted her. "Mother, sorry to disturb your evening. Esther, June, and I finished planning Alice's baby shower. It's next Sunday, and we are really hoping you'll attend."

"*Harrumph!* You don't need me. Is Mrs. *Butt Her Nose Into Our Family Business* Lupinetti coming? And that hoity-toity country club mother-in-law?" Olive hissed the names at Harriett.

"Yes, Mother, along with Alice's friends, a few neighbors, some DAR members, and—"

Olive feigned a gag. "More hoity-toity women. Have you joined the DAR snobs too?"

"Oh, Mother. Sometimes you are incorrigible. Those women are a delightful, service-oriented bunch. I work when they hold meetings, but someday I intend to join." Harriett turned to leave the doorway. "They are good friends to Alice, June, and Esther, and could also be your friends if you'd allow them."

Olive called after Harriett, "I don't want friends." She paused then called again. "Harriett, come back."

Already through the family parlor, foyer, and into the dining room, Harriett retreated. With her hands on her hips, she asked, "Yes, Mother, I'm back. What do you want?"

"Take that attitude with me, and I'll be asking you to leave again!"

Harriett clenched her teeth but remained silent.

Olive continued, "Your father let it slip; you got a raise." Olive snickered. "Two months ago! I want more rent."

The hair on the back of her neck stood at attention. Harriett failed to see how the woman remained callous and unforgiving her entire life.

"How much do you want?"

"Twenty dollars a month will do nicely." Olive turned back to her book in dismissal.

"And what shall I tell Esther about the shower? Are you coming?"

"If I can find a dress. Now leave me alone."

Exasperated, Harriett retreated to her bedroom, prepared for the next day's work, and planned an exit strategy from her parents' house. She decided to write a letter to Eddy, knowing she'd feel better discussing her problems with her husband, even if it was via long distance.

Dearest Eddy,

I miss you so! Spring blossoms will be popping out soon. I bet your weather is perfect, being right on the water in Italy. There must be something wrong with the mail delivery because it's been three weeks since I received a letter from you. I long for news about your wellbeing.

If it's all right with you, I will start watching for real estate. I know buying a house is something we should do together...I promise to keep you informed and wait for your reply, but I don't think I can tolerate living with Mother another three years. You know what she's like! I think I have money for a down payment and school, so there's no financial problem.

My new job is great. I love the extra responsibility, and I have the best assistant in Miss Coil. I'll finish my bachelor's degree in three more semesters, not counting summers. By December next year, you'll be married to a college graduate. Goodness, that sounds marvelous!

Considering all of that, do you mind if I watch as houses come on the market? Please say it's okay.

I parked your car at your parents' house this winter as we discussed, but now that conditions are safer, I'm going to ask Albert to teach me to drive. It's silly letting the car sit when I can be using it. Don't worry, I'll take the bus to work, but there are times when having a vehicle will be handy.

Eddy darling, please don't wait to write. I hope you enjoy receiving my letters. I surely miss not hearing from you and hope they resolve whatever issues your mail service is having.

Love you with all my heart and soul.

Forever yours,

Harriett

Harriett performed her perfuming and kissing ritual of sealing the letter, stamped the envelope, and placed it on her dresser to post in the morning. Rummaging through the ribbon-tied stack of six letters from Eddy, she noted the most recent postmark of February 25, 1951, three weeks ago. Before beginning her studies, she vowed to inquire about the delay with the local post office.

∞ ∞ ∞

Sunday morning arrived to find all Olive and Tabs' children and grandchildren decorating the Campbellsville Social Hall for Alice's shower. Albert climbed a ladder to hang flying storks with fold-out honeycomb bodies from the ceiling while Harriett covered long rectangular tables with pink or blue paper table-cloths. Toby, Heddy, Susie, and Lloly placed a favor consisting of sugared almonds wrapped in netting, tied with ribbon, and a folded paper napkin printed with a baby rattle at each seat.

Albert dangled crepe-paper streamers from the ceiling, alternating five pinks with five blues, across the expanse behind the food table to divide the spacious room into a more intimate party area. The head table filled one side wall while the gift table spanned the opposite side wall, with tables for guests in between, all perpendicular to the food table.

Mr. and Mrs. Lupinetti arrived after Mass with all the food, thirty minutes before the event—including fried chicken and potato salad from Esther, and tossed greens, a Jell-o fruit salad, and coleslaw from June. Although the Lupinettis were to provide pasta and a sheet cake, Mr. Lupinetti carried tray after tray of chicken parmesan, gnocchi, fettuccine alfredo, meatballs, sausages smothered with onions and green peppers in tomato sauce, and finally a sheet cake the length of an entire table, decorated with pink and blue icing flowers.

According to the state's Blue Laws, Teddy closed the apothecary at one o'clock and then picked up Alice. She wore a blue maternity dress dotted with pink flowers. Her rounded belly protruded below her glowing face, framed with bouncing, short blonde curls. The couple arrived to find the social hall awash in pink and blue stripes and filled with the pungent aroma of garlic and sauces.

Waddling through the front entryway, Alice gasped at the sight. Tears flowed instantaneously.

"Goodness, this is beautiful." She touched her bulging belly. "You are going to be such a spoiled baby."

Teddy whiffed the air, snorting several sniffs. "You ladies sure know how to throw a party. It smells delicious. When do we eat?"

Mrs. Lupinetti ran to greet the couple. "My darling Alice and her husband, we delight in our first grandbaby," she said as she rubbed Alice's baby bump.

Alice hugged Mrs. Lupinetti, kissing her cheek as Olive and Tabs arrived. Esther grimaced, watching Olive approach. Before she could chastise the Lupinettis for not being real family, Tabs swooped in and caught Olive's arm.

"Esther, June," Tabs called. "Where is the place of honor for your mother to sit?"

Harriett jumped to the rescue. "Over here, Papa. We have Alice and Teddy in the middle, you and Mother on Alice's right, Mr. and Mrs. Jenson on Teddy's left. Then Teddy's sister, Deanna Jacobs. Oh Mother, you'll like speaking with Mrs. Jacobs; she owns a dress shop in Pittsburgh. Albert is seated beside you, Papa. The Lupinettis, Esther's family, June's family, and I shall sit at the next table, followed by the rest of our guests." Harriett motioned to the appropriate chair, then added, "Mother, you look lovely in your new hat and dress. Your shoes are stunning."

Olive harrumphed and took her seat, placated that the Lupinettis were given a lesser table. Esther and June exhaled a sigh of relief as their shoulders relaxed, each flashing Harriett silent thanks.

As Olive sat, Harriett gestured to Tab's apparel. "Papa, are you wearing a new suit?"

"I am. I put my foot down. It's time I had some new clothes. You're not the only one she pushed hand-me-downs on. I've been wearing them my whole life." Tabs smiled. "I went shopping all on my own."

Harriett giggled as she smoothed the shoulder of his tweed jacket. "Bravo, Papa, bravo! You need to do that more often."

Alice and Teddy stood, greeting entering guests.

"Teddy, may I introduce my Aunt Tildy, Mother's sister. And her daughter, my cousin Lizzy. They are members of DAR."

"Pleased to see you." Teddy smiled as he shook hand after hand of his regular customers, unaware he had so many relatives.

"Teddy, you remember our new neighbor, Laurena

Williams, don't you? She moved into the old Clawson house across the street."

"Teddy, I'd like you to meet—"

The introductions continued until all the tables were filled.

The last to arrive, Mr. and Mrs. Jenson and Deanna, took their places at the head table. Olive glared at her counterpart, who was immaculately dressed, bejeweled, and groomed. Her prematurely snow-white hair was beautifully coiffed under a stylish hat.

Olive remained physically attractive for almost fifty years, still tall and lean. However, her blonde hair, peppered with gray, lacked luster and sheen. The once curly locks, no longer bouncing, were limp and lifeless waves. Her resemblance to Alice's youthful loveliness was evident, although constant frowns and scowls accented Olive's development of sagging jowls. A single strand of pearls circled Olive's neck. Time and bitterness had robbed Olive of her once commanding presence in a room.

Esther began by saying a prayer. June invited everyone to eat while the food was still hot, announcing games and gifts to follow.

While Harriett filled plates for Olive and Tabs, Olive leaned over to Alice. "Alice, it seems very odd that you've invited men. This is an old hen's social."

"Yes, Mother, but I wanted Teddy, Papa, Mr. Jenson, Albert, and Papa Lupi to attend. I thought the best way to make them feel comfortable was to include other husbands. Some came, some did not."

"Hmmm," Olive said. Her frown sunk into the creases around her mouth.

After the guests finished eating, Toby, Lloly, Susie, and Heddy collected plates to stack and wash.

Esther clinked a knife to her glass. "Attention. Attention

everyone." The chatter subsided. "We're going to play several games. Please use the paper and pencil in front of you. I'll ask a series of questions. Please write an answer. Okay? Question number one. If Baby Jenson is a little boy, what name have Alice and Teddy chosen? Same question for number two, but if Baby Jenson is a little girl."

After giving everyone time to answer, it was June's turn to MC. "Okay, let's hear your answers to number one and number two questions. Just shout out what you wrote."

Charles, Theodore, James, Paul, Franklin, and Mark were some boy names. Harriett heard a voice saying, "Tony."

Addressing the group, Harriett asked, "Who said Tony?"

Toby raised a hand holding high his answer sheet.

June glanced at both her sisters. "We have a right answer. Teddy and Alice shall name their little boy Anthony Theodore Jenson, in honor of Lupi and his generous family. Toby wins a prize."

Olive grunted her disapproval.

June continued, "Now for the girl's name?"

Elisabeth, Sally, Ruth, Mary, and Margaret were shouted. Again, a crackling voice on the verge of puberty said, "Polly."

Harriett stepped in again. "I heard a Polly. Who said Polly?"

Tears flowed from Olive's eyes. One hand instinctively moved to protect her neck from the strangling fingers of her reoccurring nightmares. The other hand touched her pearls, given to her by her father. Her mother, the original Polly and owner of the necklace, died when Olive was three years old.

Toby raised his hand a second time as the other guests chattered approval.

"Toby, my goodness! How do you know all these answers?" Her face beamed as Alice grabbed Teddy's hand.

Toby went to Alice. Hugging his seated aunt, he said, "Because I love you, Aunt Alice." His embrace failed to reach around the baby bulge. "You are the nicest grownup in town. And Uncle Teddy is really smart. Almost as smart as Aunt Harriett. I need to listen to you."

"Well done, Toby, you get a second prize." Harriett handed the blushing boy his reward a fountain pen to compliment his first prize, a writing journal.

Esther continued facilitating several more games. Finally, the time arrived to open gifts. The table on the far side of the room overflowed with packages and envelopes. The children carried them one by one to Alice and Teddy for opening while Harriett recorded the items. Cloth diapers, bottles, little dresses and pants, hand-knit blankets, and bonnets filled the smaller boxes. With all the gifts on the table opened, Dave and Albert carried out a highchair and crib from the Jensons.

Surprised, Alice gasped as she untied the ribbon surrounding the crib. "This is beautiful! But why did you go to the expense? Esther has perfectly intact nursery furniture that I can use."

Mrs. Jenson scoffed. "Alice dear, I'll not have my grandchild wearing or using hand-me-downs. We just don't tolerate that in our family."

The crowd hushed to hear better. Olive sneered.

Teddy frowned. "Mother, please don't offend my new family."

"Theodore, you're a Jenson, of the Massachusetts Jensons! Remember your standing in society! You are a pillar of this community." Mrs. Jenson's nose pointed toward the ceiling. "Have you lost all family pride?"

"No, Mother, I have not. But life in Campbellsville is— simpler, less pretentious." Teddy reached for Alice's hand. "I like this lifestyle, Mother. So, I'll ask you again to be civil."

Turning to her husband, Mrs. Jenson said, "I see. Well, I think this is time for us to leave. Alice dear, I expect you to respect my wishes by accepting this gift. Come, Deanna." She flashed her daughter a commanding glare. "Alice, you'll have a proper shower in Pittsburgh next week, Dear. No silly games or crepe paper streamers."

Olive smirked, watching the exchange with interest as the Jensons rose and kissed Alice and Teddy to hurry out the door.

Esther and June stared at each other, faces red from the insult. Harriett pursed her lips, glaring directly at the female Jenson, then reached out to comfort June.

Dropping her head, Alice whispered to Teddy. "I don't think I can handle both of our mothers displaying such attitudes." Her eyes rolled back into their sockets, exposing white balls etched with red.

Teddy wrapped his arm around his wife's bulging waist, offering little solution. "We'll manage together. At least mine lives one hundred miles away!"

During the exchange, Tildy strolled over, slipping into a seat beside her sister Olive. A dark-haired beauty in her time, she was now totally gray, with rounded, arthritic shoulders slumping forward.

"That was interesting. Poor Alice, but it looks like she has a fully stocked nursery. By the way, Olive, you look lovely."

Olive stared blankly at her sixty-five-year-old sister but didn't say a word.

"Olive! Are you not speaking to me?" Tildy asked, her usual sarcastic edge smoothed by time. "I'm thrilled to know your children through DAR."

"Matilda Elizabeth Jamison. I don't remember you ever being thrilled about anything other than yourself and Tommy Jamison!" Olive quipped.

"Oh Olive, those days are long gone. With what we've had to endure—the Depression, two world wars, now Korea—it's time to let by-gones be by-gones. Your only daughter I haven't met is the youngest. I hear she's a whiz, just like you." Tildy smiled, motioning for Lizzy to join them. "How many grandchildren do you have?"

Olive continued a silent, dumbfounded stare.

Tildy ignored Olive's pause. "Sister, dear. We really must get together and catch up. Why don't I invite you, Bessie, Ingrid, Nellie, Lizzy, your daughters, and any of the other Westchesters still living in the area out for a luncheon? Please tell me you'll come." Tildy squeezed Olive's hands.

Regaining control of her emotions, Olive thrust her arms backward, breaking Tildy's grip. "Tildy, I don't know what they've done to you! But I swore off on everything Westchester the day Father died. I want nothing to do with you, your daughter, or the rest of the sniveling bunch."

A small group of guests closest to the sisters stopped conversing and gaped at Olive, watching her spin on her heel and walk toward the exit.

Olive called to Tabs. "Tobias Bailey, take me home immediately. I've had enough people for one day!"

Alice groaned. "Please, Mother, this is supposed to be a happy day. Must we endure outbursts from both of you in one day? Are you trying to best Mrs. Jenson?"

Tabs' head swiveled between his daughters and his wife. Benny Westchester, Olive's nephew, intervened.

"Uncle Tabs, I'll drive Aunt Olive home. Ingrid is feeling peckish, so we are leaving now, anyway."

"Olive, will you go with Benny? I need to help Alice and Teddy transport all these wonderful gifts home."

Olive scowled. "You have sided with those children our entire marriage, at my expense. Do what you wish, old man. I washed my hands clean of you over twenty years ago."

Alice sank into a chair, her white face sweating. Esther rushed to pour her a glass of cool water as Mrs. Lupinetti fanned her with a paper.

Tabs bravely smiled and turned his back on Olive,

avoiding her exit. Harriett was the first daughter to reach him.

"Papa." She hugged his neck. "I know it's not the same as a wife, but you have four daughters who simply adore you."

Tabs struggled to prevent the water in his eyes from dripping down his face. "Thank you, Janie, dear. Yes, I am blessed."

The remaining guests were stunned back to reality as Toby's vacillating voice began to sing. "Mule train! Hyeah! Hyeah!" He flung his arm as if cracking a whip, in time with the popular song. "Clippity clop!"

Giggles morphed into gut-wrenching laughter as the tension in the room dispersed.

Alice summoned her nephew. "Toby darling. You are wise beyond your years. Come here; that deserves a second hug!"

8

MIRAMARE

MARCH 1951, TRIESTE, ITALY

*T*he rendezvous code perfected, Eddy and Rosa met nightly, despite Romano's surveillance. Back alleys, remote churchyards, and darkened corners became routine haunts. Several weeks into their affair, Rosa and Eddy snuggled behind a stone wall on a warm spring evening, engrossed in each other.

"You are so beautiful," said Eddy as he playfully nibbled on her ear. "I can't believe you're mine."

Rosa hummed a lullaby as she nestled into Eddy's embrace. The scent of blooming trees drifted on a soothing breeze. Then, Rosa abruptly pulled away from his arms. Her ear turned toward the pathway. She swatted Eddy, pushing him back.

"Hey, come here!" Eddy protested as he tugged at Rosa. The ribbon tying her hair loosened, sending her dark locks across her shoulders.

"Shh. I heard something," she said as she placed her finger in front of Eddy's mouth.

Eddy pulled it into his mouth, making sucking sounds. "Yum. You are tasty."

Rosa cooed. A second noise prompted another objection. "Eddy, I'm serious. I heard something coming from over there." She pointed to a clump of trees. "We should leave."

Eddy nuzzled her neck. "The only thing I hear is my heart beating. I'm not leaving until I've had my fill of you." His lips surrounded hers as he thrust his tongue into her mouth.

A snapping twig and the soft swish of movement halted Eddy's advance. He pushed Rosa back. "I think you're right. I just heard it too." He stood. Pulling Rosa to her feet, he tugged at her hand. "Come on; there it is again. Let's move."

The form of a sprinting man wearing a fedora burst from the shadow into the glimmering moonlight. It rushed directly toward the couple.

Rosa pointed and gasped. "Eddy, there! I know that hat; it's Carlos. One of my father's thugs. Hurry. He's nasty."

Eddy clutched her wrist. They ran, hand in hand, through a garden as their assailant gained on them.

Carlos screamed, "Rosa, I know that's you! Stop now!"

Eddy picked up the pace, tugging on the girl. Her foot skidded on gravel as Eddy yanked her around a corner, pulling her off balance. She fell to her knees. Eddy's arm jerked free.

"Ouch." Wincing in pain, she tried to stand but collapsed onto the ground.

"Rosa, are you okay?" Eddy retraced his last steps as he watched the gap between them and Carlos close. "Come on! He's gaining on us."

"I can't, I'm bleeding." She dabbed her legs with her handkerchief as she sobbed. "It hurts to stand. I'll stay here; Carlos will carry me home. Oh, I'll have hell to pay."

"Oh no he won't! I'm in love with you; *I'll* get you out of here."

Rosa's body fluttered at the word "love."

With ease, Eddy scooped the girl into his arms. Tossing

her upward, he repositioned her weight. Carlos was three yards away as Eddy dashed, carrying Rosa between a chicken coop and a garage. He darted into the garage, barricaded the door, and dropped behind an old tracker as the hinges rattled.

"He's here," Rosa whispered nervously. "What shall we do?"

"Be quiet." Eddy lay her on the floor. "Don't move. I'll surprise him at the door if he gets in."

"Eddy, no. Be careful. Stay here to protect me."

He kissed her quietly. "You are always safe with me. I won't let any harm come to you, never. Do you understand? Never! I'll always be there for you."

Eddy picked his way back to the door. The handle turned as the door shook in its frame, but it remained closed. After several more attempts, the noise stopped.

"I think we're safe." Rosa rubbed her knees, red from blood and bruises. "How am I going to explain my injuries?"

"I don't know yet." Eddy paced the perimeter, listening for sound. Hearing none, he retrieved Rosa, opened the door, and looked outside. "All clear," he announced.

Just then, a shadow pounced from around the corner. Rosa threw herself to the ground—a punch connected with Eddy's jaw. He ducked, avoiding a follow-up jab. Eddy looked for a weapon. Grabbing a rock, he swung at Carlos, only to miss. Carlos lunged at Eddy.

"Shit! Get off me, you goon!" Eddy screamed.

A hand clutched onto his shirt. He raised his knee and caught Carlos in the groin, melting him to the ground. Eddy turned the corner, dashing down the street, Rosa in his arms.

"There!" Rosa pointed to a stopped trolley.

Eddy looked back—no chase. He bounded up the step onto the trolley. Placing two coins into the slot, he whispered, "Don't pay attention to their stares."

Rosa relaxed on his lap as he sat on a bench. She snuggled

her head into his chest; closing her eyes, she drifted asleep. Soon, Eddy slept as well.

"Last stop," announced the driver.

Eddy bolted upright. He looked around at the unfamiliar surroundings.

"Rosa," he said, shaking her awake. "We have to get off. Can you walk?"

Rosa held onto the bench as she placed weight on her leg. To their surprise, she only wobbled slightly before moving forward.

"Looks like it."

She hobbled off the trolley with Eddy in tow, at the ready.

The vehicle pulled away. "Where are we?" Eddy looked at the groomed gardens in front of massive stone walls. "That looks like an orchard. And those are roses."

He pointed first to the right then to the left.

Rosa deliberated for several moments. Then, with full recognition, she answered. "I believe this is Miramare Castle. Look over there. I can see a turret shimmering against the water."

Eddy scanned the area; they were alone. He kissed her neck. She purred. He lifted her gently into his arms and carried her into the rose garden.

Placing her tenderly on top of a velvety tuft of grass, he cleaned the injuries on her legs. "Good as new, almost. The bruises will darken tomorrow. Maybe cover them with makeup?"

He stroked her disheveled hair out of her face, then wiped a smudge from her cheek.

"Kiss me, Eddy. I'm sure my knees will stop hurting quickly," she uttered into his ear.

Eddy eagerly complied. His lips engulfed her mouth as his hands set out on an exploration of her body.

Rosa moaned. "Eddy, you make me tingle."

"My darling, tonight I'll make you burn." Eddy curled next to Rosa's body where they lay entwined, on a bed of rose petals, until sunrise.

9

DOUBLE ANXIETY

APRIL 1951, CAMPBELLSVILLE

*H*arriett slipped in behind her desk, then rubbed her eyes. Sleep evaded her last night as she tossed and turned, worrying about Eddy. Her inquiry with the post office confirmed all deliveries were on schedule. Why did Eddy not write?

She hung her jacket on her coat tree and walked to the break room, mug in hand, for her first coffee of the morning. Returning to her desk empty-handed, since the cafeteria staff was yet to arrive, she scanned the contents of her top file folder.

Around ten o'clock, Kathryn phoned. "Harriett, Mr. Roland would like to see you in his office. Immediately."

"That sounds serious. Is he angry?"

"He's not happy, I can tell you that much, but I don't know what he wants."

"Okay, I'll be right up."

She tucked a steno pad and pen under her arm and bounded up the two flights of stairs to the executive floor.

Kathryn blushed at her friend as Harriett stood, waiting to be called into Roland's office.

"He's ready for you," said Kathryn as she screwed her lips into a forced smile. Harriett smoothed her skirt, straightened her back, and entered, head held high.

"Mrs. Kepler. Thank you for seeing me on such short notice. Please have a seat." Roland studied a paper, avoiding eye contact. "I have begun the fiscal year-end preparation. I came across an office expense that you need to explain. Here."

Roland pointed to a line item titled "Corporate Construction," listed as "upkeep" on the maintenance report.

"Why are we spending ten thousand dollars for construction? What is to be built? Why did you approve this expenditure?"

Harriett glanced at the report, then at Roland's face. "Mr. Roland, sir, I don't know what that is about."

"Why not? As General Manager, all expenses over one hundred dollars require your approval. All expenses over five hundred dollars require executive approval. I pulled the purchase order." Roland presented Harriett with a second sheet of paper. "It contains your signature."

Harriett studied it. "I've never seen this before."

"Mrs. Kepler! This is unlike you. I never expected you to deny wrongdoing." Roland stood and paced the room, hands clutched behind his back. "You disappoint me. Lying to my face, forgoing company policy, overstepping your authority. I fear I made a big mistake promoting you. You are neither ready nor capable of this level of responsibility. What am I to do about it?"

Harriett's face turned bright red as she felt the heat travel through her body. "Mr. Roland, I'm sorry. I am telling the truth. I have never seen this before. I did not and never would approve a ten-thousand-dollar expenditure."

"Mrs. Kepler, don't take me for a fool. I compared signatures from others coming from this department. They match exactly."

Harriett bit her lip. *Exactly?* she questioned silently. "Mr. Roland, do you have carbon copies of the report? May I have one to research this?"

Roland sighed. Pausing briefly, he handed Harriett one copy of the triplicate form. "I'll give you some leeway since this is your first offense. But Mrs. Kepler, it's an *expensive* first offense that will dramatically impact Dugan and Co.'s bottom line. I must warn you; your job is in jeopardy."

"Mr. Roland, please give me a few days to investigate before taking this to Mr. Dugan. I promise to provide answers by week's end."

∞ ∞ ∞

Harriett clicked off the ceiling light in her office around seven that evening. She gathered a stack of five file folders; after placing them in her tote, she trudged down the street to the bus stop. Today marked two first-time events for her life: the first time she skipped class, and the first time she was scolded by someone other than her mother. Closing her eyes, she leaned her head back to relax and think. She struggled to focus, thankful to be riding and not driving.

Tabs threw a concerned glance as she entered the back door. "Janie. Why aren't you in class?"

She flopped into a chair, arms dangling down. "Oh Papa, I had a terrible day. I think I'm going to lose my job." Tears dribbled over her cheeks.

"Did you get fired?" Tabs asked, grappling to steady his voice. "What did you do wrong?"

She buried her head in her hands. "Nothing! I did nothing wrong. I don't understand what is happening." She sobbed freely.

Tabs pulled a chair beside her and slid his arm over her shoulder. "Go ahead and cry for a minute, Janie. When you're finished, tell me all about it. Maybe I can help."

Harriett regained composure within five minutes. She sipped some tea. Folding her hands on the table, she relayed the day's events to her father.

Tabs listened intently. "So, you say it matches your signature, but you never signed."

"Yes. But it matches *too* perfectly." Her head bounced backward. "I think it's forged, Papa. Someone copied it."

"That's a substantial sum of money. What is it to be spent on?"

"The executive order doesn't say. But I pulled the file detail. It's a contract with a design firm to refurbish the executive and junior management offices." She shook her head. "I don't know why. Our offices may be masculine and a little crusty, but they are quite functional."

"I suggest you start at the beginning, by checking out the decorator. That may lead you to a quick answer."

Harriett exhaled. She wrapped her arms around Tabs' neck. "Papa, I love you. You are always here for me. For all of us. What would we ever do without you?"

Tabs chuckled and kissed her forehead. "You'd survive. But I'm happy to provide comfort. I love you too, Janie. Now, get some rest. You need to sleuth in the morning!"

∞ ∞ ∞

As promised, on Friday, Harriett scheduled a meeting with Thomas Roland. Carrying her tote bag, she sat across the desk.

"I think I found an answer," she began.

"For your sake, I hope you have."

"I pulled all the details surrounding this order. The

contract is with Kelly Jarvis Designs, a relatively new decorating company." Harriett paused before continuing. "Kelly Jarvis, originally from New York City, is a beatnik, hipster type. Very Avant-Garde, especially for Madison."

Harriett stopped when Mr. Roland cleared his throat. "Please continue."

Harriett glanced at her notes. "She moved to Madison last fall and opened her business in November."

"What is your information source?"

"Library microfiche copies of newspaper articles." Harriett waited for Roland to nod then moved on. "The Dugan and Co. purchase order came from our supply manager, Glen Garland. I spoke with Mr. Garland, and he said…" she hesitated.

"Go on, please."

"I don't like accusing folks until they have a chance to defend themselves, but…he said Stan Kirk from advertising gave Mr. Garland the order. According to Mr. Garland, Mr. Kirk handed him the purchase order and told Garland that I asked Kirk to deliver it directly. When Mr. Garland questioned the lack of executive signature, Kirk threatened to report him to Mr. Dugan."

Roland stared at Harriett. "Mrs. Kepler, this sounds a little farfetched. Why would Mr. Kirk risk his career on something like a design contract?"

"I wondered the same thing, so I went digging deeper. Turns out, Mr. Kirk and Kelly Jarvis are dating. Recent issues of The Madison Gazette printed photos in the society section of the pair together at several charity events. They are supposedly an 'up-and-coming couple.'" Harriett met Roland's gaze as she traced air quotes. "I think Mr. Kirk is trying to impress his sweetheart by providing her business."

Roland scratched his chin. "Can anyone corroborate your story?"

"Yes. Jim LaMantia, who works for Mr. Garland, witnessed the exchange and helped me research. He said Mr. Garland gave a good fight, but was outranked by Mr. Kirk in the end. Mr. Garland's wife just had a new baby, and he was afraid of losing his job if he continued to question Kirk's authority."

"Please return at two this afternoon. I want time to check out your story. Plan on facing Kirk, Garland, and LaMantia. I'll bring all of them in."

∞ ∞ ∞

At lunch, Harriett listened as Kathryn repeated her question. "What's up with you today? Usually, you multitask without effort, but today you're miles away. Does this have anything to do with Mr. Roland's meeting schedule?"

"Huh? I'm sorry." Harriett wrapped and discarded her half-eaten sandwich. "I have something on my mind."

Carolyn coughed. "No kidding! Cheer up, kiddo. You're not getting fired."

Harriett's face drained of all color. "What did you say? You don't know that for sure."

"Holy Helen! What did *Little Miss Perfect* do to put her job in jeopardy?" asked Mary Payne, Mr. Dugan's secretary.

"Don't call me that! I'm not perfect." Harriett stood and gathered her belongings, ready to depart.

"Sit down," Kathryn urged. "You're as close to perfect as it gets."

"If that's the case, I should have prevented my problem."

"Just what is your problem?" asked Carolyn. "Honey, tell us."

"I can't. Not until I have this issue resolved. I'll know this afternoon. And if I fail, well, I'll be cleaning out my desk." Harriett's body quivered as she walked to her office.

It's my word against Kirk's. Man versus woman. Geez Louise, I'm doomed!

∞ ∞ ∞

Three trips to the washroom finally calmed her stomach. At two o'clock, she gathered her notes and climbed the two flights of stairs. Mr. Roland sat at the head of the executive conference table. Stan Kirk sat on his right, Glen Garland on his left. Kathryn sat behind Roland to record the meeting.

"Harriett, please have a seat." Roland pointed to the opposite end of the table.

She swallowed, clearing the lump in her throat as she took her seat of interrogation.

Roland began. "For the record, this meeting concerns a questionable contract between Dugan and Co. and Kelly Jarvis Designs. I have spoken to all three persons in this room individually. Miss White, please indicate Mr. Stanley Kirk, Mr. Glen Garland, and Mrs. Harriett Kepler." Roland paused to drink some water. "I shall start with Mr. Kirk. Please state your case, Stan."

Harriett cringed at Roland's familiarity with Kirk. Glen Garland dried his hands on his trousers.

"Thank you, Mr. Roland. As I stated earlier, this has nothing to do with me. I…"

Garland interrupted. "That's not true! You're…"

"Mr. Garland, you'll have your turn to speak." Roland facilitated. "Kirk has the floor."

"Again, thank you, Tom," Kirk said. "My advertising department has nothing to do with supply. I should not be here."

Harriett tried to disguise her disdain at Kirk's smirking face.

"Mr. Kirk," Roland said. "Are you sure you have nothing to add?"

"Absolutely. I'm wasting time sitting in this room." Kirk stood and slid his chair under the table.

"Where are you going?" Roland clenched his jaw. "I didn't dismiss you."

"Come on, Tom! I have work to do. I'm leaving."

Roland stood, towering over the six-foot-tall Stan Kirk. "Sit down, now."

Kirk crumpled into his chair as if punched in the stomach.

"Mr. Garland, I would like to hear your version of this story," Roland asked.

Harriett watched Garland's shoulders tighten before he spoke.

"Mr. Roland, sir. I was wrong not to take this to you, but you see—Mr. Kirk gave me this contract personally. He said that Mrs. Kepler signed it and asked him to deliver it. The signature is Mrs. Kepler's." Garland hesitated. Clearing his throat, he continued. "I know company policy states that any order over five hundred dollars requires an executive signature, but, you see, Mr. Kirk insisted."

Kirk flattened his hands, slamming them on the table. "Glen, why are you making up this story? Is it because your wife just had a baby, and you're afraid of losing your job? This is nonsense!"

Roland glared at Kirk. "Mr. Kirk. I afforded you a chance to state your case. It's now Mr. Garland's turn. Please refrain from future outbursts."

"Tom, this is a bullshit meeting." Kirk stood again.

"Mr. Kirk. Watch your language in front of the lady. You try to leave one more time before I adjourn the meeting, and you'll be leaving the *company*. Do you understand?"

Kirk sat without a reply.

"Please continue, Mr. Garland."

"That's the whole story, Mr. Roland. Kirk hand-delivered this contract, and I ignored protocol…" Garland met Kirk's gaze. "…and it was because he outranks me. I was afraid that I might lose my job. I *do* have a new baby."

Roland looked at Harriett. "Mrs. Kepler, it's your turn. Why did you forgo company policy on such an extravagant contract?"

Harriett stood, placing her hands flat on the tabletop. She raised her head to engage all three men. "Mr. Roland, thank you for the opportunity to defend myself. I did not forgo company policy—"

"Double bullshit! Only *your* signature is on the contract." Kirk scoffed.

"Mr. Kirk. One more outburst, and you are fired."

"Mr. Roland, I neither saw nor approved this contract. I never asked Mr. Kirk to take it directly to Mr. Garland. The first time I saw this was when you questioned me earlier this week." Harriett grasped the edge of the tabletop to steady her nerves.

Kirk chortled. "Her word against mine. And it is an exact match of her signature."

Harriett managed a grin. "Yes, it is, Mr. Kirk. In fact, if you compare it to my signature on the last advertising purchase order, it is meticulously the same. It looks to be traced." She waited for Kirk to finish laughing before she resumed. "I contend that Mr. Kirk concocted this ruse. He forged my signature and threatened Mr. Garland to proceed."

"For God's sake Tom. I've heard enough!"

"Mr. Kirk. My patience is waning. Sit down and shut up." Roland scrutinized Harriett. "Mrs. Kepler, do you have a theory as to why Mr. Kirk would pull such a foolish stunt?"

"I don't know for sure, but according to newspaper accounts, Mr. Kirk and Kelly Jarvis, the designer, are an item." She wet her lips. "It's speculation on my part. But Mr. Roland, I know nothing about this order."

Roland nodded to Kathryn, who left the room, only to return moments later with Jim LaMantia, Mr. Garland's young new employee. Kirk's face went white.

"Mr. LaMantia, what do you know about the design contract with Kelly Jarvis?" Roland asked. Garland relaxed, and Harriett exhaled as she took her seat.

"Mr. Roland, I was outside Mr. Garland's office the day Mr. Kirk delivered this contract. When Mr. Garland insisted Mr. Kirk provide an executive signature, Mr. Kirk threatened to report him to Mr. Dugan. Mr. Kirk went on to say that Mrs. Kepler signed the form and that it was *her* funeral if she didn't follow policy." LaMantia waited for Roland, who pursed his lips.

"Anything else, Mr. LaMantia?"

"No, sir. Except, I don't think Mrs. Kepler knew about this. To me, it sounded like Mr. Kirk initiated the whole thing." LaMantia sat down and waited a moment, then added, "Oh, I don't know if this means anything, but Mr. Kirk and Miss Jarvis are a hot couple. I've seen them together, several times out and about in Madison."

Roland regarded his four employees. "Mr. Kirk, do you have anything to add? I'm giving you a chance to defend yourself."

"Nothing Tom. It's their word against mine. For all I know, Harriett pressured Garland, who in turn threatened LaMantia with his job to swear to her story. Like I said before, this is a bunch of crap." Kirk sneered at Harriett. "Are you going to believe this social-climbing corporate imposter woman, or are you going to believe an established man?"

Roland stood. Walking to the windows, he turned his back away from the table as he gazed outside at a cherry tree covered with pink blossoms. It reminded him of a tree in his backyard, where he had hung a swing for his daughters. Those very girls would be scratching and clawing to make their way in a male-dominated world.

Deliberation finished; Roland spun around and walked back to the table. "Mr. Kirk, please clear out your desk. You are hereby fired. No severance. I want you gone immediately."

"Tom!"

"It's *Mr. Roland* from now on. Miss White, please ask security to accompany him to ensure he only takes *personal* property." Roland waited while Kirk fumbled with his papers. "Let's go, Kirk. You're out and tell your girlfriend the contract is null and void."

"You'll lose your deposit!" Kirk laughed. "A thousand dollars."

Roland cocked his head. "What did you just say?"

"I said, Dugan and Co. will forfeit one thousand dollars deposit."

Harriett marveled at the smug grin on Kirk's face.

Roland gasped. "So, you admit to knowing the terms of this contract? Thank you for confirming my suspicions, Mr. Kirk. The sooner you are gone, the better."

Kirk and Kathryn left to exhales from Harriett, Glen Garland, and Jim LaMantia. Roland was the first to speak. "That wraps things up for today. Thank you all for your candor. I have suspected Stan Kirk of past nefarious behavior but could never prove it. He tried one too many stunts—and against the wrong foe." Roland smiled at Harriett. "Mrs. Kepler, I trust you learned a valuable lesson today?"

"I have. And thank you, Mr. Roland, for giving me a chance."

Before Harriett finished, Kathryn burst into the room. "Harriett, you had a phone call that the operator forwarded to me. Your sister Alice just gave birth to a healthy baby girl!"

Kathryn ran to her friend. The two women hugged, jumping up and down in celebration.

"What a splendid ending to a very turbulent week. Congratulations, Aunt Harriett," said Roland as he dismissed the meeting.

10

THE FLU

JULY 1951, TRIESTE, ITALY

Sixteen-year-old Rosa Romano awoke to discover she was still sick, the fourth consecutive day. Rolling over to the edge of the bed, she grabbed the bucket and vomited. Taking a sip of water from the glass on the nightstand, she rinsed her mouth of the foul taste. She rang the bell for her lady's maid, pulled the down-filled comforter around her ears, and snuggled back into her pillow, only to have her head back in the bucket moments later.

"Miss Rosa, not well again today?" asked her maid in Italian.

Rosa groaned. "No. Ask Mama to call Doctor Bellini. I think I have the flu."

Yearly flu cases, Spanish or otherwise, continued to claim the lives of the elderly and children. They were taken very seriously. The house servant reported to Rosa's mother, Sofia Romano, and finally to the cook to send toast and tea for Rosa's breakfast.

Sofia sat on a chair in her daughter's bedroom, wringing her hands. Rosa looked pale, perspiration clinging to her neck and wrists. The servant dabbed Rosa's forehead with a damp cloth while waiting for Dr. Bellini.

A general practitioner, Dr. Giorgio Bellini had been the Romano family physician for many years. Although midwives usually delivered babies, Giovanni Romano insisted that his wife be attended by a doctor while giving birth, so Dr. Bellini witnessed Rosa entering the world.

Sofia rushed to greet Dr. Bellini's arrival. "She's in here, doctor," Sofia said as she escorted him to Rosa's bedroom. "Shall I stay?"

Dr. Bellini smiled reassuringly, "No, Mrs. Romano. I shall call for you after I examine Rosa."

Reluctantly, Sofia turned to leave, then spun around, having second thoughts. "I prefer to remain."

"Sofia, please allow me to examine her in private. She is a modest young woman and shall be afforded some privacy. I promise to bring you in when I'm finished."

The doctor waited until he heard Sofia's footsteps fade away. "Alright, Rosa, would you like to don a clean dressing gown? I'll turn my back. Please indicate when you are clothed."

"Thank you, Doctor. This gown is smelly and sweaty." After several minutes Rosa continued, "Doctor, you may turn around. I'm changed."

"Rosa, have a seat on the edge of your bed," Dr. Bellini said as he sat in the bedside chair. "Now tell me, how many days have you been sick?"

Rosa paused to think. "This is the fourth day of vomiting, but I was queasy for several days prior. At first, I thought I had eaten a bad piece of fish, but today I haven't even eaten breakfast, and I vomited twice already."

"I see." Bellini took the girl's pulse; slightly fast. Then her temperature; normal. "Rosa, I'm going to listen to your heart and your lungs. Now lay back onto the bed. I want to palpitate your stomach and bladder." Bellini did so, then continued, "You're doing just fine. I need to ask you some questions..." He hesitated. "Of a personal nature. Is that okay with you?"

Rosa shrugged her shoulders. "If it helps you diagnose my disease, then absolutely."

The answers to Dr. Bellini's questions led to a different type of exam.

Finally, Bellini called out, "Mrs. Romano, you may join us again."

Sofia scampered down the hallway, bursting through the door. Out of breath, she asked, "What is it, Doctor?" She ran to Rosa's bed, took her hand, and squeezed.

Dr. Bellini inhaled slowly, then let out a long sigh. "I'm afraid I have some disturbing news for both of you. Sofia, you need to be seated for this, please."

Sofia nearly fainted as she sat. "Doctor, tell me! Is my Rosa going to die?" Sofia burst into tears.

"Mama!" Rosa began crying. "I'm too young to die!"

Dr. Bellini tried to stifle a smile. "Ladies, no one is dying. There is nothing wrong with Rosa that nine months won't cure. I'm afraid your daughter is pregnant."

A gasp, then silence filled the room. Sofia Romano, no longer crying, slapped her only child across the face with a loud resounding crack. "How dare you disgrace your father and me with this behavior! Our family is a respected pillar of the community, eminent since the first world war!"

Rosa no longer sobbed; she shrieked hysterically.

"Sofia, please, Rosa is as upset as you. These things happen; there are solutions," offered Bellini.

"The only acceptable solution is to terminate the pregnancy," Sofia screamed. "The sooner, the better. Say, tomorrow."

"Mama, we're Catholic!" Rosa began gasping for breath.

"I'll not kill my baby. It's a sin. I love the father, and he will marry me. You'll see."

Sofia turned her back on Rosa. Facing Dr. Bellini, she said, "We shall discuss the events this evening. Expect a call tomorrow and be ready to end this messy affair." Sofia stormed out of the room, slamming the door as she left.

Dr. Bellini gently took both of Rosa's hands. "Look at me, child. Take deep, slow breaths. Slower, slower." He wiped her forehead with a cold, damp cloth. "Now, don't you worry, we'll figure this out."

With the hysterical Rosa calmed slightly, Bellini showed himself out of the house, dreading the morrow.

∞ ∞ ∞

Sofia Romano left explicit instructions with the kitchen staff to prepare Giovanni's favorite dishes for supper. Rosa remained in bed all day, refusing to eat or bathe. As the dinner hour approached, Sofia burst into Rosa's bedroom.

"Up. Get out of bed, you little tramp. You'll eat with us this evening, and you'll fix your hair, make yourself presentable. Do you hear me?"

Rosa mumbled softly, "Yes, Mother."

Sofia and Rosa waited in the drawing-room for Giovanni to return home. Rosa gulped as the door opened.

"You say nothing!" Sofia ordered. "I shall do all the talking this evening."

"Yes, Mother."

Sofia handed Giovanni a cocktail as he hung his hat on the foyer hall tree. "Hello darling, how was your day?" she asked.

Giovanni harrumphed. "I despise having that army base in my town. Brings me nothing but trouble!" He took a sip of his drink as Sofia cringed.

"We have your favorites for dinner this evening. I want to spoil you today." Sofia smiled demurely at her husband.

"What are you up to? What happened? I can see through your little ruse. Out with the bad news!" His voice bellowed, echoing off the tile floor, filling the first floor of the villa.

"Come sit, dear." Sofia motioned toward a chair.

"Oh, Rosa, my darling beautiful daughter!" Giovanni embraced Rosa. She stiffened at his touch. "Are you joining us this evening? Not going out with your girlfriends?"

"No, Father, I'm not going out."

Giovanni downed his cocktail in three gulps. "Splendid. I love looking at your beautiful face." He pinched her cheeks and extended his arm. "Come, escort me into the dining room. Sofia, another martini, please."

Rosa, Giovanni, and Sofia sat in the opulent room at the formal table, waiting to be served their first course. Gilded, wall-sized mirrors flanked the space opposite floor-length windows that overlooked the gardens. Shimmers of light reflected off the ceiling and table from three crystal-tiered chandeliers. Steam rose from the gold-banded bowls placed before each diner.

Giovanni sipped his drink, snorted the fragrance of the soup, then pried again. "Sofia, I know you, Wife. What is the purpose of this meal?"

"Father," Rosa began to speak but was cut off by her mother.

"Hush girl. I'll tell him." Sipping her cocktail, she swallowed hard as she glared at her daughter.

Giovanni raised his voice. "Tell me what? My patience is waning, woman; tell me now!"

Sofia wiped the perspiration from her brow; Rosa hung her head, afraid to make eye contact. "My darling husband, your daughter has misbehaved and now finds herself *in a family way*."

Giovanni spit gin across the table. "Are you telling me that Rosa is pregnant?"

Sofia trembled. "Yes, I fear that is true. Dr. Bellini—"

Giovanni Romano stood, pounding his fist on the table; he screeched and pointed to Rosa. "Get out! You tramp. Get out of my house!"

Sofia tried to speak. Giovanni threw his hand in the air. She said nothing.

"You are no longer my daughter. How dare you disgrace our family. Who is the father?—No! I don't want to know. I assume he's a soldier from that blasted army base. Sofia, I want her gone tomorrow!" Giovanni refused to look at Rosa.

"But Father, where am I to go?"

"Sofia, please tell the slut that used to be my daughter that I don't give a damn where she goes, as long as she's out of my house! She may neither live at nor inherit Villa Romano. She is *dead* to me!" Giovanni pushed back his chair, toppling it. "How dare she tarnish my public reputation like this?!" He stomped out of the dining room

Sofia called out, "Giovanni, your supper, darling." Her head swiveled from her departing husband to her sitting daughter.

Rosa slumped into her chair, sobbing. "Mother, what am I to do? Will you intercede on my behalf?" she asked, then blew her nose on her embroidered napkin.

Sofia's eyes flashed daggers at the girl. "First, you disgrace the family; now, you use my linen as if it were a snot rag? Get to your room and pack your belongings." Sofia picked up her goblet and tossed it at Rosa. "I said go pack!"

She scurried away.

Rosa quickly gathered a few possessions, clothing, and toiletries into a satchel. She slipped out the back door, knowing that if her father's men followed her, she would never be truly safe. Walking the now familiar back alleys and side streets—the same ones used to rendezvous nightly with Eddy—Rosa headed to the train station. Wearing dark glasses and a scarf around her head as a disguise, she purchased a one-way ticket to Santa Croce.

∞ ∞ ∞

Isabella Cortina glanced at her husband Giuseppe before answering the knock at the door. She opened it to find her granddaughter, crying silent tears.

"Rosa, what a pleasant surprise. I didn't expect a visit. Come in, darling—why are you crying?" Isabella motioned for Rosa to enter. Noticing her luggage, she asked, "Do we have the pleasure of an overnight stay?"

Rosa threw her arms around her maternal grandmother. "Oh, Nonna, I'm in terrible trouble. Will you help me?"

"Of course, child. Come in, sit down. I'll get you a glass of water; then you can tell us all about your worries." Isabella kissed Rosa's forehead. Leading her by the hand, they joined her husband in the drawing room.

Giuseppe, equally delighted to see the girl, embraced her in welcome.

Rosa accepted the water from Isabella, who asked, "Tell us what has you so troubled. I'm sure it's not as bad as your sour face indicates."

Clasping her hands together, Rosa began. "Father disinherited me; he threw me out of the house. I have nowhere to go, Nonna, so I came here." Her tears fell freely as she spoke, but her voice remained steady and calm.

Isabella and Giuseppe exchanged glances. "Why would they disown you? You're their only child."

"Because I'm pregnant, Nonna. I have disgraced their name and reputation."

Smiling lovingly, Isabella sat down beside Rosa. She

wrapped her arm around Rosa's shoulder. "Is that all? Darling child, no need to be anxious. We can deal with a pregnancy. Our family has witnessed worse drama throughout its history."

Rosa looked at her grandmother. "You're not upset?"

"No, child. Perhaps disappointed you'll not have a large wedding, but I'm not upset. Now, tell me about the father."

Rosa relaxed into Nonna's arm. "He's a soldier from America. I love him so much."

"And does he love you?"

"Oh yes, he confesses his love nightly."

Rosa blushed. Isabella and Giuseppe both raised their eyebrows.

Giuseppe cleared his throat before asking. "Where do the two of you—ah—where do your *encounters* take place?"

"Nonno, we have a secret signaling code." Rosa grinned through her tears, proud of their cleverness. "His friend drives to Piazza Grande, where I wait with my girlfriends. He either flashes his headlights a certain number of times, or honks his horn, or a combination of both, to signal our meeting place. Father's men can't follow us that way."

Isabella stood, walked back to Giuseppe, and sat. "When did you meet this man?"

Rosa sighed dreamily. "In March. We see each other almost every night. We hide in the gardens of Castle Miramare and—well, you know. Nonna, I must get word to him. I know he'll leave his American wife and marry me."

"He's already married?" Giuseppe asked, his voice strained with tension.

"Yes, Nonno—and he's so handsome. If he knows I'm having his baby, he'll do the right thing. I just know he'll marry me!"

Exhaling a long breath, Isabella rose. "Come, let us find you a snack. It's late. I'll have the guestroom freshened for you. We'll discuss this more in the morning. I think you've had a stressful day and need some sleep."

Rosa kissed Isabella. "I love you Nonna and Nonno. I feel so much better now that I am here."

∞ ∞ ∞

Isabella tucked a down comforter around the girl, kissed her forehead, and sat in the chair beside the bed, watching the innocent child sleep. After several minutes, she rejoined Giuseppe.

"What are your thoughts, Husband?" Isabella squeezed his hand.

"Knowing our haughty son-in-law and pompous daughter, neither shall recant. Both are too prideful to risk embarrassment. I think it's best she leaves Trieste. Shall we put her in our little alpine hideaway outside Predmeja?"

"I have the same thoughts, Giuseppe. She can't stay here; they'll find her too easily and perhaps retaliate for us helping her." The old couple snuggled closer together. Isabella chuckled. "That cabin has seen its share of trauma over the years. It's rustic but charming and safe. Even if it's now in Yugoslavia, it's safer than her being in Italy—Remember all the stories about your cousin...?" Her voice trailed off as her eyes grew heavy.

Giuseppe yawned. "I believe we have a plan. Now, my wife, off to bed we go. I'm too old for such excitement!"

11

THE LETTER

*E*ddy paced up and down the alley, waiting for Rosa. After two hours, he entered the local bar seeking Wally, who was sitting in the corner.

Eddy waved and crossed the room. "Wally, man, are you sure you gave her the correct signal?"

Wally scowled. "Of course, I gave the right signal. I helped refine them, remember? Against my better judgment." He motioned to an empty barstool; Eddy sat.

Ordering a beer, Eddy continued grilling his friend. "This is the fifth night this week she didn't show. Have you heard anything?"

Laughing, Wally answered. "Eddy, *you're* the go-to guy, the one in the know. You'd find out faster than any of the rest of us."

Jumping off the barstool, Eddy began to pace again. "I don't get it. If her father suspected us, she'd tell me."

"Maybe they went on a vacation?"

"No, I saw Big M. yesterday in the square." Eddy gulped his drink.

"Rosa and—"

"—shhh. Don't use her name. Too many ears in this town," Eddy chastised.

"*She* and her mother could have gone away. That's how they do things over here." Wally frowned. "Keep that attitude up, and you'll be minus a girlfriend *and* a best friend."

"Stay cool, Wally. I'm worried, that's all."

Wally raised his hand, ordering another beer. "Maybe this is for the best. You're getting too attached to this little Italian. Remember, you have a wife back home."

Eddy heaved a long sigh. "Yeah, you're probably right. I should have listened to you in the first place. I'm actually in love with *her*. But I know it can't last."

Wally slapped Eddy on the back. "Then fate decided for you. This is your opportunity to break away, cut it off. You've had your fun, but it's over. Okay?"

"Sure, Wally. Whatever you say."

Wally shook Eddy's shoulders. "Eddy, focus. Look at me." Eddy met his eyes. "Cut your losses. Think of Harriett and the wonderful life you'll have when you get back home."

Eddy mumbled, "Harriett. I better write to her. I haven't sent a letter in a couple of weeks."

Wally's eyes closed to slits. "Just a couple weeks, or since you met *the girl?*"

"I don't know. Does it matter?"

Shaking his head, Wally slapped Eddy's arm. "You stupid fool. Of course, it matters. A couple weeks, you can pass off as trouble with the mail. Four months, that's another story!"

"Has it been four months already? Time flew by quickly. I've been with R—" he caught himself before saying her name. "—her, as long as I'd been with Harriett, in person. Though I've known Harriett all my life."

"Hell, Eddy, you're a real louse."

Eddy cuffed Wally's shoulder. "Come on, buddy. I'm just a hot-blooded, red-blooded American boy."

"You're a man, and a son of a bitch of one. Take advantage of your opportunity; clean cut."

"Yeah, yeah. You're right. The fates have dealt me a winning hand, and I'll capitalize on it." Eddy motioned to the barkeep. "Our next round's on me! I just fell into some good fortune!"

The soldiers continued drinking and joking until curfew, with Eddy, determined to break it off with Rosa.

∞ ∞ ∞

The next afternoon, Wally and Eddy waited for mail call.

"Kepler," yelled the mail clerk.

Harriett wrote several letters a week despite not receiving any in return. Today the clerk handed Eddy two envelopes.

Opening the one from Harriett first, he quickly scanned her report on local news, her job, school, house hunting, and her pledge of enduring love, always spritzed with perfume and sealed with a kiss. He folded the page and stuffed it into his pocket.

"Hey Wally, do we know anyone in Santa Croce?" Eddy asked as he noted the return address of the second envelope.

"Don't think so. Why?"

Eddy scratched his head. "I got mail from there. Wonder who it's from?"

Wally pursed his lips. "Then open it, you idiot."

"Don't call me an idiot!" Eddy tossed the balled-up envelope from Harriett at his friend. "Okay, I'll open it."

Eddy began reading.

Dear Private Kepler,

My name is Isabella Cortina. I am Rosa Romano's grandmother.

Rosa is now living in my alpine cabin located outside of

Predmeja. Rosa is carrying your child and will stay at the cabin until the baby is born.

Sadly, her parents, my daughter, have disowned her; family disgrace is unacceptable to them.

Rosa is on her own. My husband and I are helping; however, we must tread carefully. My son-in-law is a vengeful man.

If you genuinely love her, as she says you do, please contact me via return post, and I shall arrange for you to meet Rosa at the cabin.

Sincerely,

Isabella Cortina

Eddy stared blankly at the letter.

"Well, who is it from?" questioned Wally.

Eddy's spine melted as he collapsed to the floor.

"Call the medic!" cried a voice in the crowd.

"God, Eddy, wake up!" Wally slapped the sides of Eddy's face, then picked up his head, cradling it on his lap. "You okay, man? What was in that letter?"

Picking up the paper, Wally read while Eddy lay on the floor.

"Holy shit," was all he said.

Eddy moaned, then sat up. Looking at Wally, he asked, "What am I going to do?"

Wally sighed. "Well," he chided, "I can't say I'm surprised. I hate to say 'I told you so,' but Christ Eddy, I told you so!"

A GI handed Eddy a glass of water. "Drink something, Go-to Guy; you're white as a ghost."

"Oh, God, Wally!"

"We'll think of something, buddy. You need to decide if you want anything to do with this baby. You still have an out. Do you want to use it?"

SUMMER STORM

AUGUST 1951, CAMPBELLSVILLE

a clap of thunder followed by shrieking awoke Tabs and Harriett. Both of them sprinted down the hallway to find Olive sitting in bed, one hand protecting her neck, the other flailing about.

Still asleep, she screamed, "Stop, all of you. You are strangling me!"

Tabs caressed his wife. "Olive, I'm here, darling. Everything is fine. It's just a dream." Turning to Harriett, Tabs said, "Please get her a glass of water."

"Papa?" Placing her hand on Tabs' shoulder, Harriett shrugged, hesitating before leaving.

"She'll be fine. She's had the same dream for over twenty-five years, but she won't share details." Tabs rubbed Olive's sweaty back. "There, there, settle down, darling."

Olive lunged out of bed, charging a specter, only to find the window and her own reflection. A flash of light bolted across the sky, followed by a crack and rumble. She jumped, screamed, then dove back into bed. Tabs watched the scene with familiar despair.

"Olive..." Tabs reached for his wife again. This time Olive recognized him.

"Tabs, what are you doing?" Her voice hissed, and her eyes stared through him as if trying to burn a hole into the wall.

"It's storming, darling."

Harriett returned as Olive burst into hysterical sobs while clutching her neck.

Tabs attempted to comfort. "Dear wife, isn't it about time to share this nightmare? Perhaps it will help?"

"I can't! I don't want to relive it." Olive pushed Tabs so violently that he almost fell off the side of the bed.

Regaining his balance, Tabs calmly stroked Olive's hand. "Olive, your health is at risk because of these dreams. Please, Wife!"

Harriett sat on the opposite side of the bed. Taking her mother's other hand, she said, "Mother, you relive this dream every thunderstorm. Perhaps if you share it, it will no longer have a hold on you. Here, drink some water."

Olive paused, jerked her hands free, then sipped. "Get out of my room, both of you! I want some peace and quiet. Leave!"

Harriett's eyes grew wide, dark orbs searching her father for guidance.

Tabs gently reached for Olive's hand again. "Dear, purge yourself of this burden. I'm finally putting my foot down! I'm not leaving until you tell me what troubles you."

Her arm flung forward—the glass shattered as it crashed into the wall. Immediately, Harriett gathered shards.

Olive glared at her daughter. "Quit fussing. Let it be."

"Mother, if I don't clean now, you risk cutting yourself. I'm only trying to help."

Despite Tabs' soothing efforts, Olive's anxiety remained elevated. Her right leg and eye twitched uncontrollably as if separated from her brain, as she panted shallow rapid gulps of air.

"Mother, take slower, deeper breaths, please. You're going to hyperventilate." Harriett tightly grasped her leg to keep it steady. A shudder radiated through Olive's body; then, she kicked free.

"What are you trying to do to me?"

"We are only trying to help you through the night, Mother. You're in distress."

Her breathing slowed as her mind thoroughly roused itself from the terror. The leg quieted, then stopped.

"That's better, darling!" Tabs continued stroking her back. "Olive, the time has arrived; tell us that dream."

"Fine!" She sputtered, conceding the battle. "If I talk, will both of you stop hounding me? I don't know which is worse, the dream or your incessant nagging."

Tabs smiled, leaning toward her face attempting a kiss. "Tell us, Olive, go on."

Olive straightened her back. Forcing Tabs away, she swallowed and cleared her throat. "Fine! In my dream, I'm wearing my pearls, the ones from my mother."

"Yes. Mother, they are beautiful. You always wear them on special occasions." Harriett glanced at Tabs, raising her eyebrows.

Olive seethed, sucking air through her front teeth. "If you want me to share, then don't interrupt, Harriett."

Tabs motioned his head toward the door. Harriett complied. "Go on, Olive. This shall be between just you and me."

Olive scowled, waiting for Harriett to exit. "My father, Henderson, is on one side of me with my mother on the other side. Both are fighting over and clawing at the pearls. Then my sisters join the dream. Tildy and Ginny start choking me from behind. Sally and Bessie join in. By the time

I wake up, six people are trying to kill me, with Ben and Clyde standing in front of me yelling *tighter, tighter*." Silent tears flowed from Olive's eyes.

Tabs gasped, his mouth dropped. "Olive darling, I'm so sorry that you have suffered all these years."

He was at a loss for words. He knew the Westchester history, but never understood the depth of the rift between siblings.

"Everyone in the dream hates me as much as I hate them. But it's six against one." She slumped. "I awake before the end, but it's clear that I shall lose. They'll plant me beside Fred."

Tabs wrapped his arm around her shoulder. "Dear, you need to let go of the past, forgive your family. Absolve yourself."

Olive stiffened and hesitated. After several moments she relaxed, burying her head into Tabs' shoulder, she sobbed. "They'll never pardon me. And I don't know if I can forgive them. They made my life miserable. Father killed Freddy!"

A shudder spread through his body. "Darling, Henderson did not kill Fred. The Germans did. Henderson tried to be a good father; he raised his family to the best of his ability." Tabs waited, giving Olive time to comprehend his words. "I can't say the same of you, dear. You are brilliant; you know better, yet you willingly chose to abandon your family and ignore your husband and children. There's a big difference, Olive."

She sat motionless for several minutes. Finally, peering into Tabs' eyes, she asked, "If I'm that terrible, then why forgive me? I've been a horrid wife."

Tabs coughed. "Well—I can't argue that you are stubborn, sometimes even wicked."

Olive gasped then pulled the sheet around her upper body.

Tabs smiled. "But Olive, I love you. I always have loved you. Your children still try to break through. They would welcome some kindness and give love in return if only you allow them the chance. Don't push us away like you did your sisters and brothers."

Olive bent forward, her head in her lap, and wept. It seemed like an eternity passed before Olive finally spoke. "Perhaps I have a chance at redemption if it starts with you? I'll try Tabs; really, I'll try. I despise my miserable life. But I don't think I can change my ways. I'm too old."

"Trying is all we ask, dear. Open your heart and try." He continued to rub her back until she fell asleep. He lay her in the bed, covered her, and sat holding her hand the rest of the night.

∞ ∞ ∞

Harriett arrived first in the kitchen the following day. Heating a kettle of water, she loaded the electric toaster. She buttered toast as Tabs entered, yawning.

"Good morning, Papa," she said, glancing up. "Were you up early? I didn't see you in your room this morning." The bright morning sun on his face accented the ridges in his forehead and around his eyes.

"I stayed with your mother last night."

Tabs stretched. Pouring a cup of tea, he sat at the table, yawning. Harriett handed him a thick piece of toast slathered with grape jelly.

"With Mother? Or beside Mother?" She sat down across the table from him.

"You're too sharp, Janie. I sat in the chair, holding her hand. She slept soundly through the rest of the storm." Tabs wiped crumbs from his mouth with the back of his hand. "I think your mother is penitent."

Harriett choked. "Mother?" Crumbs sprayed from her mouth.

Collapsing back into his chair, arms dangling, Tabs asked, "Yes, Janie. Try treating her extra nice today. It's the first day of her trying to change her ways."

Suppressing a laugh, Harriett said, "Anything for you, Papa. But this I have to see!"

∞ ∞ ∞

Both Harriett and Tabs were well into the workday when Olive entered the empty kitchen. Making herself a cup of tea, she glanced at the calendar. Friday, shopping day. *I'll walk down to Lupinetti's this morning, add to my standing order*, she thought. She wandered down to the shop after her tea.

"Good morning Mrs. Bailey!" Dante Lupinetti greeted her. "My wife was just speaking of you. Wait, she's in the back, I'll get her," he said, stunned by an unfamiliar smile on Olive's face.

Mrs. Lupinetti greeted Olive with a hug. "Oh, Mrs. Bailey, just the woman I wanted to see. Dante and I are having a luncheon to celebrate our granddaughter's christening next Sunday. Will you and Tobias be our guests?"

Olive hesitated, swallowed, then exhaled. "Why Mrs. Lupinetti, we would love to. May I bring something? After all, she's our granddaughter too, although not the first." Olive forced a smile.

Mrs. Lupinetti's eyes widened. "Will you bring a dessert? May I call you Olive?"

"Yes, I shall happily bring a dessert. And yes, you may call me Olive—we're family after all. How many are attending?"

"Us, you, Teddy and Alice, and the godparents, so only eight. Alice didn't want a big to-do."

"I'll make an angel food cake for our new little angel,

Polly." Olive added eggs to her list, then handed it to Mr. Lupinetti, who was standing behind her with his mouth hanging open.

Olive walked past the apothecary on her way home. The bell rang as she entered. Seeing Alice in the back with baby Polly, she waved and called to her.

"Alice, may I hold that precious baby of yours?"

Alice and Teddy exchanged puzzled looks. "Sure, Mother. Polly is a little fussy today."

"That's alright. You were a fussy baby too." Olive cradled Polly in her arms. "Sure, your Momma was so fussy, just like you."

Alice steadied herself on the pharmacy counter. Teddy gulped for air.

"I'm glad I found you here, saves me a trip up the hill. Mrs. Lupinetti invited us to lunch after the Christening. I wanted to know which church and what time?"

Alice swooned again before answering. "The Presbyterian church, Teddy's family church. I often see Aunt Tildy and Aunt Bessie there. Christening is one o'clock after the service."

"Splendid. Your father and I shall see you then. Who are the godparents?"

"Albert. Teddy's sister, Deanna, is out of town, so Harriett will substitute. Thank you, Mother." Alice reached for Polly, who began whimpering.

"No, she just wants to walk." Olive strolled up and down the aisles, bouncing the baby. Alice's bottom collided with wood, hands clutching her head, while Teddy fetched water.

∞ ∞ ∞

Without Friday evening classes during the summer semester, Harriett arrived home shortly after Tabs to find

Olive at the stove cooking. She unbuttoned the top of her blouse and slid off her hose.

"Ah, that's better. Good evening, Mother. Geez, it's a scorcher today. What smells so delicious?" Harriett bit her lower lip; shrugging her shoulders, she regarded a smiling Tabs.

Despite a red bandana tied around her head, sweat dripped down her face. Olive wiped her brow then removed a loaf of fresh-baked bread from the oven. The aroma of warm yeast filled the room.

"You baked? In August?" Harriett's gaze drifted from mother to father.

"Yes, Harriett. I know you love fresh bread. I wanted to make something special; you've been working so hard." She fanned her face with her apron.

Harriett turned her head, eyeballing her father she mouthed, "What did you feed her? Where's my real mother?"

Olive sliced the warm loaf, buttered three pieces, and placed them on the table. "I made chicken and dumplings." She lifted the lid of the soup tureen. "Dig in."

Harriett served her mother, Tabs, and then herself. The trio ate in awkward silence until Harriett remembered. "Mother, I brought home a book from the library for you. It's the talk of the college." Leaning over, she pulled it from her canvas bag.

Olive read the cover. *"The Catcher in the Rye* by J. D Salinger. Odd name. Thank you, Harriett. You always bring me interesting reads." Setting the book aside, Olive said, "Tabs, Mrs. Lupinetti invited us to lunch next Sunday after Polly's Christening. I accepted."

Tabs swallowed hard to clear the food in his throat. "Wonderful, Olive. Will you be going to church also?"

"Of course. Do you mind if I go shopping for a new outfit? Shall I buy you a new shirt and tie?"

Harriett stood. Stretching, she said, "Please excuse me for a moment. I need to run upstairs." In the privacy of her room, she jumped onto her bed. Bursting into laughter, she rocked back and forth. "She'll never keep this up, no matter how hard she tries! This is hysterical to watch!"

Straight-faced, Harriett rejoined Olive and Tabs, who were deep in conversation.

"—they mentioned his death today at the Spring Factory," Tabs said.

Harriett cut another slice of bread. "Who died, Papa?"

"Old man Songer. You remember my old boss."

"Of course, she remembers, silly!" Olive interjected. "Everyone in town knows that beautiful house on top of the hill."

Harriett struggled to keep her right leg from bouncing. "Thank you, Mother, for this delicious meal and bread—yum! If you'll excuse me, I have some work to finish.

Back in her bedroom, Harriett took out pen and paper.

Dear darling Eddy,

I asked at the Post Office, but they said there was no problem with military mail service. I still haven't gotten any of your letters. Are you sending them to the correct address?

You would have enjoyed Mother this evening. Yes, I said Mother. After fifty years of bitter aggression, she is trying to change her ways. She's actually going to Polly's Christening and the Lupinettis' luncheon. She volunteered, did not have to be dragged. Watching her be kind is like watching a fox trapped in the hen house not eat any chickens.

Polly is just adorable. I can't wait for us to start our own family. Maybe we'll have little blonde-haired girls. I'm partial to little girls, but I know you want a son. We'll give our family all the opportunities that we never had.

Oh, I'm so excited. I may have a lead on a house. I don't want to get your hopes up, so I'll not tell you which place, but if it's not too expensive, I'll try to buy it. I'll keep you posted.

I hope you don't mind getting lots of short letters. I view them as a bit of conversation.

Please write back. I love you so much and can't wait for us to be together again.

Love and kisses,

Harriett

Perfuming routine completed, Harriett dropped the envelope into a foyer basket to be mailed in the morning.

∞ ∞ ∞

Olive's short curls blew in the warm afternoon breeze as she walked to church. Although clear, a thick veil of moisture filled the air. She searched the blue sky for rain clouds.

Tabs responded by pointing to the trees. "Yes, dear, it's going to rain today. Look at the maples; see how the leaves are curling in."

Olive shivered. Her hand reached for Tabs but fell short.

Tabs moved closer to Olive. "Don't worry, dear. If it storms this evening, I'll sit with you while you sleep."

Olive touched Tabs' hand. "You'll do that for me, even after being banned from my bed all these years?"

Tabs gently cupped her face. Leaning in, he tenderly kissed her lips. "I am still in love with you."

He gripped her hand; she squeezed in return as they continued down Maple Street.

Harriett, Albert, Teddy, Alice, and the Lupinettis sat in the front pew. Polly wore a Westchester Christening gown of French lace and Swiss cotton dotted with hand-sewn sea pearls. Tabs and Olive sat, waiting for Pastor McClain and the regular congregation to clear the sanctuary.

Recognizing the dress, Olive asked, "Alice, where did you find that heirloom? I haven't seen that since I was a child."

"Aunt Tildy had it. She offered it to me after I announced my pregnancy."

"Tildy? My sister Tildy was kind to you?" Olive's finger traced the bow-shaped lace insert on the hem of the skirt.

Alice chuckled and handed Polly to Olive. "Yes, Mother, your sister Tildy. She's a very nice woman."

The sleeping baby sucked her thumb as she gurgled. Tiny eyes fluttered but remained closed, hiding the blue orbs that matched her mother, grandmother, and great-grandmother.

Olive harrumphed. Tabs stroked her hand. "If you say so," Olive said. "Perhaps I shall take her up on her offer to lunch."

Albert disguised his choke into a feigned coughing jag. Shrugging his shoulders at Harriett, he grabbed her hand. "Alice, Harriett, and I shall return in just one minute. Godparent talk."

When they were out of earshot, Albert asked, "Harriett, what drug is Teddy giving Mother? What the heck just happened?"

"Albert, don't make me laugh. I'll pee my pants. You should have seen her yesterday. She was nice to me!"

"No!" Albert playfully pushed his sister.

"Yes! She baked bread and made chicken and dumplings."

"Okay, did you check for a lobotomy scar? She hasn't cooked since Esther and June were old enough to take over."

Harriett giggled. "She finally confessed her nightmare to Papa. That woman has tons of resentment and regrets. She promised Papa she'd try to forgive her family and be kinder. It won't surprise me if he moves back into her room."

S. LEE FISHER

"Get out of town! After twenty years." Albert struggled to keep his outburst to a low roar.

"Closer to twenty-two. He was out the day Doc Paulson diagnosed her pregnancy with me." Harriett spotted Pastor McClain walking down the center aisle. "We better get back. She's willingly going to Lupinettis and even baked a cake to take!"

Albert swiped his forehead and made the sign of the cross over his heart. "Harriett, we better start going to church. I think the world is coming to an end!"

98

13

JOY RIDE

AUGUST 1951, CAMPBELLSVILLE

*E*ddy's infamous sport coupe sat parked on the side street beside the Bailey house. Harriett waited in the driver's seat for Earl to give permission to proceed. Eddy's father, Edgar Kepler Sr., died a month earlier from what the family termed as *heart problems*; however, his slow decline in health, coupled with his lifestyle, rendered syphilis suspect. Earl transferred his job with the electric company and moved home to live with and care for his mother, Abigail.

Earl adjusted his position. "Geez, this car is uncomfortable." Harriett chuckled. "Are you ready?"

Harriett turned the ignition, depressed the clutch, and threw it in gear. "And we're off! Where am I going today?"

"I thought we'd do some highway driving today. Driving in this town is cake. Let's head toward Pittsburgh."

Harriett pulled onto the four-lane road. Driving west, they traveled the ridges of the Appalachian range, passing small towns and quaint farmland along the way. About forty minutes into the drive, Earl spotted a roadside diner.

"Harriett, pull over there. I'm suddenly famished. Allow

me to buy you lunch. I'm taking you for your driving test tomorrow. You're certainly qualified!"

The couple entered the diner laughing until Harriett abruptly ceased. She stood still, in full recognition of her surroundings.

Earl took her elbow. "Harriett, what's the matter?" His face flashed genuine concern.

She surveyed the restaurant. "I'm sorry, Earl. This is where Eddy proposed to me. I didn't make the connection from the outside, but—" She pointed to a table. "—it was there."

"We'll go. Come on." Earl turned toward the door.

"No, don't be silly. I'm overly sensitive. It's just that I haven't received a letter from him in five months. I'm worried, that's all." She dried her palms on her skirt before moving forward.

"Really? It's been that long?"

"Yes. I'm terrified something's happened." Harriett grabbed her handbag tightly as they stood, waiting to sit.

Earl gazed into her eyes, wondering how his brother could ever ignore such an amazing woman. "Harriett, if he were sick—or dead—the Army would notify you."

"Does he write Abigail? Did you hear from him when Edgar passed?"

Earl scratched his head. "I truthfully don't know. I'll ask. If we're staying, is here okay?"

He took her elbow and motioned toward the corner. He escorted her across the black and white tile floor to a booth. Placing a nickel into the table jukebox, he selected Bing Crosby. "What do you want to eat?"

"Anything except a stuffed pork chop!" She managed a smile. "That was our meal the night he proposed."

∞ ∞ ∞

Earl drove Harriett to Madison the next day. He waited beside the car, smiling at his sister-in-law. He watched as she slowly walked into the building. Harriett glanced back before entering. Within a few minutes, she returned, accompanied by a stern-looking, grumpy instructor wearing a badge engraved with the name "William Jarvis."

"You." He pointed to Earl. "Did you drive today?"

"Ah, yes, sir." Earl stammered, then glanced at Harriett.

"Wait here. This won't take long." Jarvis pointed to a bench.

Harriett's eyebrows arched as she inhaled and slipped into the driver's seat, awaiting her turn with Mr. Jarvis.

"Please proceed to the course." Jarvis scowled and pointed to a series of orange cones.

Harriett started the engine, rolled down the window, gestured with her hand that she was entering the traffic lane, and moved forward. Jarvis jotted notes on a tablet. Earl helplessly sat on the bench, watching and waiting as the car maneuvered in and out of the course. After about thirty minutes, Harriett returned, pulled into the same parking spot, turned off the ignition, and got out of the car. Jarvis remained inside, frantically writing on his notepad.

Finally, after several minutes, he got out. Turning to Harriett, he said, "Young lady, follow me."

Harriett shrugged her shoulders to Earl and followed Jarvis back into the building. Earl waited a good ten minutes before Harriett reappeared.

She walked out the double doors, slowly heading toward the car. When she was out of view of Jarvis, she began sprinting toward Earl. Lunging at him, she jumped up for a hug. He caught her in mid-air, but the thrust of her jump sent them both spinning in circles.

"I passed!" she exclaimed. "I was the first person today that he passed."

Earl chuckled as he sat her down on the ground. "That was an enthusiastic greeting. I never expected anything but a passing grade."

A blushing Harriett smoothed her skirt, then waved her paper license in the air. "Here it is! I'm a licensed woman driver. He said my three-point turn and parallel parking were near perfect."

"Of course they were. You have a great teacher!" Earl held the door open for Harriett.

She tilted her head and asked, "Do you mind if I keep the car now?"

Chortling, Earl slapped his knee. "Why would I mind? It's Eddy's car, yours through marriage. Besides, I don't need three cars parked in front of Mom's house. The neighbors already think she's wealthier than she is. Dad squandered most of his money on booze and women. Not on my mother."

Harriett cringed. "Poor Abigail. I know how she feels."

Earl scowled. "I didn't mean to bring up a touchy subject. Sorry." He scratched his head before continuing. "I asked Mom if Eddy writes. She just frowned and said, 'Not nearly enough.' It looks like you're not the only person he ignores."

With pursed lips, Harriett scrunched her nose. "He better have a good reason!"

"I agree, my little sister. I agree."

∞ ∞ ∞

Harriett dropped Earl off, crossed the bridge to the other side of Campbellsville, then parked the car on the side street. The hot August afternoon sun radiated off the vehicle.

"Papa, Mother!" Harriett called, running through the kitchen. "Come on. We're going for a ride."

Olive wandered out from the parlor, book in hand. "Harriett, how did it go today?"

"Come on! Where's Papa? I'm taking you for a ride." Olive pointed to the garden as Harriett ran through the yard. "Papa, wash your hands now. Let's go."

Tabs responded by wiping sweat from his forehead. "I need to wash more than my hands," he said as he replaced his handkerchief in his pocket. "Give me ten minutes to freshen up?"

Harriett picked up a stack of garden tools. "Absolutely! We're going for a ride!"

Olive crawled into the cramped back seat without complaint. Tabs settled into the passenger side as Harriett depressed the clutch.

"Where to?" she asked, her voice nearing a squeak. "I'm driving; this is too exciting."

"Harriett, it's your car. You are driving. You choose!" answered Olive from the rear as she wiggled, trying to get comfortable.

"Then I'm treating you to frozen custard." She shifted into first and proceeded down the street. Harriett was met with a nasty stare as she stopped at the first stop sign.

Olive noticed the woman's face. "Who was that giving you the evil eye? Those looks could kill."

"One of Eddy's old girlfriends." Harriett grinned at Lynette and waved as she pulled away. "They dated in high school. I guess she objects to our marriage." Harriett chuckled. "She's not the only one."

Finding it hard to disguise his own displeasure in Harriett's marriage, Tabs looked out the window as the trio drove through quaint, bucolic countryside on the way to Madison. The road followed a nearly dry meandering creek, past the dammed-up swimming hole and Tabs' favorite fishing spot.

Ten minutes into the trip, Harriett hit a bump. Olive bounced up, hitting her head on the roof.

"Son-of..."

"Mother, I'm so sorry. That bump came out of nowhere." Harriett grimaced. "Some of these country roads are full of holes."

"No problem, Harriett. It's not your fault—but this car is not the most comfortable ride."

Harriett grinned at Tabs, made a hand sign for turning, then pulled into the Tasty Freeze Delight ice cream stand. Patrons overflowed the parking lot, seeking a cool treat on a muggy afternoon.

Tabs got out of the car and approached the order window. He called back, "Olive, vanilla?"

The nodding head indicated yes.

"This is my treat. You just help me carry." Harriett scanned the menu board as they waited in line. "I want a banana split. Papa?"

"Oh, that sounds wonderful. Make it three. Your mother loves them too."

"Three banana splits, coming up," said the clerk.

An uncomfortably squirming Olive gave up. Climbing out of the car, she found an empty picnic table. She called when she spotted Harriett and Tabs walking toward the vehicle. "Over here. It's too hot in that blasted—I mean, *small* back seat."

Harriett handed her the sundae. "We got you a banana split, Mother. Is that all right?"

The dessert was met with wide, appreciative eyes.

Olive slurped a spoonful of whipped cream. "Are we celebrating today?"

Harriett danced, twirling in a circle. "Only me passing my driver's test. But that's as good a reason as any to get ice cream, especially in this weather."

Tabs wiped his mouth with a paper napkin. "I agree."

Melting confection mixed with chocolate syrup slipped from Olive's spoon, onto her lap. "Son of a—!" She stopped. "Tabs, would you kindly ask for a wet cloth? I need to wipe my dress. Silly me, I spilled some of my treat."

Harriett veiled her smile. "I'll get it, Mother." By the time she made it to the window and back, most of Olive's sundae had been eaten.

"Sorry I took so long. This place is swamped."

Olive took the cloth from Harriett and began scrubbing. After aggressive rubbing, a shadow of chocolate remained; however, Olive voiced no objection. They enjoyed the rest of their sundaes.

"Are we finished?" Tabs asked, reaching for the trash. "What now?"

A sheepish grin crossed Harriett's face. "Anyone want to drop in on Albert? He's just down the road a few miles. I think today is his afternoon off. He was going to take me for my driving test, but Earl insisted."

Olive sulked. "I'm a mess, but I've never been to his house. How sad." She glanced at the stain. "What the heck. Yes, let's go visiting."

Tabs tossed their trash into the can, and they sped down the road to visit an unsuspecting Albert.

∞ ∞ ∞

Albert stared in shocked amazement as he greeted the knock at the door. "Mother, Papa, Harriett, what a surprise! What brings you out today?" He glanced questioningly at his sister. "I see you passed your test."

Harriett nodded as they pushed through the door and into the living room. Olive scrutinized the space. "Isn't this a cute little house? Perfect for a bachelor, although it is rather tiny."

"It's enough for me, Mother." Albert winked at Harriett. "Come, I'll show you the rest of it."

Olive followed Albert into the kitchen, dining room, then down the hall to two small bedrooms. Finally, they explored the guest bath and master en suite.

"Well, what do you think?" Albert waved to the couch. "Have a seat."

Olive scratched her head. "It is quaint, but nicely furnished for a man's house. That was smart, turning that postage-stamp room into your office." She walked over to the couch and sat. "Who helped you decorate? Alice, I presume. All in all, I like it!"

Motioning to Tabs and Harriett, Albert said, "If you are staying, would you like some iced tea? Harriett, will you help?"

"Just water, please," Olive answered. "With ice, if you have some. God, it's a scorcher."

Brother and sister scurried into the kitchen. Harriett cracked the lever on the ice tray, placing cubes into each glass.

"Okay, Sister, spill! Has she slipped up yet?"

Harriett giggled. "Almost. She soiled her dress with ice cream and almost had an outburst, but stopped herself. It's hilarious, Albert. She is trying, but my, she struggles."

"She'll never make it. Bet you ten dollars she's back to her old ways before Christmas!" Albert removed a crisp bill from his wallet. Slapping it on the counter, he asked, "Are you game?"

"You're on. I say she lasts through the holidays, but come 1952, it's back to status quo." Harriett matched his bill.

"Hmmm. Two months? That's all you're giving me for ten bucks?" Albert poked Harriett's shoulder.

"Okay, okay, I'll go as far as Easter next year, but no

longer! The woman is doomed to fail. She's been bitter too long."

"Sucker! Thanks, Sis, I love making easy money!" Albert finished filling the glasses with water and carried the tray into the living room to his waiting guests.

14

DOUBLE CHEVRON

AUGUST 1951, TRIESTE, ITALY

Sarge stacked the envelope on top of the pile. Although he considered sorting the mail a mundane chore, little else remained to be done, thanks to Eddy. The Private's organization of supply and demand amazed the sergeant. Picking up the next mail, Sarge scanned the return address and quickly ripped open the envelope. He unfolded the enclosed letter and read.

"...per your recommendation, the private is hereby promoted to corporal. To be effective immediately."

Splendid, thought Sarge, *I can't wait to tell the boy*.

Eddy entered the room as Sarge tucked the envelope into his drawer. "Eddy, good, you're here. I need you to trot over to headquarters and pick up a set of corporal's chevrons."

"Sure, Sarge. Right away. Who's the lucky sap?" Eddy spun around, ready to make his exit.

Sarge grinned and continued sorting through the mail. "Private Edgar Kepler."

Eddy opened the door and waited for an answer. "Yes, Sarge, I heard. I'm on my way out. I understand if you can't tell me who is being promoted, except knowing a name makes it easier."

"I said, Private Edgar Kepler."

"Fine! I'm going. Geez, what bug is up your butt today?"

The door closed with a bang as Eddy clomped across the compound. Sarge smiled, allowing Eddy to leave confused, in a tizzy. About thirty minutes later, Eddy returned with the applique.

Eddy frowned as he handed it to Sarge. "I told you it was faster knowing the name! Christ, that dick took forever. When he finally found the paperwork, he smirked and handed me what I wanted. Never said a word." He turned toward his desk.

Sarge opened the package then calmly ordered, "Kepler, stand fast!" Pulling out the double chevron, he walked to Eddy and yanked on the single stripe. The stitches gave way as they pulled off Eddy's uniform shirt.

"What the hell, Sarge?" Eddy slapped at Sarge's hand. "What did I do? I was only complaining about the wait. It really didn't bother me that much!"

Sarge laughed out loud. "You dunce. I gave you the name of the soldier being promoted. It's *you*. Private Edgar Kepler, you are now Corporal Edgar Kepler. Congratulations, you earned this."

The blood rushed, burning Eddy's cheeks. "Thanks! I'm… flabbergasted! Boy, that went over my head."

He rubbed the embroidered applique between his fingers.

Sarge extended his hand. "No kidding. Nonetheless, a promotion is well deserved. How are your sewing skills?"

"Shit. But for changing to double chevrons, I'll learn how to stitch! Thanks, Sarge."

Eddy's vigorous pumping caused Sarge to grasp his arm. "Woah, boy. If you continue, you'll rip out my shoulder.

Count your shirts, and I'll order more. Now get out of here and tell your buddies!"

15

HOME IMPROVEMENT

SEPTEMBER 1951, PREDMEJA YUGOSLAVIA

*C*orporal Edgar Kepler Jr. finagled a deal with Sarge to be off every other weekend to visit Rosa. He brought food, money, and an occasional trinket to his Italian lover. Most of his free time was spent chopping and stacking wood in preparation for a long, two-week interval—the precious commodity was used for cooking and heating the cottage.

Intrepid Wally faithfully transported him back and forth from the Yugoslavian Alpine foothills. Separated only by modern time, the area was once all Hapsburg territory before WWI.

Rosa rubbed her aching back, amazed at how much her body had changed over the last several months. Smiling at Eddy through the cottage's only window, she sat and switched to rubbing her growing belly. The compact one-room cottage in the foothills of the Alps was sparsely furnished, if you could even call it that. A square, white table, two wooden chairs, a sink with a pump handle, and a single bed adorned with a quilt (which sprouted escaping stuffing) filled the room. Potato sacks hung on a rod served as curtains, providing privacy from an occasional peering squirrel or deer. An empty wine bottle filled with wildflowers decorated the windowsill.

Eddy charged through the door carrying an armful of wood. "How cold does it get up here?" He smiled at Rosa, then placed the wood on the dirt floor beside the hearth, disturbing a mouse. It scampered away. Wiping his hands on his trousers, he kissed the waiting girl. "God, you are more beautiful every day!"

Rosa purred. "Are you ready to eat, my handsome GI?" She rose and walked to the pot, which was simmering over the fire, to stir her soup. "Hand me two bowls, please."

Eddy reached, grabbing the dishes from a shelf above the sink that displayed two of each: plates, cups, bowls, and glasses. Placing them on the table, he said, "Put that ladle down. I want a real kiss before we eat." Eddy reached around Rosa and pulled her close. He inhaled the scent of her hair then passionately engulfed her mouth with his. "God, I love you."

Rosa turned out of his arms. "I love you, too. Now let's eat. I'm hungry—and eating for two, remember?"

His hand slapped her butt. "Go. I'll hold the bowls for you." But he held onto the back of her dress.

Rosa whipped around before Eddy withdrew his hand. Clutching his arm, she pulled it to her breast. "You need to feed me, lover, if these are to feed our baby." Her coquettish grin melted the toughened soldier into submission.

"Anything you say, Darling! I'm putty in your hands."

∞ ∞ ∞

Weekends passed too quickly. The hours between Friday night's arrival and Sunday's departure raced by at warp speed, with the sound of Wally's horn always distressing both despondent lovers.

Riding back to base late in September, Wally asked, "Eddy, can she actually survive in that shack all winter?"

"Hmm." Eddy, deep in thought, remained silent, looking out the window into the gully below.

Wally punched his arm. "I'm talking to you."

"What?" Eddy glanced hesitantly at the driver. "I wasn't paying attention."

"No shit." Wally stopped the jeep. Turning toward his friend, he asked again, "Can she survive the winter in that hellhole?" He punched Eddy's arm. "That place isn't fit to house cows, let alone a mother and baby."

Eddy mumbled, "I never thought about it. What do you suggest I do?"

Wally grunted. "For starters, install a floor."

"You're insane."

"No, you're the insane one. Do you realize how cold an earth floor can get? You need to do something to insulate that place, or she'll freeze to death."

"Well, how the hell am I supposed to do that?"

"Eddy, I'm not the one who knocked up the local magistrate's daughter. Use your brain instead of your dick to think, for a change."

Wally threw the jeep in gear and lurched forward. "It's about time you grow up, asshole. There are consequences to actions."

"Fuck!" Eddy pounded the dash with both fists.

"Settle down. We have two weeks to organize this. You buy some wood; get some straw or batting, and I'll get us a truck. We can reinforce the place before it snows."

∞ ∞ ∞

The following Tuesday, Isabella and Giuseppe Cortina made their monthly trek to the cabin to bring supplies to a waiting Rosa. Giuseppe carried boxes filled with canned goods into the room.

"Rosa," Isabella said as she stacked food onto an empty shelf. "Come here; I want to feel your belly."

"That's an odd request, Nonna."

Isabella rubbed her granddaughter's bulging baby bump. "I think the baby is moving. Your time is near, darling. You'd be wise to return to Santa Croce with us until the baby's born."

"But what about Eddy?"

"Mail him a note. Tell him where you are. I'll write to him as soon as the baby's born." She looked around the cottage. "We need to come up with a better plan for your housing after the baby is born. You can't live here all winter."

"But Nonna, I can't live with you. Papa will find me." Rosa frantically threw her few belongings into her suitcase. "I'll ask Eddy what he thinks. I need a place where we can be together as husband and wife, and that's not appropriate at your house, Nonna."

Distressed lines creased Isabella's face. "I agree, darling. I'll not stand for an illicit affair. Not under my roof." Isabella's face softened. "Don't fret. We'll figure out something."

∞ ∞ ∞

Back in the comfort of Santa Croce, Rosa snuggled into the feathers of her bed. Taking out pen and paper, she wrote.

Dear darling love,

I am back with Nonna and Nonno. They think the baby is close to coming. Oh, Eddy, I'm so excited about having our child. I know you want a boy, but I hope it's a little girl with curly blonde hair.

Nonna says I may not live in the cottage come winter.

And if I stay with her, then we may not be together. Eddy, that is unacceptable. I need you as my lover and as the father of my child. What are we to do? Please think of something, or I fear I shall never see you again.

If we were to get married, is there someplace on the base for wives to live? I don't know about these things; you must arrange all for us. Please!

Nonna will write as soon as our child is born. I must say, it is so much more comfortable living here. I don't have to cook, I'm never lonely, and I have a soft, warm bed. This life is better. Please find a way for us to live it.

I love you, my dear,

Rosa

The letter arrived on base the following Monday. Eddy scanned it then began writing his own list. Bigger bed, feather mattress, floorboards, insulation—the list filled an entire sheet of paper. He tucked it into his shirt and began doing what he did best—well, second-best—merchandise procurement.

Wally's job was to ensure a large enough truck to transport Eddy's stockpile. At seven in the evening on Friday night, he parked the truck behind Sarge's supply warehouse.

Wally honked the horn, and Eddy opened the door to expose a stack seven feet wide and at least five feet high.

"Good God, Eddy. What's all this?" Wally scratched his butt as he exited the truck. "You don't expect the two of us to load this, do you?"

Two prominently muscled men stepped from behind the stash. "No, I don't. Tonight, we have reinforcements, but once we get to the cabin, then we take it out as we use it."

Wally sighed in relief. "Thank goodness. Then I guess we better pack carefully. Let's get at it. Kepler, you owe me a beer."

"Hell, I owe all of you beers for the evening." Eddy grinned the Kepler smile.

After about thirty minutes, the last items were placed in the truck bed. All four men were sweating and short of breath.

Wally wiped his forehead with the back of his sleeve. "Come on. Close up the back. I'll park this monstrosity and get us a jeep for tonight. Be back in ten minutes."

Four men sauntered into the bar to find Sully waiting at a table. He called out as Eddy walked through the door. "Kepler, here." His big hairy arm waved them over.

Eddy motioned to the waitress. "We need two pitchers and four more mugs. Thanks, darling."

She blushed and smiled at Eddy's attention.

"Kepler, do all women faint over you?" Sully asked as he shook his head from side to side.

"Yep. Always have. Always will."

Sully decided to change the subject to the business at hand. "Hey, did you get everything you needed?"

Eddy nodded. "Just about. The place will be much more livable after this. I never really noticed the condition of things." Eddy's face reddened. "I was always too busy looking at her beautiful body. But that cottage is pretty crappy. And I guess she gets lonely during the week."

Wally choked on his beer. "You think? Kepler, I can't believe what an ass you are. Of course, she gets lonely. Hell, she's a young girl. Did you think to get her a few magazines or books?" Wally punched Eddy's shoulder. "You might be engaged in bedtime activities for your visit, but what the hell do you think she does alone all week?"

Eddy pouted. "Don't blame me. Her grandparents put her there. And they visit her once a month."

Sully stood. "Yep, you're an ass. It's your fault the kid's knocked up and has to deal with this. All you had to do was sheath it, or keep it in your pants, and all of her troubles would have been avoided." Sully searched the bar for a different table. "So, this poor child has company six days a month, and you don't think she's lonely the other twenty-four? Kepler, you're a disgrace to men."

Both hands flew to his hips. "I'll have you know, I already collected several magazines, books, and I even got her some yarn and knitting needles. Besides, once the baby comes, she'll have plenty to do."

"Go to hell, Kepler. You don't deserve either your wife or your child lover." Sully stormed off to sit at a different table.

"What's his beef?" Eddy scratched his head.

Wally glanced at the three men. "I shouldn't say, but Sully got some disturbing news about his daughter. She's in a similar situation to Rosa."

The three moaned in unison. "Ooooh."

∞ ∞ ∞

The next day, Wally and Eddy returned to find the cabin empty.

"Geez, this place is dismal with her back at her grandparents." Eddy roamed aimlessly for a moment. "I can't believe it's almost time for the baby to arrive." Eddy dropped his head, moping to the truck.

"We're in luck, with her gone. I'll stay this weekend and help you get this place fixed up. And I won't have to travel back and forth."

"Fine and dandy for you, but I don't get to see Rosa."

"Good god, Eddy! She's getting too close to the end for sex. Is that all you think about?"

Eddy grinned. "Ahh—yes, don't you?"

"No, you idiot. I don't." Wally shook his head. "I swear you're hopeless."

The friends quickly emptied the cabin of all furniture and began the arduous job of preparing for winter. An insulated floor came first. Eddy spread a thick layer of straw over the dirt. They constructed a supporting frame out of two-by-fours, filling in with more straw. Next came a base of plywood. The pile in the truck dwindled as the men worked.

Surveying their work, Wally felt for drafts. "I think the linoleum will do the trick. I can barely feel any radiating cold. You may be a prick, but you are good at finding things!"

Balancing the rolled flooring on his shoulder, Eddy glanced at the space. "This is much better. We'll do the walls tomorrow, and we can stack more wood."

"All well and good, but what's for supper? I'm starving."

"Shit. I can't cook."

"You better learn, my friend, because I'm cheap labor, but I do require food as payment."

Eddy rummaged through the jars in the cottage. Finding dried pasta and tomato sauce, he cranked the sink pump, filling a kettle with water.

"Wally, will you at least start a fire? It's getting chilly in here now that we're not moving."

"Yeah, yeah." Wally grabbed an armful of logs and threw them on the newly installed plywood.

"Hey, don't make a mess. We still have the linoleum to install."

"Shut up and feed me." Wally slumped onto the floor then slid off his boots.

"Wally, Move that wood. While this place is clear, we should unroll this tonight so that we can move the furniture back inside."

"Hallelujah! You're finally thinking!" Wally picked up his newly deposited firewood. "I wondered if you'd figure that out on your own."

They unrolled an imitation brick linoleum floor, secured it to the base, and sealed the edges.

Wally retrieved a broom and swept the scrap into a pile. Walking toward the door, he said, "We'll know if this worked. I'll sleep on the floor tonight, and if I wake up stiff, not only are you short a worker, but you'll know you failed at protecting her from the cold."

Eddy smirked. "Oh, that's nice!"

"Where do you throw trash?"

Eddy pointed through the window to a hole in the hillside. "I dug a pit for rubbish. Over there beside the latrine."

"That brings me to my next question. You better do something to clear her path to the outhouse. Snow-covered ground might be treacherous. God forbid she falls."

Eddy shuddered. "Wally, are you always so negative? Now my head is filled with all kinds of bad visions." Eddy scooped a spoon of sauce. Throwing it on the noodles, he handed a bowl to Wally. "Shut up and eat. We still need to bring in the furniture."

The pair sat on the floor, eating quietly. Eddy thought of Rosa's warm body while Wally thought of lonely, cold winter nights.

After collecting their dishes, Eddy piled them in the sink. "It's getting dark. Let's hurry."

Back outside, Wally climbed into the truck. Throwing aside a large covering, he exposed a bed frame, mattress, and armoire.

"Eddy—a belated wedding gift."

Eddy jumped into the truck. Fingering the bed frame, he asked, "Where did you get these? It's perfect!" He spun to face Wally. "I looked for a double bed, but couldn't find one."

Wally's face beamed. "You're not the only person with skills. I have some too. I also found a suitable pair of fancy curtains. Women like that stuff."

By the time they got the furniture in place and Wally unpacked his bed sack, he was exhausted. Eddy climbed into the new bed, testing it by bouncing up and down. "Wally, this is great. Nice spring action."

"Shut up, Kepler, and go to sleep. Morning will come too quickly, and we have tons to do yet." Wally was asleep within minutes.

Eddy closed his eyes and smiled, dreaming of Rosa.

16

ALL GROWN UP

SEPTEMBER 1951, CAMPBELLSVILLE

*H*arriett enjoyed flaunting her new driving skills, although the nasty looks from the town's women became increasingly uncomfortable.

One late September Wednesday, Harriett commented while eating lunch, "Now that winter is coming, I really should look for a car with a heater."

Kathryn looked up from her salad. "You mean that infamous vehicle doesn't have heat?"

Harriett giggled. "No. I guess Eddy and companion made enough heat on their own." Her smile faded.

"He hasn't written yet, has he?" Caroline's motherly face peered at the young executive.

Harriett shook her head. "No. I don't want to talk about it."

"Harriett, you need to face facts; this man has left you high and dry!" Kathryn said sternly. "But what you *can* do is sell that precious car." She grinned. "Call it poetic justice."

Mary Payne glanced at Kathryn. "Isn't Mr. Roland selling his Buick? Harriett, ask him if he'd sell it to you instead of trading it in."

Kathryn agreed. "It's a beautiful car. He gets a new vehicle every two years. Mary, that's a grand idea. I'll schedule a meeting for you this afternoon. His calendar is open today."

Harriett bit into the second half of her egg salad sandwich. "Geez, I don't know. Can I do that? Legally?"

"You're his wife. I'm sure either Mr. Roland or Mr. Dugan will know a way around the system. Leave it to us. You make your deal with Mr. Roland, and we'll see to the rest!" Kathryn grinned. "And then we can go on proper adventures in your new Buick."

Placing both hands on the table, Harriett pondered her friend's words. After several moments she said, "You're right, Kathryn. He is my husband, even if he is ignoring me. Serves him right to miss out on that piece of junk. That car is fine for a young kid, but not for an adult. I'll talk with Mr. Roland. Thank you."

∞ ∞ ∞

Saturday of the next week, Harriett drove to class in Madison instead of taking the bus. Her concentration waned as she listened to her economics professor discuss the effects of World War One on the US dollar and the gold standard. Absentmindedly she took notes, scribbling in her steno pad. The three-hour class seemed to be never-ending. Finally, the clock struck noon. Grabbing her books and handbag, she raced to the restroom. She pulled off her skirt, replacing it with a pair of clam-digger slacks, slipped out of her pumps, and donned a pair of Keds, still wearing her sweater and silk neck scarf. She folded her skirt, placed it into her bag, and ran to the parking lot.

The light green Buick Roadmaster sedan, with its smiling chrome grille and sleek, curved, chrome side stripe, was parked in the student parking lot. It looked more likely to be owned by a faculty member than a student. Harriett unlocked the door and sat behind the steering wheel. She caressed the tan leather dashboard and adjusted the power seat to accommodate her short stature.

"Now *this* is a car," she said out loud as she smiled at her purchase.

Throwing the car's automatic transmission into drive, she headed north.

Kathryn waited on the sidewalk in front of her apartment building with a picnic basket by her side. She whistled as she climbed into the passenger seat.

"This car suits you! I packed sandwiches, chips, and fruit. Where are we headed?"

Harriett looked up from her map. Folding the paper, she said, "I thought we'd continue heading north. It's such a lovely day. Let's go to that state park with the covered bridge. They have walking trails, picnic tables, and the leaves should be starting to turn. Maybe not the best color yet, but we should have a nice fall display of foliage."

"I wore my flat shoes. Let's go."

The drive through country roads, dotted with oranges, reds, and yellows, was breathtaking. Kathryn and Harriett comfortably chatted about work, passing the hour.

Kathryn pointed to the sign as Harriett slowed. Flicking on her turn signal, she waited to cross traffic before pulling onto the lane that led to the park. The tires crunched on the gravel as they headed down the road.

"How do you know about this place?" asked Kathryn.

"Papa told me about it. He used to visit here as a young man with his cousin Wyeth before he married Mother." Harriett untied her neck scarf and wrapped it around her hair, tying the ends behind her head. "I'm starving, but let's walk first.".

Kathryn grabbed two apples. Tossing one to Harriett, she

locked their basket in the trunk before heading toward the covered bridge. A placard nailed to the side of the bridge outlined its history.

Kathryn's eyes widened as she read. "Geez, this was built one hundred years ago. Looks to be in good shape."

Harriett moved under the arched trusses. "Reminds me of Ichabod Crane. I wouldn't want to be here on Halloween." She laughed out loud. "I can hear hooves clip-clopping on the wooden floorboards, galloping toward me."

Kathryn followed Harriett, who stopped midpoint through the ninety-five-foot expanse.

The women leaned over the railing, watching as the water gurgled and slurped, bouncing over rocks as it slipped downstream. Yellow leaves from a maple tree drifted down on the gentle breeze and floated into a small estuary, where they circled, then shot out to continue their journey.

Looking back at the entrance, Kathryn commented. "This is as long as a football field."

Harriett turned her head to hide the tears welling in her eyes. "I'm sorry. Everything reminds me of Eddy. He was a football star—should have gone to college on scholarship."

"Why didn't he?"

Harriett sighed. "I've never been told the actual story, only bits and pieces from several different people—but from what I can tell, he literally dropped the ball."

Kathryn guffawed at Harriett's analogy.

"I gather that Coach Reven—you know, my tennis teacher —provided him the necessary paperwork. Eddy needed to complete the personal section and send it in to the college sports conference, or something like that."

"Sounds like he was set up for success." Kathryn gazed at the babbling brook beneath the bridge.

"Yes, it does. But for whatever reason, Eddy never

followed through." She sighed again. "Seems that ignoring responsibility is Eddy's status quo."

Wrapping her arm around her friend's shoulder, Kathryn urged. "Let's continue our walk. I'm starving too; the apple doesn't quite fill my tummy."

They strolled along the stream for another fifteen minutes, delighting in the crisp air and musky smell of autumn, before heading back to the car. Harriett spread a checkered tablecloth over the picnic table and Kathryn unpacked the basket. A group of teenage boys strutted past, whistling catcalls as the women ate ham and cheese sandwiches, washed down with bottles of warm Coca-Cola.

Harriett crunched on a potato chip. "Silly kids. We're ancient compared to them."

"Compliments are always welcome. Besides, you're gorgeous."

Harriett flushed. "Don't make me blush! Oh, did I tell you that I may have a lead on a house?"

Kathryn's hands flew to her hips. "No! How could you forget that detail?"

"Well, I'm not certain yet. But Papa's old boss passed away a little over a month ago. All his children moved out of town and the house is just empty. It's not on the market yet, but I'm watching and hoping." She dreamily looked at the sky. "It's the biggest house in town. Beautiful red brick, located on the highest street, reigning over the entire area. Every Christmas Mrs. Songer lit blue electric candles in the windows. They could be seen for miles."

"Wow, it sounds perfect. Can you swing a mortgage and school?" Kathryn wiped a dollop of mustard from her mouth.

"I think so. I save every possible penny. I probably shouldn't have bought the car, but—"

"Oh no you don't! That car screams 'Harriett Bailey Kepler, college graduate, future female junior executive.'"

Beaming, Harriett took a swig of cola and swallowed. "It does, doesn't it?" Glancing admiringly as sunlight reflected off of the polished car, she said, "I should have enough money for a down payment. Seriously, a mortgage can't be much more than what I'm paying Mother for rent. She may be trying to be nice, but she hasn't lowered my financial obligation."

Both women laughed. Harriett continued. "I just wish I was doing this with Eddy, even if it has to be long distance. I want him to be part of the decision making."

"Whatever his reason for not writing, Harriett, you can't just let time stand still. Life goes on." Kathryn removed a metal cake caddy from the basket. "I made chocolate cake," she said as she unlatched the top. "Not from scratch. I used one of those mixes, but the batter was good!" She smiled at her friend. "Harriett, why don't you try contacting his commanding officer?"

She thought for a few minutes before answering. "I've considered that. But no. If he deliberately chooses to ignore me, then I'm not desperate. I refuse to be the damsel in distress." Harriett bit her lip. "Kathryn, I'm going to college so that I never have to depend on a man for my livelihood. I'll not cower to Eddy, no matter how much I love him."

She blew her nose, forcing the tears to remain at bay. Moving to sit beside her friend, Kathryn slid her arm around Harriett's waist.

"You my dear, are one of the brightest, strongest women I know. You'll be fine, with or without him! I know you will. Now, let's eat cake!"

"Ha! You sound like Marie Antoinette. But yes, cake it is."

17

HILL HOUSE

CAMPBELLSVILLE, OCTOBER 1951

*H*arriett grabbed the stack of mail waiting for her in the front foyer. Bounding up the steps, she ran to her room, closed the door, and jumped onto her bed. Scanning the envelopes, she found the return address she wanted. She ripped open the seal and pulled out the letter, reading quickly as a smile inched its way across her face. Refolded and re-stuffed, she placed the correspondence into an accordion-type of paper file folder, then retrieved her bank book from the top drawer of her dresser.

Two-thousand dollars, she thought. *I never imagined having that much money, let alone spending it on a house down payment.* She grabbed her stationary before replacing the leger and began writing.

Darling Eddy,

I hope that title is still appropriate. Geez, why don't you write? Have I done something to offend you? How could I?

I found our house! I wish you were here with me, but this is too good to pass on. Mr. Songer—you remember, Papa's old boss—died this summer. His kids live all across the country and want to sell the house quickly. I made them an offer, and they accepted it. I know, I should have told you first, but...well are you even writing to me? So how am I to wait on your approval? Eddy, this house is a place I would buy with or without you at this stage in my life. Darling, it would be easier with two incomes, however, since you send no support, I have learned to rely on myself. I can do this alone. I don't want to, but I can.

Eddy, you are breaking my heart! Please put it back together by writing soon.

She stopped writing to blow her nose. Emotionally unprepared for the words that flowed so easily, Harriett trembled. A tear dropped onto her letter, smudging the ink.

Stop crying, Harriett, she chastised herself. *Are you really willing to give him up?* As she sat crying, the back door opened and closed.

"Papa!"

Seconds later, Harriett was clinging to Tabs, sobbing.

Tabs held her tightly as he rubbed her back. "Janie, dear. What has you so upset?" Gently pushing her away, he tucked a loose strand of hair behind her ear. "Come now, tell me all about it."

Harriett blew her nose while Tabs stoked the stove and put on a kettle of water. "Janie?"

"Oh, Papa. I'm so confused. I should be happy, but I'm sad."

"Honey, you're not making any sense and that has me frightened. Let's start at the beginning."

Harriett smiled; the tension broken. "Not used to me talking gibberish?" She sat at the table, motioning for Tabs to join her. "I got the Songer house. The bank approved my mortgage today."

Tabs inhaled. "Janie, I'm so proud of you. But I'm not sure how your mother will take the news."

"What do you mean? How her mother will take *what* news?" asked Olive as she entered the kitchen. Tabs and Harriett looked at each other, Harriett bit her lip and Tabs sucked in his cheeks.

Inhaling deeply, Harriett replied. "I'm moving out. I bought a house."

Olive chuckled. "Is that all? You made it sound devastating. Tabs, you're the one who will be lost without her, not me. We both knew she'd be leaving eventually. Make me a cup, too."

Harriett winced. "Well Mother, I bought the Songer house. The big house on the hill."

The blood rushed to Olive's face. She spit the words, "Songer house?!" Her fist hit the table, bouncing the cups and spilling hot tea. "You bought MY house, the Songer house?!"

Tabs motioned for Harriett to leave the room.

"No, Papa, I'm staying. Yes, Mother, I bought the house on the hill. But it was never your house. The Songer children wanted a quick sale. I have enough saved for a down payment, and the bank approved my mortgage. I sign the closing papers next Friday. Please be happy for me. It's bad enough that I have to do this alone, without my husband…"

"Without your husband! Has that no-good cad written to you yet? Yes, I know, Missy, that it's been months since his last letter. Looks like he married you and dumped you after he got what he wanted on the honeymoon."

The tears began flowing from Harriett's eyes again. "No, he hasn't written. And I'm devastated about it. But if I want this house, I need to move now. So, I'm doing it alone."

Olive flushed red. "No one thought to tell me that the house was for sale? I've waited my entire life for that place, and you scoop it away without me even knowing it was on the market! You're despicable!"

Harriett moved toward her mother, as Tabs reached for Harriett's arm. "With Songer dead why wouldn't it be for sale? Would you actually move?" she asked. "This house is your pride and joy."

"Yes, I would move." Olive swept her hand across the table, sending teacups shattering to the floor. "I used to come to town every Christmas just to get a glimpse of it. I was supposed to be the town doctor, living on the hill!"

"But, Mother, you're not the town doctor, are you? The truth is, you're Mrs. Bailey, not Dr. Westchester."

"Get out now!" Olive screamed. "If you are leaving, then go now." She pointed to the door. "Take that hoity-toity car of yours and get out. You can get the rest of your belongings when I'm not home!"

Olive spun on her heel. Opening the door, she waved toward the car.

"Go! Are you deaf?"

"Papa?" Harriett pleaded.

"Janie, go stay with Alice tonight. I'll smooth this over with your mother. Grab some things for work and I'll see you tomorrow after class." Tabs kissed Harriett's face. "I'm sorry, sweetie."

∞ ∞ ∞

Alice balanced Polly on her hip as she answered the knock at the door. "Harriett?" she questioned, noticing the overnight bag at her sister's feet.

Harriett burst into gasping sobs. "Alice," she stammered. "May I stay here tonight? Mother kicked me out."

"She what?"

"She threw me out of the house because I bought the Songer place."

Alice shook her head. "Wait, when did you buy the Songer house? My, that's only two blocks away."

"I received my mortgage approval letter today. I can close on the house next Friday. Mother went spastic when she heard."

"Geez, come, come in. Sit down." Alice repositioned Polly. "Would you like a glass of water?"

"Yes, please. Hand her to me. I'll hold her; maybe that will cheer me." Harriett reached for her goddaughter. "Hi, little Polly. Your Aunt Harriett is going to live down the street. You can come play with your cousins…" Harriett sobbed harder.

"Goodness, now what's wrong?" Alice asked as she handed a tumbler to Harriett.

"Alice, I'm a mess…"

"I see that!"

"Oh! Goodness, I'm excited about the house, but…"

Alice sat beside Harriett and hugged her. "I know. It's Eddy."

"Yes." Harriett sighed. "I told Polly she could play with her cousins…she may never have cousins, if Eddy actually left me."

"Harriett. Seriously, think about what you just said." Alice swallowed. "You are young and beautiful, not to mention smart, educated, and financially independent. What man wouldn't want that in a wife?"

"I want them to love me for me, not my bank account!"

"Certainly, they would love you for you. But what you're missing is that you are not one-dimensional, like me."

Harriett ticked her tongue against her mouth. "Hush with that talk."

"No, I'm serious. I am blessed with a pretty face and a nice body, but that's it. You have that, *plus* all the extras that go along with it. You're the complete package." Alice waited for Harriett to calm down. "Now, is Mother's issue with you moving out? Or is it because the Songer house is her coveted property?"

Harriett managed a shallow grin. "Because it's the Songer house. She can care less about me. She actually threw that in Papa's face, that he'll miss me more than she will." A chortle escaped her mouth. "Well, Albert just made ten bucks."

"Okay, now I really don't follow you." Alice scratched her head and reached for Polly.

"Albert and I bet on how long it would take for Mother to revert to her true colors. I said she'd make it through the holidays. Wrong!" Both women giggled. "It was ten dollars well spent."

"That's better. You're too pretty to cry. Now let's get you something to eat before we make up the spare bedroom."

18

NEW DECOR

NOVEMBER 1951, SANTA CROCE, ITALY

*R*osa waddled to the breakfast table, her belly stretching the fabric of her dress. "Good morning Nonna and Nonno," she said as she yawned. "Goodness, how much bigger will I get before this football player decides to join us." She smiled as she rubbed her belly. "I think it's a boy. He's very active."

Isabella swallowed a sip of latte. "I think your time is near. Rosa, do you have any baby items—clothing, diapers, and such?" Isabella glanced at her granddaughter's bump. "We need to go shopping. I have a bassinet in the attic. I think we need to prepare the nursery now."

"Nonna," Rosa said. "I spent long hours in the cabin knitting and sewing clothes for this baby. Nonno, can you make a trip back to retrieve them?"

Giuseppe stood and walked to the buffet to refill his coffee cup. "I should go close the cabin for winter anyway. So yes, Rosa dear, I'll collect your handiwork."

Rosa pouted. "Thanks, Nonno. Does this mean I may no longer live there? What about Eddy?"

Isabella's eyes met her husband's. "Dear, we have not

solved the problem of a residence for you and the child. But that cabin is out of the question."

Rosa sobbed. "I'm so emotional these days—but I can't live without Eddy. Nonna, I just can't!" She grabbed a piece of warm bread, buttered it, and retreated to her room to cry alone.

That afternoon, Giuseppe Cortina made the drive to Predmeja. He nearly dropped over from shock when he entered the cabin. A shiny linoleum floor and wood-covered walls thwarted the autumn chill. Curtains hung from the window. A rocking chair and torché gas lamp, sitting next to the hearth, were flanked with a large woven basket, filled with a feather mattress to cradle the infant. A large armoire, on the other side of the hearth, housed Rosa's and Eddy's clothing. Inside, he found baby items neatly folded and stacked.

"Heavens! Who did this?" Giuseppe questioned.

He opened a narrow jelly cabinet next to the sink to find it completely stocked with canned goods and root vegetables. Firewood was piled high beside the rocker. A new iron double bed with a thick mattress filled the corner opposite the hearth. Two fluffy pillows topped a warm quilt. A crystal-shaded lamp sat atop a small bedside table, with a covered chamber pot beneath. A third gas lamp sat on the table.

"Someone invested a lot of time and money into this place." Giuseppe whistled. "Maybe that GI does love Rosa."

Giuseppe inspected the corners, floor, and window for drafts. Finding minimal airflow, he moved his inquiry outside. The pathway to the latrine outhouse was smoothed and roughly paved. Although gaps between the wood slats remained for airflow, a toilet seat with a lid was installed over the once open hole. A large mound of firewood, heaped on the side of the cabin, ensured at least a month of heat.

"This place is livable!" Giuseppe muttered out loud as he

made his way back inside to his original mission of baby clothes.

∞ ∞ ∞

Giuseppe walked into the parlor to find Isabella knitting and Rosa sulking.

"Rosa dear, will you give your grandmother and me some privacy? We need to discuss something."

Rosa pouted but stood and shuffled back to her bedroom, mumbling as she walked.

Giuseppe handed the baby items to Isabella. "She's been busy. Her stitching is very neat and uniform. And, wife, I think we're safe allowing her to remain at the cabin."

Isabella squeezed the items tightly against her chest. "Oh, Giuseppe. I can't! They'll both freeze. That place is no more than a barn."

Giuseppe grinned. "Not anymore. I believe that GI loves Rosa. The place has been *enhanced*."

Giuseppe described his findings to his wife, who sat with her mouth gaping wide. "Well, what do you think?" he asked. "Do we allow her to remain in the cabin?"

Isabella tilted her head back and rubbed her eyes. "Perhaps so. Let's call Rosa back and discuss this with her."

Rosa swayed her way to the settee and sat. She absentmindedly rubbed her belly.

"Rosa dear, how often does your GI visit you?" Isabella asked soothingly. The late afternoon shadows softened the ridges of her face, morphing inquisition to conversation.

Rosa smiled, thinking about Eddy. "He comes every other weekend and we spend three blissful days together."

The old couple exchanged smirks. "What do you do when he's not there?"

Rosa sighed, "It does get lonely, but I don't mind because

I'm counting the days until he returns. I spend my time knitting and sewing while I have light. I have candles for the evening, plus the firelight. I'm learning to cook." She giggled. "Can you imagine that? Me, cooking!"

Isabella nodded to Giuseppe. "Rosa," she said. "Is this young man that important to you?"

"Oh yes, Nonna, he's everything!" Her eyes sparkled.

Moving to his granddaughter, Giuseppe caressed the back of her head. "Well, he obviously cares about you. The cabin is transformed into a comfortable cottage. If you truly desire to live there, you may, as long as he marries you come spring."

Rosa cocked her head to the side. "Transformed?"

Giuseppe retold of the renovations.

Rosa listened intently, as the smile grew across her face. "Thank you, Nonna, thank you, Nonno. He does love me! This proves he'll marry me!" She felt a warm gush of liquid running down her leg. Looking down, she questioned, "Nonna, what is happening?"

"Giuseppe, please call the doctor." Isabella grinned. "We shall soon meet our first grandchild!"

19

THE MOVE

NOVEMBER 1951, CAMPBELLSVILLE

*H*arriett unlocked the front door. Before entering her new home, she turned to survey expansive vistas of the valley. The Conemaugh River meandered through town, its docile pre-winter silhouette threading through bare oaks and maples. Harriett thought back to the flood of 1936 when the water raged, and her father almost drowned trying to save his work crew.

Her footsteps echoed on the hardwood floors and bounced through the spacious empty house as she crossed the threshold. The entryway alone could hold half of her mother's first floor. A large carved staircase curved upwards; beckoning *come explore my treasures.* A crystal-studded chandelier came to life as she depressed a round wall button.

Alice gasped at the light dancing off the walls. "Wow! That's some light fixture. I wonder what other surprises await you?"

Harriett only smiled and continued walking across the sizable foyer to the kitchen, where she placed her box on the countertop. "Alice, most everything belongs in here," she called to her sister. "I promise an adventure later."

Gaping at the ceiling and walls, Alice bumped into the door jamb. "Ouch. Geez, Harriett, no wonder Mother had her eye on the house. This kitchen is gigantic. Needs a little updating, but you surely have enough space to do anything with it. That corner is perfect for your laundry/mudroom and a large pantry." Alice pointed to the far end of the kitchen. "Promise me I can help you decorate and remodel this place. Please! Promise." Alice sat her box on the floor. "This house is probably the closest thing in town to the mansion where Mother grew up."

Harriett smiled at her sister's request as she ran her hand over the cold metal countertops. "I'll decorate in due time, Alice. Give me a chance to make some money first." She paused. "I don't remember ever visiting the Westchester farm."

"Most likely, you didn't. Mother abandoned the Westchesters years ago. I was little when I visited, but the place is so big, it left an impression. She has pictures of it in the parlor —at least, it's in the background. I think it's her wedding picture."

Harriett headed toward the front door. "I'll look if I'm ever invited to return." She laughed.

Alice continued to gawk on her way back to the truck. "Harriett, do you own any furniture?" A delivery van parked behind Harriett's borrowed truck as Alice uttered the question. "I spoke too soon."

Rushing to greet the driver, Harriett motioned toward the second floor. The men lugged a double bed, dresser, mattress, box springs, two nightstands, mirror, and chest of drawers up the staircase as Harriett's watchful eye guarded the woodwork. The matching bedroom set, a sleek modern designed geometric concept from Heywood Wakefield, deviated from Harriett's more traditional style. The only adornment on the otherwise stark champagne-colored birch pieces was the raised square knobs centered on each drawer.

"Goodness, Harriett. You are full of surprises. This is more my style than yours."

Harriett giggled. "I plenty of space for any and every type of furniture in this place!"

Harriett searched the kitchen for the box labeled "bed linens" and traipsed up the stairs behind the delivery men. "Come on Alice. Up we go."

Alice grabbed a stack of clothing and followed. "Harriett, this room is huge! Is that a walk-in closet? Goodness. Where do you want these?" She surveyed the master bedroom. The grand room, wallpapered in a pale blue and green silk-screened leaf design, was large enough to hold a sofa, side tables, two oversized stuffed chairs, and lamps in addition to the bedroom suite.

"Hang them anywhere. I contemplated using one of the other bedrooms, saving this one for when Eddy returns, but…"

"Oh no. You chose correctly. This is your house; you deserve the biggest room. If the thought is purchasing a suite of furniture together, this can always be moved."

Pulling the tape from her box, Harriett asked, "Shall we make up the bed as soon as it's assembled?"

She tugged at the yellow floral spread. Giving it a good shake, she draped it over a nightstand.

Alice waited for Harriett to sign the paperwork and for the men to leave before commenting. "You may want a different bed covering. Something more sophisticated. The yellow flowers are cute, but no good in here." Alice walked to one of the two front windows and looked down the street. "Hey, Sis, do you have other deliveries today?"

Harriett frowned. "Nope. This is it. Albert is delivering

his kitchen table and chairs in a couple of days. He's buying a new, smaller set. I'll be eating off the floor until it comes."

Alice laughed. "That table always was too big for Albert's tiny kitchen. It will fit better in here, but you don't need a table for your egg salad sandwiches!" Alice tugged on two tangled hangers. "Then, if that's the case, I'll carry in more clothing while you fill the drawers. At least you'll have a bed to sleep on tonight."

The women worked diligently. Within the hour they moved downstairs to unpack more boxes. Harriett fingered the items before placing them on a shelf. "I don't remember most of these things. They're wedding presents. It's been a year, already."

Alice sighed as she unwrapped a crystal vase. "Well, when he comes home, he better be buying you roses every day for a year. They'll look beautiful in this!" She handed the vessel to Harriett.

Harriett strolled into the dining room. Built-in cabinets with glass upper doors flanked one entire wall. The other three walls were papered in what looked to be silk fabric, printed with cherry trees, full of blossoms. A second crystal chandelier hung from the center of the ten-foot-high ceiling.

"Someday," she called to Alice. "I'll own a big mahogany table with twelve chairs and a matching buffet sideboard. We'll hold all our family holiday meals in this room!"

Poking her head through the doorway, Alice laughed. "Then you better learn to cook, or you'll be catering every event."

Harriett placed the vase in the cabinet before throwing a piece of wrapping paper at her sister. "You're just down the street. You can bring the food!"

"Ha. Fair enough." Alice glanced at her wristwatch. "Geez, I better head home. Laurena Williams, my neighbor in the little house across the street, is watching Polly, and I have to make supper for Teddy." She headed toward the entryway to retrieve her coat. "Harriett, why don't you join us tonight? Meet Laurena. She's a free-spirited independent woman like you."

"Thanks, Alice, but no. I'll boil a couple of eggs. I'm at least good at that."

∞ ∞ ∞

Harriett rubbed her arms to shake the chill. She never thought to check her thermostat earlier. Moving and lifting kept her warm. Harriett flicked the light switch and proceeded into the basement, flashlight in hand. Instead of a monstrous coal burner, she found a medium-sized box gas-fueled unit. Harriett shone her light on different sections before finding a door labeled "pilot light." Nothing. No flame, no instruction.

I guess I'll layer with blankets tonight and check the furnace tomorrow.

After replacing the covering, Harriett moved from the basement to the bedroom. She lay down on her new mattress.

Goodness, this is much more comfortable than the one at home. I'll be super productive with a good night's sleep, she thought.

Unfolding a fitted sheet, she slipped the corners around the mattress. After tucking in the bottom of a flat sheet and slipping pillows into cases, she sprayed it with a solution of lavender water. Her only chore left was to find her woolen blanket and top it off with the spread.

That should keep me warm enough.

Her thoughts were interrupted by a chime. Bounding down the front stairs, she flicked another switch and hoped her lightbulbs lit. She peered out the door to see Alice's husband.

"Teddy, what are you doing here?" Harriett motioned for him to enter.

"Alice sent a dinner plate. Said you couldn't possibly live on eggs alone." Teddy gazed at the large empty space. "Going to take a while to fill this place."

Harriett inhaled. "Mmm, that smells good. Ah—Teddy, may I ask a favor? I intended to ask for help, perhaps tomorrow, but you're here now."

"Sure, what do you need?"

"The pilot is out on the furnace, and I don't know if I can simply light it or if I need to throw a lever first."

Teddy unwound his scarf and removed his hat. "Absolutely. Come with me, and I'll show you how."

"I'm right behind you. I may have more than I can handle with this house."

Teddy shook his head. "Nonsense. You'll catch on quickly. Between Darrell, David, Albert, and me, we'll teach you everything you need to know."

"Papa is retiring soon." Harriett grinned. "I'll enlist his help, too!"

The tutorial complete, Harriett was instructed on the workings of a modern gas furnace. The blower turned on, and warm air was forced through the registers.

"Okay, Harriett, you're all set and should be warm by bedtime. Alice will be furious that you didn't eat while your food was still hot!"

"I'll not tell her, so she'll never know. Thanks, Teddy." Harriett kissed her brother-in-law on the cheek. "I don't know what I'd do without my family."

∞ ∞ ∞

After three intense years of work and school without a break, Harriett capitalized on her professor canceling class by scheduling her first week of vacation. The industrious woman had transitioned immediately from high school to secretarial college, where she graduated early with an associate degree to begin working. She then pursued her bachelor's degree, all while working full time. Time off was long overdue.

She awoke the following day after a deep, dreamless sleep. Stretching her arms, she yawned and cuddled back into her pillows.

Just ten more minutes, she thought.

Five minutes later, she was in the bathroom searching through a box for her grooming supplies. She unpacked, filling the shelves of the built-in medicine cabinet before brushing her teeth. Back in the bedroom, she dressed in old slacks and blouse, patched leftovers from her high school days. Making her way to the kitchen, she surveyed the large empty house.

I really should buy at least a stuffed chair, or maybe a desk.

She filled her new kettle with water and turned the knob on the gas stove. A flame appeared instantaneously.

Mother really needs to get rid of that old coal stove, she thought.

Before she could pour milk on her bowl of cereal, she heard the doorbell chime.

Cup in hand, she answered the door. "Earl, this is a surprise. Come in."

Eddy's brother, Earl, smiled. "Good morning. I can't stay, I'm on my way to work, but there is something that I wanted to mention to you."

"Sure—can you at least have some tea?"

He nodded. "A quick one."

They walked into the kitchen. Harriett offered him a cup, then looked around, laughing. "I do have a table coming, but it looks like I can't offer you a seat. Oh wait—there's a window seat in the study. No cushion yet, but let's talk there."

She led the way to a dark wood-paneled room off the main hallway. A large fireplace, surrounded by Delft tile boasting an overbearing mantle, was flanked on both sides with empty bookcases. A bare seat fronted the large, double, floor-to-ceiling window, adorned with wooden mullions that overlooked the side terrace and street.

Earl whistled. "Goodness Harriett, this is some house. What are you going to do with all this space?"

Harriett frowned. "I hope to fill it with lots of little Keplers, but...what's on your mind today?"

Earl looked out the window before meeting her eyes. "I'm worried about you living alone in this mansion. I think you need a phone, just in case. Using my employee discount, I can get you a private line at the same price as a party-line. What do you think? Can I put in the order today?"

Harriett tilted her head to the side. "That's probably a good idea. There's so much I don't yet know about owning a house. Are you sure it's the same cost as a party line? I don't mind sharing, and I really need to watch my money."

He nodded. "Definitely. So...if I can ask, what did you end up paying for this place?" Earl felt the blood rushing to his face as soon as he uttered the question.

Harriett returned the blush. "Ten thousand dollars. Twenty percent down. Can you imagine! I can't believe it's mine."

Earl sucked air through his front teeth. "I can see why you're watching your pennies."

"For the mortgage, plus..." Harriett motioned with her hand. "I really need a couple of pieces of furniture."

"Ah, at least one or two." Earl chuckled and stood. "Then I'll place the order today. You'll have a phone by Friday." He leaned over and kissed her forehead. "I feel better already."

Harriett walked Earl out, then returned to the kitchen and the remaining pile of moving items. She grabbed a broom, dustpan, bucket, and mop, then headed toward the front living room. By noon she worked her way through the parlor, entrance hallway, and dining room, the front third of the first floor. The wood floors, walls, and windowsills sparkled. After throwing several eggs on the stove to boil, she collapsed onto the floor. She closed her eyes, allowing her mind to drift into Limbo. Hearing the water bubble too soon, she exhaled a long groan then stood. Removing the saucepan from the flame to allow the eggs to cook in hot water, she rubbed her back then headed up the back staircase to explore the second floor.

The steps emptied into a small room, presumably a servant's room, due to the set of labeled chimes.

Heavens, what did I get myself into?

She opened the door to find a closed door and another staircase leading up.

That's for another day.

She shook her head, walking down a long hallway to the curving front stairs she descended.

Her stomach growled, reminding her that eggs awaited her on the stove and a bowl of uneaten cereal was getting stale on the countertop.

Must eat for strength!

She intended to clean for two days, then explore nearby secondhand shops for a few essential furniture items. Her budget was already stretched too thin to allow for anything new. The butler's pantry and study were next on her list to tackle. She repositioned the borrowed step ladder and began scrubbing the wooden walls, using a brush to clean the crevices of the carved moldings. Scouring architectural details consumed the afternoon. At six, she found herself back on the kitchen floor, eyes closed, rubbing her back.

A loud moan escaped her lips as the door chimes sounded again. *Harriett, you never had visitors at home; this place is like a bus stop.* Rolling over, she jumped to her feet.

"Teddy?"

He handed her a foil-covered plate. "You better eat this hot tonight. Alice will kill me if you don't."

Harriett forced a smile. "Teddy, I'd offer you some refreshment, but I have nowhere to sit. Is it okay if I take the food and say goodnight? I'm exhausted."

His hand moved forward. "Of course. Before I go, would you be interested in my stuffed leather armchair? Alice says that it's too big and clunky. It 'doesn't fit the sleek modern décor of the rest of the house.' I have to discard it, whether or not you take it."

Harriett ran her fingers through her hair. "I would love to. How much do you want?"

"Nothing. Don't be silly. I was going to put it out for the trashman. Shall I bring it later tonight, or tomorrow?"

Harriett grunted. "Ugh." She rubbed her neck. "Tonight. Tomorrow, I may be dead."

A loud guffaw escaped Teddy's lips. "Little Harriett, your muscles aren't used to such strenuous exercise. But knowing your past fitness routine, you'll be back in shape in no time." Halfway down the steps, he called, "I'll be back in thirty minutes, and I expect a clean plate in return for the chair."

"It's a deal. Please thank Alice for me!"

20

BAPTISM

DECEMBER 1951, TRIESTE, ITALY

*E*ddy continued to make his twice-monthly visits to the cabin in Predmeja, capitalizing on the opportunity to continue enhancing the décor, chopping wood, and stocking shelves. His entire paycheck was dedicated to making Rosa's life more comfortable. Wally, always at his side, offered suggestions and hints. Eddy remained uncreative when it came to a young girl's needs.

In mid-December, the friends sauntered into the mess hall upon their return to the base.

Eddy piled his plate full of mashed potatoes and meat covered with gravy.

"I'm starving," he said as his stomach growled.

Behind in the chow line, Wally scooped a spoonful of sickly-looking pale green orbs. "I think these are brussels sprouts."

Eddy glanced at his friend. "Those look disgusting. I need *substantial* food!"

"Is that what Rosa feeds you?" Wally chuckled.

Frowning, Eddy piled limp carrots on top of the mountain of potatoes and gravy. "Shut up about Rosa. I haven't seen her in two and a half months, and she doesn't write. I'm afraid we did all this work for nothing. The baby should be here by now, but her grandmother hasn't written yet."

"That's odd. But again, Eddy, you may have an out." Wally tossed wilted lettuce onto his tray. "You're one of the luckiest SOBs I've ever met!"

Eddy walked to a table, sat, and shoveled food into his mouth. "Yea, I may have another out, but I still wish I knew the sex of that baby," he said with a mouthful of food.

As they talked, a private approached. "Corporal Kepler. Corporal Eddy Kepler?" he called.

Eddy raised his hand. "That's me, Private. What do you need?"

The private screwed his lips together. "Ah—Corporal, I can't explain it, but I found these three letters addressed to you under a stack of papers in Sergeant Hill's office. Ah, I'm the sergeant's clerk. Don't know why they were there, but I figured I should get them to you ASAP."

Eddy took the envelopes from the private. "Thanks, Buddy." He waited until he was out of earshot. "That son-of-a -bitch. Hill did this on purpose!"

Wally spread his lips revealing clenched teeth. "Probably did. What's the return address, Santa Croce? Do you get other mail?"

"Yeah, yeah. Harriett writes every week. She bought a house, so I get an update on her latest purchase or cleaning episode every week. I couldn't care less." Eddy swung his arm in dismissal.

Wally pursed his mouth and blew out a gust of air. "Geez, that's harsh. She *is* your wife."

"I know, I know. Maybe I feel just a little bit guilty. Maybe I'm just worried about Rosa."

"Then open your letters. Find out what's going on." Wally waited for Eddy.

Eddy pushed his tray to the side. Opening the oldest first, he read.

Corporal Kepler,
    You have a son.

Tears filled Eddy's eyes. He looked up from the correspondence. "Wally, she had a boy. I have a little baby boy."

Wally grinned. "Congrats, my friend. Everyone healthy? What else does it say?"

Eddy read on.

Rosa gave birth on the twelfth of November to a healthy, eight-pound baby boy. Mother and child are fine, but missing you. My husband discovered the improvements made to the cabin. We assume you made them for Rosa. We would not have permitted her to take a child there to live for the winter; however, in light of your enhancements, we have agreed to allow her to stay after his Christening, provided your interest in this relationship continues. I know that you are married. Please know that Rosa is madly in love with both you and your son. I shall write informing you of his baptism as soon as the arrangements are made.

    Sincerely,
    Isabella Cortina

The second letter was dated a week later.

Dear Corporal,
    Rosa had hoped for a return letter. Receiving none, I fear your interest in my granddaughter is over now that responsibility is involved. This letter is to inform you of the baby's christening date. It is scheduled for Sunday, December sixteenth at five in the afternoon, at The Church of the

Blessed Heart. It's a small chapel located on the Strada Costiera, above the Castle Miramare. I believe you are familiar with the castle. Giovanni and Sofia Romano neither know of nor shall attend the baptism. You shall remain free from reproach from my husband and me. However, Rosa will be heartbroken if you are not there.

Cordially,

Isabella

The third letter contained only three lines.

The christening is Sunday at five. Rosa is devastated that you abandoned her. I'm sad to say, her father was correct.

Eddy folded the paper. Looking at his watch, he swore under his breath. "Wally, hurry. I have an hour to get there. Damn that Hill, I'll kill him!" Eddy barked, then shoveled several spoons of slop into his mouth and swallowed without chewing.

Heads turned toward the threat.

Wally grabbed Eddy's arm. "Get where? Slow down, what did that letter say?"

Eddy hurriedly dumped his food in the trash. He called to Wally as he headed for the door. "Change into your dress uniform. I need you to be a godfather. Hurry, get a jeep and pick me up in ten minutes."

Eddy was dressed and waiting for Wally within ten minutes. The spit shine of his shoes reflected a frown as he stood in front of his barracks. Five minutes later, Wally arrived, driving an open-top jeep.

Eddy glanced at his wristwatch as he climbed into the vehicle. "What took you so long?"

"I was only gone fifteen minutes. Lighten up. You demand

too much from friendship!" Wally shifted and sped toward the front gates.

The jeep headed west toward the port and center of town, then turned north onto Viale Miramare, traveling along the coastline toward the Hapsburg Castle. The green-blue waters of the Adriatic glistened in the late afternoon sun. A light breeze blew from the east.

"I love it here," mumbled Eddy as he stared at his watch.

Sensing Eddy's agitation. Wally depressed the gas.

"Woah, slow down, Buddy." Eddy grabbed hold of the door. "Up ahead the road forks, go right. If you go left, you'll end up at the castle."

Wally eased off the gas and shifted into third gear. "How do you know so much about this road?"

Eddy blushed as he pointed to the approaching turn. "Rosa and I rendezvoused at Castle Miramare many nights." He chuckled. "That's probably where she got pregnant." He pointed to the sign indicating the split. "Take Strada Costiera, there."

The jeep veered right as the road turned inland, away from the coastline. The Church of the Blessed Heart was several miles up the road on the left. Wally parked as the church bell chimed five times.

The men entered the sanctuary. Rosa, Isabella, and Giuseppe stood before the priest, who removed the covering from the baptismal font. Four heads turned as the men entered. Walking down the center aisle, Eddy wiggled in beside a beaming Rosa.

Her face glowed as Eddy slipped his arm around her. "You came!" she whispered.

Isabella squeezed her husband's hand. "Thank God!" She made the sign of the cross.

"Of course, I came. I just found out, but I'll explain later." Eddy leaned over to peak at the baby.

Rosa lifted the blanket uncovering his face. "Meet your son. He looks just like you." She caressed his head. "This is your Daddy."

The round head, with a tuft of curly blond hair peeking out the front, was covered with a lace bonnet. His eyes fluttered open, then shut immediately.

Tears flowed freely from Eddy's eyes. He kissed Rosa on the cheek as the priest's arms crossed in front of him, patiently waiting to begin the christening.

"Are we ready now?" asked the clergyman.

"*Si.* So sorry, *Padre.* We are ready," said Rosa. Eddy stood crying, shaking his head.

"What name in Christ do you give this child?" asked the priest.

Rosa looked at Eddy, then at her grandfather. "I name my son Joseph Edgar Kepler. Is that okay, Eddy?"

Eddy touched the soft skin of the baby's face, who cooed with the caress. Eddy was in love for the second time in his life. "Yes, darling, that is perfect. Everything is absolutely perfect!"

BLOW BY BLOW

*E*ddy burst through the door of the outer office. Sergeant Hill looked up from the anterior room.

"Private, what is all the commotion?" Hill yelled to the stunned clerk, who stood watching for Eddy's next move.

Red-faced, his fists squeezed into tight balls, Eddy bellowed, "Hill, come out here, you bastard!"

The private stepped into Eddy's path. "Corporal, I'm sorry, but Sergeant Hill is currently occupied."

"Hill!" Eddy pushed the private aside. "I'm coming after you."

Hill moved to the door's threshold. "Let him pass, Private. I want to hear what this piece of crap is screaming about."

Eddy confronted Hill, chest to chest, nose to nose. "Why the hell did you hide my mail, you pile of shit?" Eddy pushed Hill backward.

Hill reached out and grabbed Eddy by the shirt to keep himself from falling. "What are you talking about, Kepler?"

"My letters." Spittle splashed Hill in the face. "I've been worried sick about her. Do you know what it's like not knowing? I didn't hear a word for over six weeks. I was crazy, out-of-my-mind sick, you asshole."

Hill smirked. "You don't deserve her, Kepler! She should be *my* woman, not yours. You already have a wife in the states. You don't deserve Rosa!" The blood rushed up Hill's neck.

"You're jealous?" Teeth clenched; Eddy wound his arm and punched Hill in the jaw.

Hill flew backward. He lifted his leg as he fell. The heel of his boot connected with Eddy's groin; the rigid sole compressed soft flesh. Eddy went down, groaning and grabbing his body, then vomited as he collapsed to the floor. Two MPs barged in to find both men prostrate.

"Sergeant Hill," the MP asked. "Are you okay? Shall we arrest the corporal?"

Hill rubbed his chin, laughing. "Hell, I have a glass jaw! Not today. This is off the record, between Kepler and me. Personal matter. You're dismissed."

The MPs glanced at each other knowingly, trying to hide their smirks as they exited.

Eddy, a crumpled mass of pain, rolled onto his side into a fetal position. Hill kicked his rump. "Kepler, get up and get out of here. And stay away from Rosa. Next time, I won't be so generous!"

The stars disappeared, and Eddy's head stopped spinning. Looking up at Hill, he grinned.

"Joke's on you. She had my baby; I have a son. I'm going to marry her. Your loss, Sergeant Hill!"

The knowledge of Rosa bearing Eddy's child was more lethal than the blow to the chin. Hill gasped, the air knocked out of him. He was rendered helpless, sinking into his chair. He watched Eddy climb to his feet to slowly hobble out.

22

WE THREE

DECEMBER 1951, SANTA CROCE, ITALY

*R*osa sat quietly in the back seat, bouncing a sleeping Joey on her lap. The baby stirred to the sound of a honking horn but quickly drifted off, secure in his mother's arms.

"Nonna." Rosa leaned toward Isabella Cortina. "Thank you again. Do you think Eddy will be waiting for us?"

"Granddaughter, if he's not at the cabin, that means he has no intention of marriage and you are returning home with us. I shall not permit you to winter alone up there with a newborn. This may be the last time our little car can make the trip until spring."

"But we have lots of supplies in the boot. Surely they will take me through spring."

Isabella frowned. "You are young, naïve, and in love. I do not wish to ruin your homecoming, but dear…"

Rosa rolled her eyes. Sitting back into the seat, she began singing to the sleeping infant. "Daddy loves you. Daddy loves me. How happy we'll be, just we three."

The car wheels sputtered and spun over loose rocks as they climbed to the plateau at the base of the mountain. Rosa peered dreamily out the window. Her heart jumped as the cabin and Eddy came into view.

"Nonna, he's here." Her voice was barely a whisper.

The back door of the car swung open as Giuseppe shifted into park. Eddy ran to Rosa, embracing the girl as he stroked the head of the tiny creature in her arms.

"It's only been a week, but he's grown so big!" Eddy's voice filled with awe. "I can't believe we made him."

Giuseppe cleared his throat. "Sorry to interrupt this moment, but I have a car to unload, and I need to get back to the city before dark."

Eddy reached for a box of jars.

"Corporal," Giuseppe said, "may I have your pledge that you'll care for Rosa and Joey? Marry her come spring. Otherwise, they are not staying."

Eddy glared at Giuseppe. "I am offended to be asked that question! Of course, I will. They are my responsibility, and I'll see to their well-being. I already consider her my wife. Bet on that, old man!"

Eddy emptied the rest of the cargo without a word. With the last bag in his arm, he slammed the trunk shut. "I'm done, and I want some time with my bride if you don't mind. Time to head home!"

Rosa's head moved from Giuseppe to Isabella. Her eyes filled with tears as she hugged her grandmother.

"Nonna, I love you. Thank you for taking care of me." She kissed her cheek.

Isabella reached for Joey. "Let me hold him one last time. Next time I see him, he'll be so big! These winters can be long and hard, dear; please be careful and be safe. I love you too."

After handing the baby back, both Giuseppe and Isabella stood beside the car, unwilling to depart, staring at their young granddaughter and great-grandson. Finally, after several long minutes, Giuseppe broke the spell.

"Come, Isabella, it's time."

∞ ∞ ∞

Eddy cut boughs of pine from the forest and placed them in a vase. A warm holiday atmosphere was created by the scent of crackling burning wood mixed with the fresh pine cuttings. Rosa hummed *Venite Fedeli* as she changed Joey's diaper.

A whiff drifted to Eddy's nose. "Yikes! How does someone so tiny make such a big smell?"

Rosa giggled as she deposited the soiled diaper into a covered pail. She waved her hand to placate Eddy. "He's too small to be stinky. I'll take this out in the morning. It's too cold to switch out the water tonight."

"Don't worry. I'll do it in a minute. Right now, I want you to come over here. Sit beside me on the bed."

"Eddy!"

"No, not that, though it's not a bad idea." Eddy grunted as he patted the quilt. "Here. I won't be back until after Christmas. Tonight is our Christmas eve."

With Joey safely tucked into his basket crib, Rosa rested her head on Eddy's shoulder. "Are you sure you can't come back next weekend?" She circled his lips with her finger.

Frowning, nose scrunched, Eddy answered, "No. My deal is every other weekend, just like before." He reached into his pocket and pulled out a fabric pouch. "Here, Rosa. Merry Christmas, darling."

Rosa untied the top and turned the pouch over to dispense a modest strand of graduated-sized pearls. The necklace fell onto the colorful quilt.

"I know they're not the beautiful big pearls given to you

by your parents, but they're the best I can do right now." He clasped them around her neck. "You are so beautiful, my darling. I'll love you till the day I die!"

Rosa fingered the pearls as Eddy's lips tenderly caressed hers.

"Eddy. This strand means more to me than any gift from my father. I'll treasure them forever." She reached under the bed. "Here, I have something for you, too. Merry Christmas, love."

Eddy untied the string to reveal a woolen scarf, which he held in the air. "This will come in handy. Did you knit this yourself?"

"Of course, silly. I'm no longer the spoiled little girl from Trieste. Merry Christmas, my husband." She snuggled into his shoulder before falling asleep.

Softly, Eddy kissed her forehead. "Merry Christmas, my darling wife."

23

RETREAT TO HIGHER GROUND

DECEMBER 1951, CAMPBELLSVILLE

*N*ovember winds lost their sting to the anticipation of holiday fun. Although sparsely furnished, Harriett's large home would easily accommodate the entire family celebrating Tabs' retirement. And with everyone bringing a chair, she'd have plenty of seating.

Harriett fussed over the final preparations, then walked into her office, admiring the newly purchased, large, mahogany desk, Teddy's old stuffed leather chair, and a floor lamp. It was her only real furniture besides her bedroom suite. Looking out from the window seat, she spied Toby, Heddy, Lloly, and Susie strolling up the front steps. The scent of pine accosted her as she rushed past the living room to the outer vestibule and front door.

"Come in! Goodness, you children grow taller every time I see you. Where's Violet?"

She reached to take their coats, forcing them to deposit their treasures on the floor. She hung coats and scarves on a hall tree, a remnant from the Songers, then ushered them through the second set of doors and into the foyer.

"Mommy didn't want Violet to get in the way," Toby said as he gawked at the house.

Harriett frowned, retrieving discarded packages. "Oh, that's too bad. She's such a sweetie!"

"Aunt Harriett, I can see my reflection in the wood!" Toby said as he gazed up the grand staircase. "The ceiling even shines."

"Well, the chandelier helps to make the ceiling shine."

Harriett glanced at the pale, blue, crystal fixture. Faceted Austrian hand-cut glass teardrops reflected the light of six bulbs. Matching sconces flanked the entrance to the parlor on the left and the dining room on the right.

"What is all of this? Come, help me carry it into the kitchen."

The children followed Harriett. Toby placed his bowl on the chrome yellow table and sat on one of the six matching chairs. The set unsuccessfully filled the center of the spacious area.

"Heddy has potato salad, Aunt Harriett. I carried the fried chicken." Lloly and Susie set their containers on the table beside the bowl.

Harriett ruffled a thick tuft of hair on the top of Toby's head. "You look more and more like your namesake every day! Thanks for helping me."

"Sure thing, Aunt Harriett," said Heddy, swinging her legs back and forth.

"This is a fun day out for us," Lloly chimed in.

Susie smiled shyly as she sat, admiring her cousin.

Heddy reached inside a shopping bag that hung around her wrist. "We brought colored paper. Momma said you'd at least have scissors and glue. But if you don't have glue, Aunt Harriett, we can make it out of flour and water!"

Harriett chuckled as she opened a cabinet drawer to remove three pairs of scissors and two bottles of rubber cement. "Your mother said that, did she? She's assuming a lot. Yes, children, I am somewhat prepared. I may not own tree decorations, at least not yet, but I have glue for you to use."

Toby rose from the table. "Where is the tree, Aunt Harriett? If it's big, we should probably get started."

Harriett grabbed a plate of cookies and motioned to the center hallway. "In the front room. Follow me."

The five entered the living room to find a nine-foot-tall spruce tree centered in the front window, standing in a washtub filled with water. Several strands of lights glowed in multi-colors.

Lloly inhaled. "Gosh! I've never seen a tree so big. We'll be cutting and pasting all day!"

The children plopped down on the floor, spreading their bodies and supplies. Harriett handed them the scissors, glue, and a ruler, then sat on the floor with them.

"Susie, watch how I'm making lines." Harriett placed the ruler on the paper and drew across the edge. "Do you think you can draw lines every one inch across the paper? I know this is, shall we say, a *casual* tree, but I would like things to be uniform."

"Sure, Aunt Harriett. I'm nine, not a baby like Violet. I'll line, Lloly can cut, and Toby and Heddy can glue." Susie scrutinized the tree. "Aunt Harriett, do you have a star of Bethlehem for the top of the tree?"

Hands on hips, Harriett hummed. "Gee. I should probably buy one, shouldn't I?"

"A tree that big needs a star, don't you agree, Toby?" Susie smiled at her older cousin.

"Well, I guess so. But that's for Aunt Harriett to decide. We better get started on our paper chain!"

"Splendid, then I'll let you alone to work. If you need me, just call. I'll be around someplace." Harriett smiled lovingly at the industrious nieces and nephews. Jumping up in one move, she walked back into the kitchen. She busied herself refrigerating the food before attacking her list of chores, primarily the cursory last-minute cleaning.

Harriett listened to the distant chatter and giggles of the children working diligently. Around noon, she peeked into the room. Lloly lay on his back looking at the ceiling, legs arched, as he glued strips of paper together into a chain that reached to the entrance and back.

Stepping over their creation, she announced lunch. "Kids, let's head back to the kitchen for a snack."

Fourteen-year-old Toby's stomach growled in response. "I'm hungry," he said as he jumped up.

In the kitchen, five plates awaited them. "Take any seat," Harriett said as she placed a tray of peanut butter, banana, and grape jelly sandwiches onto the table. Toby grabbed two halves and began chewing.

"Is this Grandma Olive's jelly?" he asked as purple oozed down his chin.

"Sort of. The grapes are from her vine, but Aunt Alice made the jelly. Grandma Olive doesn't cook much." The tea kettle whistled, calling Harriett. She returned with a tray filled with mugs of hot cocoa mounded high with miniature marshmallows.

Susie squealed. "Aunt Harriett, can I come back tomorrow? You're the best cook ever!"

Harriett chuckled. "Sweetie, you're probably the first and last person to call me a good cook. Be careful; the cocoa is hot."

Harriett left the children to finish eating while she inspected their morning handiwork. Twenty feet of paper garland curled around the parlor. Harriett dragged it up a step ladder and began draping. It stopped halfway down the tree.

"Kiddos, we need a lot more chain. I think I picked too big a tree."

Heddy gasped. "Oh no, Aunt Harriett. It's a perfect tree. I can show you how to make lacy ornaments out of string. Do you have string? I can make lacy snowflakes by winding string around straight pins. If you paint them with glue, they'll hold their shape."

"No, honey. I don't."

"How about white thread? We'll need to wrap them double, but the thread will work."

"Sorry, honey. No thread either." Harriett scrunched her mouth to the side as she searched a drawer filled with odds and ends.

"Hmm. Then let me look in your sewing box. I'm sure you have something we can use."

Her belly shook in laughter. "Heddy, I don't own a sewing box."

"That's impossible." Heddy's hands flew to her hips. "Every woman owns a sewing box! Even I have my own sewing box."

"I guess I'm different. We'll have to make do with garland. I was going to bake some cookies this afternoon, but why don't I help you instead?"

Susie jumped up and down. "Goodie! Sit by me, Aunt Harriett."

Harriett squatted on the floor. "Shall we sing some carols while we work?"

Heddy scanned the room, searching the empty walls and corners in vain. "So, if you don't have a sewing box, I'm guessing you don't have a record player either."

"That would be affirmative. We don't need music to sing. Pretend we're on a horse-drawn sleigh riding over the countryside."

She made sounds of ringing bells and cracking whips. The children giggled.

Lloly crawled to Harriett's other side. "I'll start, Aunt Harriett. Dashing through the snow…"

∞ ∞ ∞

The next morning, Harriett ironed a borrowed red table-cloth. She smoothed it over the makeshift table of plywood resting on top of sawhorses set up in the dining room. *Someday*, she thought. *Eddy and I will own proper furniture.* She filled a vase with pine and holly cuttings from her back garden and placed it in the middle. The Timex on her wrist indicated thirty minutes until her sisters' arrival. She hurried back into the kitchen to begin filling the borrowed platters and trays.

The knock at the front door came too soon. Wiping her hands on her apron, she hurried to greet much-needed help. She hugged Esther, Toby, and Heddy, then beckoned them in.

Esther pulled Harriett aside to whisper. "I don't know what you did, but all those kids talked about last night was Aunt Harriett this, and Aunt Harriett that. You sure charmed them."

"Well, I'm a lot closer to their age than you, Sis. It wasn't a stretch to get into their minds."

"Heddy," Esther addressed her second-born. "Don't you have something for your aunt?"

Heddy grinned ear to ear as she handed Harriett a brown bag. "I worked late last night, Aunt Harriett."

"What do we have here?" Harriett surveyed the bag's contents.

Heddy blushed. "I made you some lace decorations."

"Oh!" Harriett removed one of the intricate string creations. "They're beautiful. Why don't you and Toby hang

164

them on the tree while your mother and I work? But mind you, do not climb on the ladder." They skipped into the living room to begin a sibling discussion concerning strategic tree placement of the new adornments.

Esther and Harriett worked, filling the table. Thirty minutes later, Alice, Teddy, and Polly knocked, followed by David, June and Susie, Darrell, and Violet, and finally Tabs. Olive was dragged up the stairs, under protest.

"Papa! Happy birthday and happy retirement!" Harriett threw her arms around her father's neck. "Where does the time go? You can't possibly be turning sixty-two!"

"Janie, darling, my leg tells me every day that I lived every second of those sixty-some years!" Tabs scanned the group. "Where's Albert?"

Olive harumphed as she scowled, looking around the house, then at Harriett.

Albert burst through the door, followed by Laurena Williams. "Sorry I'm late. You remember Laurena don't you?" he asked as Alice's young neighbor blushed bright red.

Alice greeted Laurena. "This is a surprise." Turning to her brother, Alice punched his arm. "What are you up to, brother? Keeping secrets from me? I didn't realize you were dating anyone."

"Ouch." Albert grinned sheepishly. "I met Laurena at your baby shower, sis. By the way, I'm twenty-six. Old enough to date!"

Olive turned her attention from the carved wood trim of the entranceway to conversation.

"Albert, you're like your father—starting late. Laurena, how old are you?"

A cacophony of gasps escaped. "Mother!" Alice defended her friend and brother. "That's none of your business."

"I say it is my business if she's dating my son." Olive

moved closer to Laurena, whose wide eyes pleaded with Albert for help.

Albert pursed his lips. His gaze was intent on his mother's eyes. "Mother, you couldn't be further from the truth. You lost control of me the day you pushed me into enlisting." Albert reached for Laurena's hand. "Come on, Laurie, let's help in the kitchen. This is Papa's party, not hers."

Tabs' cousin Wyeth arrived moments later, as well as non-family guests such as Campbellsville's mayor, Doc Ralph Paulson Jr., and Dante Lupinetti and his wife. Benny and Ingrid Westchester joined soon after, as well as Esther's in-laws and Earl Kepler and his mother, Abigail. At the same time, Olive sulked and snooped through the house, checking out each corner and molding for dust. Harriett tried to ignore her mother's probing exploration, but she knew Olive was judging every inch of the coveted house.

Harriett greeted her guests, ushered them into the dining room and then into the living room as they carried plates full of food. Her neck glowed red as she offered seats on folding camp stools and lawn chairs. Four oversized Adirondack chairs from Tabs' garden were the only comfortable seating.

Once they were all assembled, eating, and chatting, Harriett addressed the group. "May I have your attention, please?" Voices hushed. "We are celebrating, today, the birthday and retirement of the most important man in my life." Albert and Alice glanced at each other as Harriett continued. "Tobias Bailey is retiring from the Campbellsville Spring Company on his sixty-second birthday. This is a huge loss for the business, but an equally huge gain for his family. We now have the pleasure of his company all day, every day."

Heads turned toward Olive as she let out a loud groan. "Good god."

Harriett continued. "Mother may not be happy, but I know that I speak for the rest of us when I say we are thrilled

166

to have Papa all to ourselves." She glared at her mother. "I, for one, can use a hand." She waved her arm around the room as the crowd chuckled. "So today, let's celebrate this special man, his work, and his life!" She raised her glass high. "To Tobias Bailey, my Papa!"

"To Tabs."

"Congratulations!"

"Bravo to a life well spent!"

The crowd cheered as Albert began singing "For He's a Jolly Good Fellow."

∞ ∞ ∞

The afternoon sped by quickly as the group filled their stomachs, offered congratulations, presented tokens, gave gifts, and pumped Tabs' arm with good wishes.

Wyeth Bailey was the last to leave. Harriett scooted around, collecting dirty dishes as she watched him shake Tabs' hand.

"Cousin, it's hard to believe all we've lived through. I don't blame you for going early. I'm out next year, as soon as I turn sixty-five."

Tabs slapped Wyeth on the back. "My leg won't last that long, with the war and the flood. Too many injuries to one spot. I must admit, Wyeth, I am sincerely sorry that our relationship is so distanced."

Wyeth grimaced. "Tabs, as much as I care for you, I feel equally strongly *against* your wife. Truthfully, I can't stand that woman. She was a precocious youngster but is downright intolerable as an adult." Wyeth waited for Tabs' response. "I'm sorry if I offend, but I can't pretend otherwise."

Tabs embraced his cousin and childhood companion. "No offense taken, Wyeth. She was a beauty. Too bad the personality never matched her looks." The entryway echoed with male laughter. "Despite all her faults, I love her."

Moments later, the door opened and closed.

Alone in the foyer, Tabs wandered into the kitchen, searching for Harriett. "Ah, there you are, Janie." He kissed his daughter on the cheek. "Thank you for such a wonderful party."

Harriett finished stacking dirty dishes in the sink before responding. She then hugged her father. "Papa, your entire life has centered around others. It was time for you to have one special day celebrating you."

Tabs wiped his eyes with the back of his hand, then turned on the hot water tap.

"Oh no, you're not helping with the clean-up! Alice is coming back later to help me. She went home to check on Polly, but she's returning."

Squeezing a squirt of Joy into the sink, Tabs ignored Harriett's objection by picking up a dishcloth. "Talk to me, Janie."

"Of course, Papa." Harriett stopped to screen her father's face. "What's on your mind?"

Tabs inhaled. "I love her, but I'm not sure I'll be able to handle your mother full time." He laughed. "I'm happy to retire. My leg is shot. But Olive, all day? I don't think even the good Lord can handle that!"

Harriett's lips sputtered. "I'll not give you an argument on that point. She's still furious with me. She barely spoke to me today. I think she came just to go on a private expedition of my house. I saw her descending the back stairs." She motioned to the staircase that emptied into the kitchen. "If she thought no one would see her, she's losing her mind."

Tabs winced.

"Papa, I didn't mean that she didn't want to celebrate you." Harriett exhaled and grabbed more dishes.

"I understand. But you're probably correct."

The pile of dirty glasses slowly declined as the pair worked and talked. Tabs inspected a cabinet door as he placed the glasses inside. "I was thinking, maybe I can help you get this place in shape. At least until Eddy returns."

Harriett frowned. "Papa, do you really think he's coming back?" She sniffed. "I'm ready to give up on him. We've been married for over two years and have not spent a Christmas together. I got a card from him last year, but he hasn't written since March."

"Janie, I don't know what to say. I feared you were making a mistake, that he would break your heart. But honey, it was your mistake to make, not mine." Tabs huffed. "Hell, I've made enough of my own errors in character."

Harriett threw her sponge into the soapy water and wrapped her arm around Tabs' neck. "Oh Papa. We're a pair, aren't we?"

"Cheer up, Janie." Tabs drew the edges of her mouth into a smile. "Why don't you make a list of chores and projects, and I'll spend my days fixing things for you while you work?" Tabs managed his own smile. "I'll be glad to see you more often, and to escape your mother."

"It's a deal. It won't be hard to keep you busy, especially come spring when I attack the gardens." Harriett sighed. Handing Tabs a house key, she said, "In the meantime, you can start by tightening that cabinet door you were inspecting."

∞ ∞ ∞

Christmas day was a madhouse, the whole family descending on June. Excited children ran wild. After helping clean up, Harriett excused herself, collected her gifts, and walked up the hill to her empty house. She deposited her presents under the tree, then opened each one for the first time, not wanting to take time away from the kiddos, earlier.

She chose the largest box to open first; the card read, *love The Clines*. Inside, Harriett found a stocked sewing basket, complete with dressmaker's shears, assorted colors of thread, cord, elastic, thimble, straight pins, and various other gadgets.

"Sweet girl, Heddy. Thanks for telling your mother that I'm hopeless."

Other boxes contained clothing items from her other siblings, all suitable for work. The last package was not in a box. A small rectangular block was covered in newsprint. *Papa*, she thought. Removing the wrapping revealed a hand-carved replica of her double front doors hanging on a string. On the transom was carved "1951."

"Oh Papa, my first real Christmas ornament." She clenched the ornament to her heart, then cried herself to sleep, lying on the floor in front of the tree.

24

AWOL

JANUARY 1952, PREDMEJA, YUGOSLAVIA

*T*he screeching of tires and a screaming voice pierced the frosty night air. Unexpected, scattered snowflakes filled a starless night, and a bora wind teased of a cold night and morning to follow.

The voice from the jeep yelled, "Eddy! Come on, let's go! We'll never make it back in time. We only have twenty minutes before lights out."

Standing in only his standard-issue boxers and t-shirt, broad shoulders and muscles exposed, Eddy looked around the cottage, full of the glowing warmth of the fire and the woman he loved. The entire contents of his footlocker were stuffed into his army duffel, which was thrown on the new double bed.

His eyes met those of the petite girl clearing their meager meal of polenta and dried pork from the center table. Her dress was clean, a tattered remnant of past prosperity. It was cinched at the waist with a shawl. Her long locks were piled loosely on top of her head; one wisp of jet black hair curled across her round face. She was beautiful. She tried to hold back her tears as she began sobbing.

She turned her head away. "Eddy, please get dressed. You must go. We don't need trouble." She sniffled.

"Wally, go. Head home without me!" Eddy bit his lip. The horn beeped three times. "Go now," Eddy yelled, "before I chicken out."

Eddy wrapped his arms around the weeping girl. Drawing her near, he kissed her tenderly.

"Shh, *amore mia*. I'm staying."

Rosa gasped, her misty eyes glowing. "Eddy, you can't, can you? We can make a good life for our little family, yes?"

Eddy released the girl and picked up the three-month-old infant, wrapped in a thin blanket. The baby cooed at his father's touch.

I'll be a good father for him, he thought.

Eddy kissed the child's forehead. "Rosa, you and little Joey are my family. I love you both so much." He whispered into her ear, "I'm never leaving again."

The horn honked. Eddy stuck his head through a slit in the open door. "No, Wally. I'm staying. Promise not to tell anyone where I am!"

At that moment, Eddy Kepler willingly abandoned his country, his unit, his wife, and all creature comforts to live in an Alpine cottage with Rosa Romano and baby Joey. The jeep sped away, leaving Eddy Kepler AWOL.

25

DAY ONE

*E*ddy stretched, rubbed his eyes, then reached for the bedside chamber pot. Rather than inhaling the smell of urine, he smelled freshly brewing coffee.

"Rosa, aren't you sleeping?" he asked the smiling woman stoking the fire.

"Good morning, sleepyhead. Joey and I have been up for several hours already. Didn't you hear him crying?" She shook her head in disbelief. "That boy wants his breakfast!"

"Like father, like son." Eddy patted the bed beside him. "Come back in here. I want to celebrate the first day of the rest of our lives together."

He flashed her a playful smirk, then rolled onto his back to expose a strategic bulge in the blanket.

"Oh my!" Rosa giggled when she made the anatomical connection. "Are you going to disrupt my morning routine every day?"

"You bet I am. Now come over here!"

∞ ∞ ∞

The couple lay entwined in each other's arms, both spent, while Joey slept, his belly filled.

Eddy finally broke the spell. Pulling on his trousers, he reached into his pocket to pull out his entire wad of cash: twenty dollars.

"Hmm. This isn't going to buy much." He frowned. "Rosa, I think I need to find a job. Are there any small towns close by?"

"Not where you can find work. But the train station is about five miles away. It's a tough walk in the winter, no clear path, but it's walkable." She pointed east. "You could catch the train to a larger city, closer to Ljubljana."

"Well, tomorrow, I'll search. Today, I luxuriate in your arms." He laughed. "I'll chop some extra wood too."

∞ ∞ ∞

The walk to the train station took Eddy a little over an hour. Although only four or five miles, the terrain was rocky, hilly, and without a trail. Eddy waited inside the small, two-room station house for the next train heading north.

"Hey buddy," he asked the station master. "How often does a train come to and from Ljubljana?

The man warily looked up from his desk and shook his head without answering.

Eddy tried again. "Do you speak English?"

Head down, the clerk grunted. "Not many words."

"Well, isn't that just perfect? How the hell am I supposed to communicate?" Eddy stared at a schedule written in Slovenian before kicking the wall. "Son of a bitch!"

A grin spread across the clerk's face.

Eddy's outstretched arms rested on the desktop. He leaned forward. "Why you bastard! You do speak English."

"Morning train leaves at five, evening train arrives at seven," he mumbled.

"Good God! Just two?"

"That's what I said." He proceeded to stamp a stack of waiting papers. "My English is perfect."

Eddy said, "I'll be back in the morning," only to be answered with another grunt.

He wandered another twenty minutes into a tiny town to find several cottages and a blacksmith. The smithy greeted Eddy with a blow of his hammer on metal.

"Buddy, is there any place around here to find work?" asked Eddy.

The hammer continued pounding.

Eddy considered his question. "Okay, I get it, but where can a fellow get work?"

His answer was echoing metal clashes of the swinging tool.

Retracing his step to the station, Eddy popped his head in the door. A familiar *thump, thump* greeted him as the station master glanced up.

"Yeah, it's me again. Where can I find work around here?"

"Godovic." A finger pointed northeast

"You have a train going to Godovic?"

"Five in the morning. Train to Ljubljana."

"Shit." Eddy turned toward home.

∞ ∞ ∞

"Rosa, it won't be every other week. I'll be home every weekend." Eddy pranced around the table, watching his weeping lover. "There's no way in hell that I'm getting up every morning at four, walking an hour to the train, riding another ninety minutes, working eight hours, to reverse the process to come home at eight every evening. I'm not doing it!"

"But Eddy, I'll be alone again, all week. I want to be *with* you." She wiped her nose on the back of her hand.

"As soon as I can afford a place for us to live, we'll move there together!" Eddy stomped his foot. "Rosa, I'm not trying to be difficult. I spent all my money fixing this place up for you. *For you*! That schedule, every day, is too much to ask of any man!"

"Oh, but you can ask *me* to stay here, all by myself, to look after your child!"

Eddy's face glowed red. "Rosa, don't fight with me. I know what's best for the three of us." He lowered his voice. "I promise to move you to Godovic as soon as possible, but that's not right now. Understood?"

Rosa sniffed as her sobs slowed. "Yes, Eddy. Understood, as long as you promise to be home every weekend."

Eddy glared at Rosa. "If I say it, I mean it!" Grabbing the diaper pail, he stomped out of the cottage to the outhouse.

26

HALF KILO

JANUARY 1952, GODOVIC, YUGOSLAVIA

*E*ddy trekked early the following morning to the train station. Boarding the five o'clock train to Ljubljana, he flopped into a lumpy seat; slumping forward, he fell immediately asleep. The screeching of air brakes and the conductor announcing in Italian and Slovenian, "Godovic, next stop Rovte" woke him, interrupting the jarring ride. Eddy managed to understand the word Godovic. He jumped up and raced to the door, sneaking through at the last minute.

The rural train station reminded Eddy of Campbellsville. It was the first time Eddy had thought of home in months. With a pang of guilt, he wondered how his mother was getting on now that his father was dead. He even thought about Harriett.

As much as I love Rosa, he thought, *Harriett's a better meal ticket.*

The narrow main street led him into the center of town. Godovic looked like any other tiny European village, with houses built up against each other and shuttered windows sporting empty flower boxes awaiting spring blooms. A channel ran through the middle of the sloped, narrow-cobbled street to carry away sewage and water.

He trekked through town looking at the variety of stores, stopping in front of a butcher shop. Peering inside, he saw a line of customers ten deep waiting to be served. Without hesitation, Eddy strolled behind the counter, washed his hands, donned an apron, and yelled, "Next!" startling both butcher and customers.

The bewildered butcher, too stunned to act, gazed at the blond man standing beside him.

Eddy motioned to a waiting customer. "Sprechen Sie English?"

Regaining his senses the butcher asked, "German or American?"

"American. Next in line, please. What do you need?" Eddy asked in English as he scrutinized the waiting patrons.

Several customers chuckled; others rolled their eyes.

One man answered in broken English, "We're Slovenian, not German and not Italian! I'll take half-kilo pork chops, silly American."

Unabashed, Eddy looked at the butcher. "This scale calibrated in kilos?"

"Si. You want a job, American?" Luigi Rizzo asked as he stacked meat on the scale.

"You Italian?" Eddy, pointing to a row of pork, waited for his customer to respond.

"*Si*. Italian living in Yugoslavia who is fluent in many languages. Yes or no, American? You want a job?" Rizzo asked again. He wrapped the meat and handed it across the counter.

"Yes, yes. I want a job." Eddy grinned the infamous Kepler smile.

"Then you're hired. American, you have a name?"

"Eddy Kepler, sir. I'm Eddy Kepler. You know where I can

rent a bed?" He rested his hand on the counter, close to the deli slicer.

"Watch your finger! Yes, Eddy Kepler. You can sleep in the attic with my two youngest sons. Now, who's next in line?" Luigi asked, grinning from ear to ear.

27

PERENNIALS

FEBRUARY 1952, CAMPBELLSVILLE

*T*he knowledge that her father was in her home, even if she returned late without seeing him, dispelled some of her loneliness, but not enough. Harriett spent the Christmas holidays of 1951 alone in the big house. Christmas Day dinner, hosted by June and David—with all siblings, spouses, and children, including Albert and Laurena, attending—provided minimal comfort. Even Olive showed, bedecked in new attire from head to foot, although she remained somewhat reclusive of the otherwise festive, chaotic celebration.

Harriett visited Earl and her mother-in-law, Abigail, on Christmas eve. Neither Earl nor Abigail received communication from Eddy, and neither event substituted for an absent husband. Eddy sent no card, no gift, no letter. As far as Harriett knew, Eddy Kepler evaporated into thin air.

Harriett sulked, rolled into a ball crying alone each night, missing her delinquent husband. New Year's Eve and Day were no better. She was glad to be off work to allow her red, puffy eyes time to clear.

Determined to overcome her depression, Harriett devoted

her energy to school and home improvement, adding items to her "to-do" list weekly, which Tabs crossed off as completed. An unexpected holiday bonus culminated with the purchase of a new, upholstered couch and matching chair for the living room. A coffee table, two matching end tables, and two lamps from the thrift shop supplemented her décor, resulting in an attractive casual room for one lonely woman.

Two rooms started, eight to go! Maybe I can count the kitchen table as semi-done, she thought to a cadence of echoing foot-steps. *I should buy some area rugs!*

As the temperature headed into the forties, the last significant snowfall of the month melted and Mother Nature teased spring's arrival. Tabs spent the day exploring the vast planted garden areas of the property, around the front, side, and back. He waited in the kitchen for Harriett, placing a kettle of water on the stove when he heard her unlock the front door.

Harriett entered the kitchen, surprised to see her father. "Papa, still here? You're usually gone by the time I make it out of the office." Flinging a canvas tote filled with paperwork onto the table, she rubbed the back of her neck.

"Janie, I made you tea. Have a seat. I want to talk about my discoveries." He motioned to a waiting cup, steam curling into an upward stream.

"Papa, what are you up to?" Harriett kissed him in greeting. "I think spring will arrive soon, despite the groundhog's prediction of six more weeks of winter."

She dug to the bottom of her cookie jar to find two snick-erdoodles and handed one to Tabs.

"What kept you so late today?" Harriett asked.

Tabs shrugged and stirred sugar into his cup. He then bit into the cookie.

"Janie, are you baking?" He continued, not waiting for an answer, "Punxsutawney Phil is wrong this year. Spring is almost here. I've been over every inch of your property today. You have a variety of bulbs peeking through the ground. You'll have a splendid Easter display and beyond."

"I remember how beautiful Mrs. Songer's front gardens were, but I never saw the back. Which areas did you explore?" She walked over to stare through the back door at the groomed yard and woodlands beyond.

"You have tulips surrounding the side terraces. Probably the safest place to avoid any munching deer." He chuckled. "I may come shoot one next hunting season! The pines in the back are edged with forsythia and daffodils. Should be a pretty contrast of yellow to the evergreens. There are lilies, both day and oriental, beside the front steps leading up to the house. I'm sure Songers planted many perennials not yet sprouting. I spotted some hyacinth and the tips of what I think are irises. Of course, azalea, rhododendron, verbena, and weigela bushes will add color as well."

Harriett interrupted him. "So basically, the entire property is planted. Ugh. Lots of weeding."

Tabs smiled. "That's why I waited for you today. I'm almost finished with your inside list, at least until you decide to decorate some other rooms. But with the weather warming, I can continue working in your gardens—I can weed, transplant as needed, and trim."

"Papa, what about Mother?" Harriett poured them both a second cup of tea.

"I'll still have time to plant my garden well enough so your mother doesn't complain. My woodland walks are limited. The leg objects." His eyes sparkled as he rubbed his shin. "So, can I start outside? I'd love to plant a cutting of my climbing rose bush. Pass it on to you."

"Papa, you don't have to ask. You're welcome to do whatever you wish. This place is as much yours as it is mine."

Harriett let out a big chuckle. "Geez, I'd be happy to have you move in."

"Don't tempt me, Janie, don't tempt me. After thirty-two years with Olive, I should look for an escape route!" He guffawed. "I guess I'm in it for the long haul. Hell, only the Lord above knows why, but I still love her." Tabs walked to deposit his cup in the sink. "Good. I'll make my plans for your plantings and, with a little luck and elbow grease, your yard will sparkle like the inside of this house."

She tightened her arms around Tabs' neck and sighed. "Papa, I'd be so lonely if it wasn't for you. I love you so much!"

28

BURNT POTATOES

CAMPBELLSVILLE, MARCH 1952

*H*arriett channeled her despair into her studies. Two more months and she would be a college graduate, the proud owner of a Bachelor of Science degree in finance. Despite being first in her high school class, her many accomplishments continued to lack cooking skills. The tiny woman tried her hand at baking, triumphing over snickerdoodle cookies and cinnamon raisin bars—however, egg salad sandwiches remained the staple of her evening meals.

One Sunday afternoon, Harriett dialed Abigail's familiar phone number.

"Earl, it's Harriett."

Earl's laugh crackled over the line. "Yes, Sister, I recognize your voice. What's up?"

She cleared her throat. "I was wondering if I might come over for a visit this afternoon?"

Earl stammered, too quickly, "Absolutely. You don't have to ask. Our door is always open."

"Good. Abigail's home, isn't she?" Harriett asked. "If so, I'll be over shortly."

Hesitating a moment, Earl replied, "You're welcome even

184

if Mother isn't home. If you're worried about appearances, well, you're family now. Sister-in-Law, I promise you are safe with me."

Relieved her beet-red face was screened, Harriett stuttered, "Ah...oh...yes, Earl, I know. Ah...I was hoping Abigail would give me some cooking tips.

Her statement left Earl speechless. Several minutes passed before Earl recovered, just as Harriett clicked the phone receiver.

"Earl, you still there? Earl?"

"Yes, Harriett. I'm here. Come over as soon as you can."

∞ ∞ ∞

The car door shut fifteen minutes later, and Harriett walked to an open front door and a waiting brother-in-law. An awkward hug from both occupants greeted her.

Abigail ushered Harriett into the kitchen, where she began fussing with utensils, saucepans, and recipes. "Harriett dear, I'm so happy to pass on my kitchen skills."

A coughing Earl interrupted her.

Shaking her finger at her oldest son, Abigail continued. "Like I was saying, I'm delighted to share all of Eddy's favorite recipes with you."

Harriett gulped a deep breath then released it slowly. "Abigail, has Eddy written to you at all?"

"No! He's a no-good son."

"Mom, you're talking to his wife." Earl cautioned.

Her hands went to her hips. "Well, he's a no-good husband if he hasn't written Harriett either."

Harriett's arm attempted to circle Abigail's generous waist. "Not since last March...but let's change the subject. I'm sorry for asking. I'm here to cook. What's for supper?"

Abigail looked over her recipe cards. "Let's have roasted

potatoes and pork chops! Harriett, why don't you join Earl and me for Sunday worship services each week?" She bit her lip. "Knowing the Lord was always a comfort to me when Eddy's father behaved as he did."

Harriett paused. "I'll consider the invitation. Maybe next week." Harriett picked up the recipe and read. "Where do we start?"

Abigail giggled as she retrieved the card. "It says to turn the oven to four hundred twenty-five degrees."

Harriett cocked her head to the side. "Geez, that seems high but okay."

With the prep work complete and the food in the oven, Harriett, Earl, and Abigail retired to the parlor with iced tea.

After an hour, the pleasant conversation was interrupted as a haze drifted into the room. Harriett sniffed. "Do you smell that? Ugh. It smells like burning flesh."

Earl inhaled deeply as Abigail sat chatting away. "I think that's our dinner!" He looked at Harriett and motioned with his head. "Shall we?"

Earl and Harriett ran into the kitchen as a cloud of billowing black smoke filtered into the dining room.

"I'll open the doors and windows," called Harriett, waving a towel in the air as Earl charged through the smoke to turn off and open the oven door. Another puff of black char mushroomed out.

Coughing and gagging, Harriett said, "I do believe the temperature was too high."

Earl snorted as he removed the roasting pan. Three shriveled potatoes the size of charcoal nuggets and three flaking pieces of leather were fused to the bottom of the pan. "You think so?"

He tossed the pan and contents onto the porch. "I have an idea! Why don't I take all of us out to dinner?"

Harriett rocked from leg to leg as she doubled over,

holding her belly. "Oh my. I'm laughing so hard I must pee. I'll be right back—but this was my idea. I'm paying for dinner." She dashed out of the room past a stunned Abigail.

Earl called after her, "No, you're not paying! I should have warned you Mother can't cook!"

By the time Harriett rejoined Earl, Abigail had wandered into the dining room. "Goodness, what's all this?"

"Mom, you need to adjust your recipe. We're going out for dinner."

Abigail giggled. "Oh, I wasn't sure if that temperature started with a three or a four. Must have been a three." She reached into the cabinet above the stove. "I keep baking soda up here, just in case. Puts out fires fast!"

Harriett burst into laughter. "Mother Abigail, how often do you need to extinguish fires?"

Abigail tilted her head and thought. "Every time I cook?"

Harriett punched Earl in the shoulder. "You knew!"

"I confess, I did. But this was fun watching." Earl began closing the windows. "Come on, let's close up and go get some food. I'm starving."

"If you know she can't cook, what do you eat?"

"I stock the cupboards with lots of canned goods. She does best when she only has to heat things up." Earl opened the door to expose shelves filled with cans of soup, stew, and even spaghetti. "Plus, I eat out every chance I get."

Harriett scrunched her nose. "But I still need to learn how to cook!"

"Harriett, you are so talented. So what, if you can't cook yet? Give it time. You'll learn."

She bit her lip. "I can ask Alice. She's fabulous in the kitchen."

Earl's stomach growled. "See how fast you solved your problem? Now let's go, before I die of malnutrition!"

Harriett's face glowed with the compliment. "I'll drive. Abigail, grab your coat."

Earl smiled sheepishly. "You drive only if I pay. Sorry, little sis. Prank or not, it was worth it just seeing your face. My little brother found a gem in you!"

SLALOM

MARCH 1952, PREDMEJA, YUGOSLAVIA

*R*osa endured long, lonely weeks of boredom, tending only to a growing baby. Her entire life revolved around weekends and Eddy's return. Weekends were blissful for Eddy, who enjoyed conjugal visits and pulling his chubby-cheeked son on a rickety cart, converted into a sled with a pair of broken skis. After each ride, Joey grunted with arms upstretched, indicating, *another ride, please, Daddy*. The baby was the image of his father: blond, wavy hair, piercing eyes, and an infectious smile. However, after several weekends, Eddy soon grew weary of the rigorous work necessary to provide a week of heat.

Every weekend Rosa pleaded, "Please, Eddy, stay with me throughout the week!" And every weekend, Eddy answered, "The answer is no. Such travel is too much to ask of a man!" She grew thin and pale, too depressed to cook for just one. But she was dependent on Eddy for food, money, and precious firewood. The weather prohibited Isabella's visits and supplies. Rosa's only surplus came from Luigi, who contributed extra slices of bacon and soup bones weekly.

Eddy fell into step as the new Godovic butcher. Village

girls and homemakers stretched their budgets to have the handsome young American cut an extra piece of meat. Eddy did not disappoint, dispensing broad smiles and winking eyes with every package. Luigi Rizzo enjoyed the additional income. When a late winter storm blanketed the town with several feet of snow, Luigi plotted a family ski excursion.

Luigi surveyed the line of patrons with a smile. "Eduardo, come here. I wish to speak with you."

"*Si. Si,*" answered Eddy, who was shocked that his Italian and Slovenian vocabulary increased daily since he considered high school English class a foreign language. He wiped his hands on his apron and turned away from the counter. "Everything okay, boss?"

"My family is taking a skiing trip tomorrow. Would you like to join us?" asked Luigi. "You've been working very hard, and I think you deserve a treat." The butcher's fatherly tone pleased Eddy.

"Who will watch the shop?'

"My brother. He broke his leg in the last war. Can no longer ski. How about it? You won't miss your weekend with sweet Rosa?"

Eddy grinned. "Yeah. I earned a break. This endless work is tiresome." He turned back to the counter before remembering his manners. "Oh—thank you, Luigi."

That night, Eddy slept soundly to be awakened early by his roommates anxiously dressing in their skiwear. Eddy donned his Army-issue thermals under a thin pair of trousers, inadequate to cut the cold.

"Don't you have wool ski trousers?" asked one roommate.

"Nah. I'll be fine. Having fun is worth a little cold," Eddy answered with bravado. "Plus, I have this scarf," he said as he wrapped Rosa's handiwork around his neck and tucked the ends into his belt. His hand felt an unusual object in this pocket. "How the hell did these get in here?" he asked, as he pulled out Rosa's strand of pearls.

The boys and Eddy trudged down the stairs to meet the remaining Rizzo family, their skis, poles, and picnic baskets in their hands.

Luigi handed Eddy a pair of skis. "Try on these boots. My brother Paulo has the biggest feet. They may be tight."

Eddy stretched. "Thanks, man. I was hoping to save the expense of renting skis. I'll force the boots for the day!"

The family piled onto the train for a forty-minute ride to the nearest ski resort. Once aboard, Mrs. Carmella Rizzo, unpacked her picnic hamper, distributing fresh bread and cheese to break their fast. Luigi passed around a flask of wine. Eddy ate a generous portion, then settled back for additional sleep, despite the boisterous chatter of the group.

"Eduardo, wake up!" Luigi shook Eddy's shoulder. "We're here."

Eddy yawned, lazily following Luigi off the train toward the lift ticket booth.

"No, put your money away, Eduardo. My treat." Luigi handed Eddy an all-day lift pass.

Eddy grabbed the pass and raced toward the chairlift. The wind on the mountaintop blew fiercely through his thin clothing. Eddy tightened the scarf around his neck and jumped off the ride. A natural athlete, he skillfully balanced, shifting weight and bending knees from side to side as he sped down the trail. Exhilarated excitement caught him off guard.

Harriett would love this, he thought briefly, *I need to take her skiing*.

A gust of wind sucked out his breath as he remembered Rosa and Joey.

Eddy made three trips up and down the slope, reviving memories of his carefree youth as Carmella completed her first run. She slid over to her waiting family, who gathered around an open fire.

"Momma, is it finally time for lunch?" asked one of the youngsters in Italian.

"Yes, come, bring the hamper." Carmella pointed to the rented locker containing a basket full of food. The family packed into a pavilion, a warming hut. Carmella spread a tablecloth on the wooden table as Luigi rubbed his stomach. "Hurry, Carmella. We are hungry and want to ski! You're wasting daylight."

Eddy managed to understand the gist of the rapid chattering in Italian.

"Patience. I'll not place my good food on this dirty slab of wood." A collection of groans filtered through her objection. Finally, the table was set with sausages, cheese, olives, pickled eggs, dried fruit, biscotti, and wine. Luigi and Eddy hungrily attacked the provisions.

"Mrs. Rizzo, this sure hits the spot! But with all this wine, I need the latrine." Eddy winked as he turned toward the main chalet.

As he approached the building, he spotted a group of American soldiers, all officers, standing around a fire and warming themselves. They glanced in his direction, then one pointed directly at Eddy, who turned quickly to the right to avoid recognition.

One of the sergeants slapped another on the arm. "Hill, is that *Kepler* over there?" he asked as he pointed to the back of Eddy.

A grin spread across Sergeant Hill's face. "Sure looks like him. Check this out. Kepler!" Hill yelled.

Eddy instinctively turned at his name.

Sergeant Hill burst into laughter. "Stupid moron! I knew he'd fall for that." Sergeant Hill addressed the lieutenant standing beside him. "Sir, that man is AWOL. He's Corporal

Edgar Kepler. Went missing a couple of months ago. He needs to be arrested and taken in."

The lieutenant tipped his head. "Then arrest him, Sergeant. Why are you asking me?"

Hill looked at his companion. "Let's go get that son-of-a-bitch!"

Eddy ran. At the corner of the chalet, the ground sloped upward. Cold, cramped toes slid, tossing Eddy headfirst into a drift. His neck jerked backward as he hit the hard-packed surface. Front teeth pierced his lip, blood spurted. Thrusting a handful of snow on his mouth to stop the bleeding, Eddy winced as the pain radiated through his jaw into his ears. He managed to stand and run.

Both sergeants chased the red trail created by every heartbeat as Eddy headed into the lodge. Past the lobby and gawking skiers, he ran down a long hallway that led to rooms for rent. Running pressed his full bladder against his prostate. Spotting the sign for a bathroom, Eddy darted inside as Hill turned the corner, close behind. The stop to relieve himself proved critical and slow.

Come on, Eddy urged his bladder to empty. The stream of urine seemed to be never-ending. Hill burst through the door as Eddy rezipped his trousers.

"You are under arrest, Corporal!" Hill yelled as he lunged at Eddy, who ducked, punching Hill in the midsection. "Not only are you AWOL, but you just assaulted a superior officer. Turn around."

Eddy swung a second punch as Hill's companion charged into the room. He caught Eddy's upstretched arm. Hill retaliated with a punch to the gut before yanking Eddy's arms behind his back and cuffing him. Hill pushed Eddy forward as the other sergeant pulled on his shoulder.

"You're in a pile of shit, soldier." Hill laughed. "I'll make sure I wipe that smirk permanently off your conceited face."

Eddy Kepler was escorted to the waiting Army officers, a sergeant on each side, as a stunned Luigi Rizzo and family watched in disbelief. Eddy looked in their direction, eyes pleading.

Eddy stood helpless as a lieutenant officially charged him. Sergeant Hill extracted a log from a stack of firewood, whacking Eddy on the side of the head and causing him to drop.

"Sergeant Hill! That was unnecessary. Kepler is constrained, going nowhere," screamed the lieutenant. "Apologize immediately."

"Sorry, sir."

The lieutenant scowled. "Not to me, you imbecile. Apologize to Kepler."

Sergeant Hill's face contorted. "Sir, I have no intention of apologizing to that piece of shit, sir."

"I suggest you do as ordered, Hill, or you'll occupy the cell next to his."

Hill glowered at Eddy. "Sorry Kepler, you asshole. That last whack was payback for Rosa."

"Sergeant Hill?"

Hill's face turned red. "Fine. Kepler, I'm sorry," he said, as he kicked snow with his boot.

Eddy smiled as he watched Sergeant Hill saunter away from the group. He knew Hill was on the verge of another confrontation and repercussion.

∞ ∞ ∞

Carmella tugged at her husband's shirt sleeve as she asked. "Luigi, why do those soldiers have Eduardo?"

"I wish I knew Carmella. But it doesn't look good for Eddy, and it doesn't look good for business." He frowned. "I fear all those extra sales will disappear with our handsome American."

The woman gasped. "What about his young wife and baby?" She moved toward the soldiers. "Eduardo, your wife!" Her voice faded in the wind.

Luigi grabbed her arm, pulling her back. "Carmella. We can't get in the middle of this. If Eddy is in trouble, we don't want to bring it on us."

"But the child!" Carmella's face drained of all color.

"I'll try to figure out where the wife and child live and send them some money, dear."

THE BRIG

MARCH AND APRIL 1952, TRIESTE, ITALY

*E*ddy and company arrived back at the base to awaiting MPs, who placed Eddy under arrest for the third time that day. After an official arraignment, he was thrown into a cell and refused visitors.

Eddy shook the bars of his cell.

"Rosa," he screamed over and over. After an hour without water, his voice faded from a bellowing baritone to a rasping squeak. "Rosa, someone contact Rosa!"

Exhaustion overwhelmed him. He melted to the floor, drifting into a fitful slumber.

The following day, Eddy, shivering on the ground, his mouth parched, awoke to Sergeant Hill laughing outside his cell.

"Kepler, you don't look so smug now. The fat lip is attractive!"

Eddy lunged at Hill but was stopped by metal. "Hill, if you care for Rosa at all, you'll get Wally Stuart in here. He's the only one who knows where she is."

The sound echoed from deep in Hill's lungs. "You are a stupid idiot, Kepler. You signed away all visiting privileges yesterday at your arraignment. Wally can't visit, even if he wants. You, asshole, are headed for four weeks of solitary confinement before your court-martial. See you later, you son-of-a-bitch!"

Hill walked away as Eddy continued to yell, "Rosa, I love you! Hill, help her." To himself, he thought, *Harriett, how do I get out of this mess?*

∞ ∞ ∞

Eddy spent four weeks in solitary. Every day the cry to Rosa went out. Every day he was met with a barrage of "Shut the fuck up!" from other prisoners and guards. Finally, in April, he was transferred back to the regular prison population and an awaiting visitor.

Relief flooded Eddy's face when he spotted Wally. The guard brought the shackled Eddy into the room and chained him to the table.

Wally shook his head. "Good God, Eddy. You've done it now!"

Eddy interrupted his friend. "Wally, I need you to go out to the cabin now. It's been four weeks, and Rosa doesn't have any food, money, or firewood. Please! She could be starving. Oh God, It's still winter up there."

Wally sighed. "I can't believe you put that poor child in this predicament."

"Wally, blame me some other day. Right now, I need you to take her food, cut some wood, and bring little Joey some milk and cereal. He's growing so fast." Eddy grabbed both sides of his head. "Oh God, Rosa," he repeated.

Wally stood and paced. "Calm down. I'll go out this afternoon. But you my friend, are in big trouble. You're going on trial for desertion."

"I'll worry about that tomorrow. Just make sure you come

back later to report. And Wally, tell her I'm so sorry and that I love her. I'll make this right."

∞ ∞ ∞

At eight o'clock, about an hour before lights out, Eddy was ushered back into the visitor's room. He hurriedly shuffled to the table and waited for the click.

Exhaling, he said, "Wally, thank goodness. How was she? Did she forgive me? How's Joey?"

Wally bit his lip. "Slow down, Eddy. Now, don't accuse the messenger, but she wasn't there."

All color drained from Eddy's face. "What do you mean, she wasn't there?" Eddy reached for Wally's chest, but constraints prohibited the move.

"Buddy, I mean just that. She wasn't at the cabin. When I opened the door, the place was cold and empty. Looked like the fire was out for some time. I stacked wood and left the food on the table, just in case, but I don't think she's coming back. Mice were scampering all through the cabin."

Eddy hung his head. "Where would she go? You must check her parents' house. Tomorrow."

"Eddy, you strain a relationship, don't you?" Wally wiped his hands on his trousers. "I want nothing to do with Giovanni Romano—*but* I'll do this for her sake. I feel bad I helped her get tangled up with you."

Tears streamed down Eddy's cheeks. "Rosa! Oh, my darling Rosa." Running his shackled hand through his hair, he screamed, "Guard! Take me back to my cell. I'm going to be sick."

∞ ∞ ∞

Wally returned the next day at noon. The guard grumbled

as he ushered Eddy back to the table. "Kepler, you're making up for four weeks with all these visits."

Eddy ignored him. "So, Wally, how are they?"

Wally frowned. "I talked to the guard at the Romano gate. She hasn't been at the villa since last March, when Romano kicked her out."

"Son of a bitch!" Eddy slammed his fist on the table. "Where is she?"

"My guess is with the grandmother. I suggest you write her a letter."

"I don't know her last name. You'll have to go to Santa Croce."

Wally sighed. "What do you mean you don't know her last name? She wrote you letters, didn't she? It should be on those."

"I didn't keep any of that stuff. I burned all of it. Too afraid that the Army would be able to trace me if they got hold of it."

"Geez, Eddy, think! Do you remember a street address? We only went to the church."

"I have been thinking. What the fuck do you think I'm doing all day other than thinking. She's just a kid."

"I told you that a year ago. Shit, she could be a dead kid with a dead baby."

"Shut the fuck up, Wally. I don't want to hear it."

"Someone has to drive the truth into that bone head of yours. You stupid shit. They're going to court-martial you and send you back home. And to what? Harriett? Do you actually think she'll take you? Or are you going to try escaping into Yugoslavia again?"

"Okay, you're right. How do I get out of this?"

"You don't get it, do you? *You don't get out of this!*" Wally stood and called for the guard. "Maybe if you plead to go to Korea, they'll send you there to be slaughtered. Good luck with that!"

Wally slammed the door behind him, and Eddy waddled back to his cell.

∞ ∞ ∞

Eddy was dragged before an Army tribunal three days later. His appointed lawyer, Lieutenant Gary Moser, a young kid of twenty-four, conferred with Eddy before entering the meeting room. Moser, inexperienced, had been licensed for only six months before being drafted

The presiding officer, Colonel Paul Bernabo, pounded his gavel. "This court-martial is now in session. Will the defendant please stand?"

Eddy and Moser stood. The scraping of chair legs on the wooden floor echoed through the empty room. Eddy glared at the Colonel.

"You are charged with desertion, absence without leave. How do you plead?"

Moser swallowed to wet his mouth. "Guilty, sir."

"Then I sentence you to be dishonorably discharged and transferred to Lev..."

"Sir, if I may approach?" Moser cleared his throat, hoping for the chance to present Eddy's idea to the officer.

Colonel Bernabo scowled. "Approach. Make this quick, son."

"Sir, will you consider sending Corporal Kepler to the front line in Korea instead of a dishonorable discharge? The corporal is remorseful, regrets his actions, calling them immature and stupid. You see, there is a girl and baby involved..."

"Yes, I, along with most base personnel, are well aware of the circumstances of this case. You present an interesting offer." Colonel Bernabo interrupted Moser and pounded his gavel again. "We shall adjourn for fifteen minutes. Gentlemen," he said, looking at the other two presiders, "please join me in my office."

Eddy grabbed Lieutenant Moser's arm. "Well, did he buy it?"

"I don't know, Kepler. Why should they? It's a stupid cockamamie idea, just about as dumb as going AWOL. I can't believe they are even discussing it." Moser tapped his papers on the table to straighten the edges before placing them in his briefcase.

Eddy flushed, squinting his eyes. "Get your nose out of the clouds, college brat."

"Geez, you are incorrigible. I'm the only thing standing between you and Kansas, yet you insult me." Moser stood, ready to leave.

Eddy rubbed his neck. "Where are you going? You can't go!"

"Just watch me. This should have been in and out, open and closed case. You're wasting the tribunal's and my time."

Eddy grabbed Moser's arm. "Fine. I'll be nice. Just get me out of this mess."

Ten minutes passed before Colonel Bernabo and colleagues returned. Eddy and Lieutenant Moser stood as the gavel sounded.

"We accept your idea, Lieutenant, of replacing the discharge with front-line service. In light of his previous service and a glowing report from his sergeant, I'll show some leniency. There are few women, where he's going, for our infamous Corporal Kepler to denigrate, and our troops need constant replenishment. In addition to transfer to Korean active duty, Corporal Kepler is immediately stripped of rank. The transfer is to become effective next week. Private Kepler shall remain in custody until that time. That is all. Dismissed."

The gavel echoed. Eddy grinned at Lieutenant Moser. "Good job, college kid."

"I'd wait to thank me. Those fighting boys in Korea are getting slaughtered. I may have arranged for your early grave."

"Suits me just fine. I can't find Rosa and Joey, and I don't want to live without them."

31

SPRING BLOOMS

MAY 1952, CAMPBELLSVILLE

*A*n array of plant life, fueled by April rains, burst into a glorious display of color and shape. The gardens of Hill House, high above the valley, dazzled Campbellsville. Tabs' handiwork resulted in crisply edged, groomed beds of perennials, shrubs, bushes, and trees. Two large cement urn planters, filled with colorful pansies, flanked the top of the large, sweeping, front stone staircase that led to the covered porch entrance, while yellow jonquils and daffodils lined their length. From the back terrace, dark green pines and evergreens edged with yellow forsythia and purple, red, and orange azaleas provided a splendid backdrop to the property line. Yellow and red tulips poked through the side of the terrace. Both town and country-dwellers deliberately trekked to the top street of Campbellsville to view Hill House's beauty.

Hard work and perseverance rewarded Harriett with an earlier than expected graduation. In one week, she was to be the first college graduate of either the Bailey or the Kepler family.

Harriett's phone rang late on Thursday afternoon. "Harriett, I know it's late, but Mr. Roland and Mr. Vincent were hoping for a short meeting. Can you come up now?"

"Sure. What's up?"

"This time, I don't know."

Harriett bounded up the two flights of stairs to greet her friend. "Any big weekend plans, Kathryn?"

"Nope. Not one. They are waiting in the conference room. Oh, Mr. Dugan is there too."

Harriett's hands began to sweat. "Mr. Dugan? Am I in trouble?"

Kathryn shrugged her shoulders. "Only way to find out is to go in."

Harriett knocked on the door before entering. The three corporate executives sat around the conference table, a folder in front of each, with the fourth folder at an empty chair.

Harriett motioned to the paperwork. "Good afternoon, gentlemen. I assume this is for me?"

Mr. Roland smiled. "Yes, please have a seat, Harriett. We have a proposition."

Harriett smoothed her skirt as she sat. She placed her folded hands on the table, waiting to be told she was free to open the file.

Mr. Vincent spoke next. "Harriett, you are an exemplary employee. How long have you worked for me now?"

"About a year and a half, Mr. Vincent. I was promoted in January, 1951." She fingered the paperwork but kept it closed.

Mr. Dugan observed her movements. "I see that Mrs. Kepler is curious."

Harriett chuckled, then frowned. "Well, yes, Mr. Dugan. Of course, I am curious. I have never been in a meeting with the three of you other than as a secretary taking shorthand."

Mr. Roland opened his folder. "Please, Harriett. Feel free to glance through that file." He nodded toward her folder.

"Take a few minutes to peruse, and then we shall continue this conversation."

Opening the file, Harriett tried to hide her anxiety. She read and reread the first page before glancing up at the three men, who were all smiling.

"I don't understand. Why am I listed as an officer on the letterhead?"

Mr. Roland grinned. "Harriett, you receive your BS next week, correct?"

"Yes."

Mr. Dugan interrupted. "Mrs. Kepler, I don't play games. I am retiring at the end of the fiscal year, on June thirtieth. This is my family company, so I shall stay as Chairman of the Board of Directors; however, Mr. Roland is replacing me as CEO. Now, do you understand?"

Harriett inhaled; her mouth hung open slightly. "Truthfully, no."

"We are promoting you to CFO, Harriett." Mr. Roland chuckled. "You'll be Dugan and Co.'s first female senior executive. You'll spend half of each day training with me in the next two months, and the other half training your replacement. Then, you'll move into my office and I'll take the big one in the corner."

"I...don't know what to say?" Harriett continued to leaf through the paperwork. She stopped when she got to the compensation package. Covering her mouth with both hands, she asked, "Is *this* my salary?"

All three men laughed out loud. "Yes, Harriett. I hope it is adequate. You'll be eligible for a raise in six months."

Mr. Vincent handed her a single sheet outlining her new responsibilities, then added, "I'll be taking over the head of personnel along with my duties as COO. My job got much easier when we promoted you as Operations General Manager."

"Which brings me to my next question," added Mr. Roland. "Is Miss Coil ready to replace you?"

Harriett pursed her lips in thought. "Not really. She's more than a head secretary, but she's young and inexperienced. Not ready for such a big job." Harriett blushed before continuing. "Who am I to make that assessment? I'm pretty young and inexperienced myself."

"I disagree with your self-assessment. Plus, your degree is a big win for you. Do you have any alternate suggestions?"

"I do. That new junior exec from supply, Jim LaMantia, will be a great operations manager with the help of Miss Coil. You remember he's the one who witnessed at the Stan Kirk debacle. I believe he's a Pitt graduate."

"You see, Dugan, I told you she was a born leader." Mr. Roland handed Harriett another single sheet of paper. "I have another idea. Mrs. Payne is ready to retire. How do you feel about bringing Miss Coil along as your secretary/assistant? I'll replace Mary with Kathryn. Don't want to break in someone new." Roland grinned then waited for Harriett's reply.

"But LaMantia will need help acclimating to his new responsibilities." She straightened her papers without looking down.

"Mary is willing to remain until the end of August, giving LaMantia two months of half days with you and three complete months with Miss Coil. That is plenty of time, if the man is worth his salt—considering I threw you blindly into the position. I know you and Kathryn are good friends, but you should have no problem using her until Mary is ready to go."

Harriett thought for a moment. "Am I trying to micromanage?"

The men smiled at their new executive fledgling. Mr. Roland stood, extended his hand to shake. "Welcome to the corporate executive world, Mrs. Harriett Bailey Kepler. You'll adapt quickly."

The other two men followed suit, ushering Harriett through a quick rite of passage.

"I suppose I need to update my wardrobe." Harriett frowned as she touched her cotton blouse.

"You can afford to buy silk, if you wish, although your current dress is appropriate. Maybe add a few basic expansion pieces."

"Why, Mr. Roland! I didn't realize you had such fashion sense."

"Dear Mrs. Kepler. I have a wife and three adult daughters. My house is overrun with female apparel."

Four laughing Dugan & Co. executives ceased conversation as they exited the room. Mr. Dugan handed Harriett an envelope. "Mrs. Kepler, I almost forgot. Here's a little something from the three of us to commemorate your graduation. Buy yourself something extravagant. And a sincere congratulations to you!"

Kathryn, deliberately remaining late, glanced up from her reading. "Harriett, do you have a minute?"

Harriett turned to the men. "I'll gather all parties tomorrow at a two o'clock meeting for Mr. Dugan's announcement." She reached to shake hands again, grasping firmly. "Thank you again for your trust."

"It was earned. Any woman with your brains and firm handshake is worthy." Mr. Roland turned to Kathryn. "Miss White, please schedule yourself for a meeting with me tomorrow morning at ten."

"Of course, Mr. Roland," Kathryn noted the time before looking at Harriett.

Three office doors closed, leaving the two women alone. Kathryn reached for Harriett's arms. "What the heck was that all about?"

"Oh, Kathryn. I'm not at liberty to say, not yet. The company announcement is tomorrow afternoon, but you'll know tomorrow morning." Harriett tucked her paperwork under her arm. "Back to the weekend. Want to go out for dinner and a drink tomorrow night?"

"Drive and stay overnight then?" Kathryn paused before adding. "There is one condition. You fill me in on what was just discussed!"

"You'll know everything I'm free to share."

∞ ∞ ∞

Harriett drove past Alice and Teddy's on her way home. Earl's car was curiously parked on the street outside their house. Wondering why Earl was visiting the Jensons, Harriett pulled the Buick into her single-car detached garage and climbed the steps to the house. In the kitchen, she opened the refrigerator and tossed two eggs into a saucepan.

I really need to learn to cook. I'll be clucking soon, she thought.

While the water boiled, she opened the gift envelope. An embossed card and a check for one thousand dollars fell out.

Harriett inhaled. *Geez, Louise! That's almost one-tenth of my new salary.*

Harriett placed the check on the table. Taking the eggs out of the water, she decided on eating them soft boiled with toast. She crunched numbers as she chewed the bread. After dinner, she roamed the house, surveying each room while jotting ideas down on paper. Still in need of furniture were two empty bedrooms, a maid's room, and a bathroom on the second floor.

Harriett rattled the doorknob leading to the third floor. Locked. *I really need to call a locksmith to unlock that door. Skip the attic*, she thought. *I'll go up eventually.*

Formal dining room, butler's pantry, more kitchen items,

partial living room, powder room on the first floor, side terrace, back patio outside. Her journey ended in the office at her desk. She sighed. What a long list. Removing stationery from her set, she began writing.

Dear Eddy,

What is the problem? Please help me understand why you don't write. I have more good news. Besides getting my degree next week, I also got a promotion. I know! My second within two years, and this one is a doozie! I'm to be a corporate officer of Dugan and Co., their chief financial officer. Can you imagine that? A female executive—and at my age!

Eddy, it's been so long since your last correspondence. If you are still alive and have any feelings for me, please write.

She began to sob. Writing the words made her thoughts a reality. Salty tears dripped, smearing the ink, but she continued to write.

I am now capable of providing for myself. Correction—I did that before. I am now capable of *comfortably* providing for myself. I'm making twelve thousand dollars a year. I know, it's so much money! Mr. Roland also promised me a possible raise in six months. I never imagined making this much.

Another tear plopped onto the page. Harriett laid her pen down to allow the ink to dry. She paced around the room for several minutes before continuing.

This is hard for me to say and do, but if you want your freedom, I'll give it to you. Although, you must be the one to provide the grounds for divorce. I may have a failed marriage, but I won't tarnish MY reputation for your sake. You may do that on your own.

So, you see, Eddy, leave me alone if that's what you want. I'm okay. Goodness. Saying that hurts. I still love you so much. But I refuse to be treated as an afterthought. Tell me, and we will end this now. If I must live without you, I'm doing it on my terms.

Harriett.

She blew her nose. *Geez, Louise, I'll have so much to tell Kathryn tomorrow.*

∞ ∞ ∞

The next evening, with umbrellas raised, Kathryn and Harriett walked out of the building together. The rain blew in sheets; Madison was soaked clean.

Kathryn yelled above the howling wind. "Harriett, I insist you stay the night. It's too dangerous to drive far in this rain."

The duo walked to Harriett's Buick. "Jump in. I intend to stay. I packed a bag after listening to the weather report last night. I'm hoping you might go shopping with me tomorrow."

Kathryn removed her rain bonnet then shook her umbrella before tossing it into the back. "What are we shopping for? I'm afraid your beautiful car got a bath."

Harriett turned on the automatic defroster. "Some furniture and a television." She handed Kathryn a small towel. "Here, dry off."

Kathryn wiped her handbag. Turning to Harriett, she gulped, "A real television? Goodness Harriett, did you inherit a fortune from a long, lost relative? On your mother's side?" She chuckled.

"We'll talk about it over dinner and drinks, but there is more to Mr. Dugan retiring and Mr. Roland being promoted."

Kathryn rubbed her hands together. "Oh, I guessed correctly! You're being promoted too, aren't you?" She reached over, giving her friend a soggy hug. "You're to replace him as CFO, aren't you? Goodness, my best friend is an executive!"

"Wow. I've never been anyone's best friend." Harriett giggled as they drove slowly out of downtown Madison towards Howard Johnson's restaurant. Ten minutes later, the women sat in a booth, drinking coffee.

Harriett clutched her mug, warming her hands. "Spring rain can be chilling. About as cold as my marriage."

"That was harsh. But you were so in love with Eddy."

A frown crossed Harriett's face. "I am still in love with him, but..." She hesitated, working up the courage to continue. "I wrote yesterday to tell him about my promotion. I offered to give him a divorce, with the stipulation that he provide the grounds."

Kathryn grabbed Harriett's hands. "I'm so sorry. Has he contacted you at all?"

Harriett dapped her eyes and sniffled. "Not since March of last year. Fourteen months without any communication is brutal." She blew her nose. "My life with Eddy seems like a fleeting dream. If he truly doesn't want to be married, I want to end this on my terms. I can't control his feelings, but I can control how I move forward."

"Oh, Harriett, I am so sorry." Tears began welling in Kathryn's eyes. "You manage to hide your feelings. You are so chipper at work."

Harriett bit her lip. "I must mask them." She released a long sigh. "I refuse to allow Eddy Kepler to ruin my career and my education, along with my marriage. He only gets the one."

"Honey, I'm so sorry. Do you think something happened to him?"

Harriett shook her head. "No. I would have heard by now. I asked Papa, Albert, and even Earl the same question. They all agree that I would have been notified by the army." The talking stopped when the waitress approached. "I need a few more minutes, please...when Lupi was killed, Alice knew within three weeks of his death. No, Eddy's alive. This is deliberate."

"We better look at the menu. She's lurking in the corner waiting for us." Kathryn opened her menu to the daily specials.

The friends ordered their meals then resumed. "Let's change the subject. I'll not allow him to ruin our night. What's on your shopping list beside a television?"

Pulling a list from her handbag, Harriett read aloud. "A dining room table and chairs, a new bedroom set, patio furniture. I want to look at china and crystal patterns, maybe start collecting. If I have a formal dining room, I need formal dishes." She smiled then continued. "Let's see, the TV, kitchen items. I got some wonderful wedding gifts that I intend to keep, with or without Eddy. But I need baking supplies."

"Goodness, where'd you get all the money?"

Harriett blushed. "It's a graduation gift from Mr. Roland, Mr. Vincent, and Mr. Dugan. I was told to buy something frivolous, so I'm decorating a portion of my house."

"Well, I can't wait to help you spend that money. I know a couple of good secondhand stores. I think I'll live vicariously through you, my friend."

The waitress delivered their meals. Kathryn raised her water glass in a toast. "To the first female college graduate and first female executive at Dugan and Co.! Congratulations, dear Harriett. You are truly amazing!"

32

SUMMA CUM LAUDE

MAY 1952, CAMPBELLSVILLE

*S*aturday, the next week, Alice and Teddy waited in the living room for Harriett to finish dressing. The three were driving together to Madison College's graduation ceremony. Unlike the previous weekend, it was a glorious spring morning. A warm, gentle breeze from the southwest tossed branches of budding trees to and fro.

Harriett hurried down the staircase, cap and gown in hand. "I'm sorry. I'm never late."

Alice grabbed her coat as they headed for the door. "It's okay. Now, don't make plans, Teddy and I are having you over for dinner tonight."

"I promise." Harriett smiled at her sister. "I have butterflies." She grabbed a homemade canvas tote bag. "Can't forget my speech!"

Teddy drove the trio to Madison, where Harriett donned her cap and gown and was draped with cords indicating her *summa cum laude* status. She was not first in the overall 1952 graduating class, but she was in the top five percent. Regardless, the faculty chose her to speak to her peers as a thriving contemporary. While she was one year older than her classmates, who were just beginning their careers, she, contrastingly, began post-grad life a deeply riveted maven.

Alice and Teddy joined Tabs, Earl, Abigail, Albert, Laurena, June, Dave, Esther, and Darrell who occupied the fifth row from the front.

"Where's Mother?" Alice asked her father as she opened her program.

Tabs frowned. "She threw a fit. Said she refused to watch Harriett fulfill someone else's dreams." Tabs ticked his tongue. "As if Olive were the only person allowed aspiration of a college degree. That woman frustrates me!"

Esther laughed. "Papa, I don't think I ever heard you speak badly of Mother."

"Gosh, after all these years, I've finally lost patience."

Albert whispered to Laurena, "It's about time! He should have never married her."

"But then you'd never have been born!" Laurena squeezed his hand. "And that is an unthinkable thought."

Earl interrupted the Bailey tittering. "Alice, is Harriett still in the dark?"

"Yes, she thinks we are eating back at our house tonight."

"Perfect. I hope this pleases her. She is an incredible woman!"

Albert and Alice glanced at each other; eyebrows arched at Earl's compliment. The crowd hushed as the graduates entered the auditorium and marched to their seats. Speeches began with the College President, followed by the Dean of Students. Harriett was the fifth of seven scheduled speakers. She climbed onto a wooden box behind the podium, to the chuckles of spectators and classmates.

The tiny woman adjusted the microphone and began. "Greetings dignitaries, distinguished faculty, classmates, friends, and family. Today we celebrate individual achievement. As the first college graduate in my family, I am truly blessed."

She continued, however, modesty prohibited self-bragging, and she made no mention of her recent promotion. Her voice resonated her message with self-confidence and control. The audience fell under her spell, listening intently to every word.

"As we prepare to begin our lives as college graduates, I conclude by sharing the thoughts of two very wise men. Consider these words of Winston Churchill. I quote, "Success is not final, failure is not fatal: it is the courage to continue that counts." Classmates, I challenge you to go into the world with the courage to dream, to aspire, and to achieve. Strive for your own definition of success. *But* bear in mind the words of Albert Schweitzer. "Success is not the key to happiness." Rather, "Happiness is the key to success. If you love what you are doing, you will be successful."

She paused, glancing at the graduates, then at the audience. "Please, I invite each of you to join me on this adventuresome journey called life to travel beside me on the road to success."

The speech lasted only three minutes in total. The crowd erupted with a thunderous standing ovation. Harriett folded her papers and stepped off the lift as a man waited to remove it for the next speaker. The last two speeches lasted fifteen minutes, to the audience's grumblings. Finally, the presentation of diplomas with individual recognition concluded the ceremony.

Students and families gathered outside at the campus's central courtyard for photographs. Teddy, the family photographer, snapped away as Harriett posed with each member and the group.

Earl reached for the camera. "Teddy, get in there with

Alice and Harriett. I'll take this one. Then, if you don't mind, I'd like one without Mother—just the two of us."

Alice poked Albert's arm when Earl slipped his hand onto Harriett's back for the picture.

As they walked toward the parking lot, Harriett stopped to glance back at the grounds. Sighing, she said, "If only Eddy were here." Then she walked on.

Earl led the caravan of vehicles out of the lot, turning left onto the tree-lined street leading into Madison instead of right toward Campbellsville.

"Teddy, he's going the wrong way!" Harriett grabbed Teddy's shoulder from behind.

Alice chuckled. "No, Harriett. We have a surprise for you. Well, *Earl* has a surprise for you."

"Is that why I saw his car parked at your house the other night?"

Alice punched Teddy's arm. "I told you she'd see the car!"

"What's the big secret?" Harriett bounced up and down on the seat.

"All in due time."

Before long, the cars turned off the road into the parking lot of Madison's premier steakhouse.

"We're eating in a fancy restaurant?" Harriett asked as she leaned toward Alice. "Mr. Dugan and Mr. Roland declared this the best meat in town."

Harriett watched Earl hand Abigail a wrapped package before helping her to the door.

Teddy slipped into a parking spot, opened the door for each woman, and unlocked the trunk to pull out another wrapped package.

"You didn't buy me a gift, did you? I told everyone not to spend their money on me!" Harriett blushed as she objected. "I don't want all this fuss."

"Too bad, Sis, you're getting it. Now cover your eyes. I'll lead the way."

The hostess ushered the group into a private dining room, decorated with floating helium-filled balloons, fresh flowers, and a printed sign saying *Congratulations Harriett Bailey Kepler*. The guests piled their gifts on an empty table.

"You can look," said Earl as he removed her hand covering her eyes.

Harriett gasped. "Geez Louise! All of this for me?"

Earl led Harriett to the head of the table, pulled out her chair, then handed her a dozen long-stem roses. "Congratulations, Harriett. I don't know your favorite flower. I hope you like roses."

"Who doesn't like roses? They are gorgeous! I've never been given a full dozen at one time." She sniffled and reached for her handkerchief. "Having my degree is reward enough. You guys didn't need to go to all this trouble."

Alice looked at Earl, who nodded. "It's all Earl's idea. He arranged for everything."

Harriett sucked on her lower lip, pausing before answering. "Earl, how can I ever say thank you? This is so kind."

"It's well-deserved. I'm so proud of you, Harriett." Earl felt his face redden. "Shall we be seated? I ordered a preset menu, starting with appetizers. Help yourselves to wine or beer with dinner. I selected a Cabernet Sauvignon. If you wish to order a cocktail, then it's on your tab! But, Harriett, feel free to order whatever you wish." Earl looked directly at Harriett. "The waitress will ask how to prepare your steak, a filet."

Darrell rubbed his growling stomach. "This was worth sitting through all those boring speeches." Esther kicked him under the table.

Five chairs lined each side of the table. With Harriett at one end and Teddy at the other, the rest alternated girl/boy as best they could. Earl sat on Harriett's left with Tabs on her right. "Janie, I'm so proud of you."

"Was Mother a witch about this?" Harriett touched her father's hand.

Tabs scratched his nose. "A *college grad* asked that question, can you believe it?" Albert and June chuckled.

"Sorry. It was a stupid question! I just hope she wasn't too tough on you, Papa." Harriett leaned in to straighten Tabs' necktie. "You look very handsome. New suit?"

"Yes, Ma'am. Special day—and I intend to look the part, now that I'm running with the big dogs."

The waitress returned with the completed drink order, then placed two large trays of assorted appetizers on the table to be shared by the twelve diners.

"What is this thing wrapped in bacon?" Darrell asked as he crunched.

"A water chestnut."

"Alice and Theodore Jenson!" said Harriett. "You conspired in arranging this, didn't you? That's why Earl was at your house?"

Earl answered first. "Do you think *I'm* familiar with water chestnuts? Me? A product of Campbellsville?" Everyone laughed. "Teddy says they serve them at the country club, so..."

Harriett leaned over and kissed Earl on the cheek. "Thank you, Brother-in-Law. I am duly impressed." Earl blushed as he gently caressed his face. Under the table, Alice kicked both Albert and Teddy.

Esther picked up the conversation. Drinks were followed with a creamy broccoli soup. Next, the waitress placed a small cup of sorbet at each place.

Darrell looked at Esther. "Okay, why am I getting dessert before my steak?"

The women giggled. Alice offered, "It's to cleanse your palate."

"My *what?*"

"Your *palate*. Clean all the taste from your mouth so that you can enjoy the flavor of your steak."

"I can do that with a swig of water. I don't need some fancy ice cream."

Esther kicked her husband again. "Darrell, for goodness' sake, have a little class. Harriett is a corporate manager. Between her, pharmacist Teddy, pilot Dave, and meteorologist Albert, the Baileys are moving up in the world! We may even achieve Westchester status!"

"That may be so, but I'm not a Bailey. I'm an ex-coal mining Cline."

While the group chuckled at Darrell, Harriett reached into her handbag. She handed each partygoer a business card that read "Harriett Bailey Kepler, Vice President and Chief Financial Officer, Dugan & Co., 725 Main Street, Madison, Pennsylvania 412-555-6767."

Alice stared at her sister. "Why does this say 'Vice President?'"

A grin spread across Harriett's face. "I was promoted last Friday. I am a corporate officer. Can you believe it?"

"Did you get a raise, too?" asked June.

"Geez, Louise! Did I!" Harriett finished her sorbet before continuing. "I'm *embarrassed* to tell you my salary, and I got a big bonus check. Next weekend I have furniture being delivered. No more hollow echo on Hill Street." She glanced at Earl. "Considering that, may I help with tonight's cost?"

Teddy jumped in. "Absolutely not! Earl and I are treating you, tonight."

Earl cleared his throat. "Teddy, we've been over this. Tonight is on me. Me alone. I want to do this."

Alice steadied Teddy's hand. "No arguing, gentlemen. Oh good, here come our steaks."

After steaks, chiffon cake with sabayon sauce and coffee concluded the meal. The women, helping Abigail, headed to the ladies' room en masse while the men lit cigarettes. Upon their return, all smoking ceased.

Earl clinked his fork against his coffee cup. "Attention, please. I'd like to propose a toast. To Harriett Bailey Kepler, our beautiful, successful executive. Congratulations on graduating *summa cum laude*—not that I know what that means. Now, it's time for gifts!"

"No, please." Harriett threw her hands in the air. "This is plenty."

Abigail rose first and retrieved her package. "Here, darling. I made this for you."

Harriett unwrapped a hand-knitted, cashmere, red-and-white scarf. "Thank you so much! Did you know these were Madison's school colors?

Abigail winked. "A little birdie told me. Like the wool? Earl ordered it special."

"We're next," Esther said as she handed over a box. Harriett tore away the paper to find a new silk slip. "I didn't know about your promotion, but I figured you wouldn't have to do laundry as much."

"It's so soft. I love it." Harriett giggled. "I don't have to go to the laundromat anymore. I have a new, matching, electric washer and dryer coming next week, too!"

The crowd oohed. Albert and Laurena gifted a silver business card case and fountain pen, both engraved with *HBK*.

Harriett filled it with her new business cards. "Perfect!"

June and Dave handed Harriett two boxes. The first contained a silk blue and white striped blouse, the second a blue and white hat.

Alice presented a white leather handbag and a pair of white shoes, sporting peek-a-boo toes.

"Before you say a word, I know! No white before Memorial Day or after Labor Day. That's why Teddy and I picked them—because you'd never buy them for yourself."

Tabs was the last of the Baileys. "This is from your mother and me." Albert sprayed coffee into his napkin.

"Don't make me choke, Dad! We all know better."

Harriett stroked Tabs' hand. "It's okay, Papa. She hates me, and I'm okay with it."

"No, Janie, she doesn't hate you…"

"No excuses for her. Not today. She hates everyone." Harriett opened the box to find a pure white linen skirt. "What a gorgeous outfit. So, who went shopping and picked the ensemble?"

June blushed as she raised her hand. "That would be me."

"Your taste is exquisite! This is a beautiful summer outfit, something I would never purchase. I don't care how much money they pay me. White is too frivolous."

Earl spoke up. "My turn!"

"No, Earl, you've already done too much."

"No, I haven't. You're remarkable. You deserve this and much more. My brother is a lucky man—and a fool." A few raised eyebrows and sideways glances were shared. "Here." Earl handed Harriett a large, rectangular, wrapped box.

She stripped the paper, handing the discards to Albert, who rolled it into a ball, giving Harriett room to open the box. Inside she found a brown leather attaché case monogrammed *HBK* in gold letters.

"Oh, Earl." Harriett opened the locks on each end to find the keys inside. "I use a canvas bag to tote things back and forth from work."

"I've seen it. This is much more appropriate, especially

with the promotion." Earl smiled reluctantly. "Carry it in good health, with corporate success."

Harriett rubbed her face. "Thank you all. What a truly memorable day this is." She hesitated before adding, "I may as well tell you now; I begin working on my master's degree in September. I've been accepted into a Ph.D. program. It's going to take five or six years to complete, but in the end, I'll be Doctor Harriett Bailey Kepler."

"Bravo, Sis!" Albert said. "That will seal your fate with Mother. Once she hears this news, she'll never speak to you again. Lucky you!"

Albert grinned at Alice, who burst into laughter.

33

DAYS OF WINE AND ROSES

*H*arriett's first week as CFO-in-training was filled with meetings, business lunches, and introductions. Mr. Roland and Mr. Dugan proudly presented their protégé to the Madison corporate world, assuring them of her capabilities. Meanwhile, Jim LaMantia proved capable; the professional young man learned quickly. By the time Friday night arrived, Harriett was exhausted, but far from overwhelmed. Walking through the empty house, she smiled, knowing tomorrow her house would transition into a home.

Alice arrived promptly at nine. Harriett abandoned her stack of paper on her desk to answer the door.

"Good morning. Want some coffee?" she asked.

"No, but I'd love some tea. Coffee irritates my stomach." Alice rubbed her belly, then grinned. "I didn't want to tell you until after your celebration, but I'm pregnant again!"

Harriett jumped up and down. "Goodness, you're as fertile as Esther. I can't believe she has four children, and she's only thirty-three."

"She takes after Mother. Looks like I'll be doing the same.

Polly just turned one." The women walked down the hallway into the kitchen. "So, what's coming today?"

The doorbell rang, interrupting their conversation. Harriett jumped up.

"It's starting. I ordered so much stuff—I'm anxious to see all of it together!"

Harriett returned with two boxes from Gimbel's department store. She cut the tape and began removing individually wrapped items.

"Oh, goody, my china. What do you think?" Harriett unwrapped a pale blue-and-white porcelain dinner plate trimmed in a gold band. "It's called 'Southern Blue and Gold' by Crown Staffordshire. I wanted something simple, but elegant."

"I think you've hit it straight on. That's a gorgeous pattern. Food will display beautifully."

Harriett broke into a roaring laugh. "Good grief, I forgot I had to be able to cook before I can use them!"

"I'll teach you. You have all this spare time over the summer. Come down, you can learn about cooking and babies simultaneously." Alice patted her tummy.

"Don't ruin today. I don't want to think about my losses, only my purchases."

The doorbell rang again. Alice gasped as the delivery men carried a rectangular, Regency-style mahogany table with ten side chairs and two armchairs into the dining room, followed by a large, matching, buffet.

"That is stunning!" Alice fingered a drawer pull on the console.

"Thanks. I didn't want anything too formal, but this room is special, with fabric walls. I went for a lower profile, but classic design." Harriett motioned to have the table centered under the crystal chandelier.

"Listen to Miss Home Decorator!" Alice touched the wall.

"Know its history?"

"Papa said this is hand-painted silk from Japan. Songer bought it long before the war." Harriett admired the pink cherry blossoms painted on white-and-blue silk, which covered the walls above framed wooden panels. "I don't know where Songer got all the money. Papa held the same position during the war and never made that much money."

Alice guffawed. "Do we know that for a fact? Mother confiscated his paychecks. For all we know, she has a small fortune hidden someplace in her closet."

"At least he's starting to stand up for himself. He bought a new suit just for my graduation."

Alice stroked her sister's face. "Harriett, he is so proud of you. We all are. Do you know he actually disparaged her last weekend?"

"No!" The doorbell rang the third time.

"Now what? How much did you spend?"

"Sister dear, more than I should have." Harriett trotted to the entry. "But I bought some shares of stock too."

Delivery number three was a Zenith television encased in a sleek walnut cabinet. Harriett placed it in the living room, plugged it in, and adjusted the antennae for best reception.

"The men are coming next weekend to install a Channel Master on my roof." She giggled. "Not that I'll have time to watch TV once school starts again."

Deliveries continued throughout the day. Alice fondled Harriett's new bakeware with envy. "Teddy needs to buy me some of this, as much as I cook and bake."

The last delivery of the day, a secondhand, blue-and-green, tufted wool, area rug was laid in the office. Harriett tossed a few green-and-yellow floral throw pillows on Teddy's discarded chair and into the window nook. A green, glass-shaded apothecary lamp sat on her desk.

"All I need are draperies and another chair, and this room

is done." Harriett smoothed the green, blue, and yellow plaid of the newly upholstered window seat as both women stared outside.

"No, leave the windows bare." Alice sighed and turned. "That old chair looks great in here. It was too big for our house, with all my new modern furniture. But in this room, it's perfect." Alice plopped into the stuffed leather chair. "Don't you dare tell Teddy, but this chair is extremely comfortable!"

The sisters talked and laughed the rest of the day, unpacking boxes of used books and consignment store treasures, partially filling shelves and cabinets.

At three, Alice slumped into a kitchen chair. "Harriett, I'm going home for a quick nap and to make supper. Laurena is babysitting Polly today."

"What's up with Albert and Laurena? Are they getting serious?"

"It wouldn't surprise me to see a ring on her finger this summer. They see a lot of each other."

Harriett yawned. "It's about time Albert gets married. Sorry I kept you so long, especially now that you are pregnant."

Alice returned the yawn and rubbed her back. "It's okay. This place is starting to look like a real home!"

A DIFFERENT HILL

JULY 1952, KOREA

*E*ddy spent the next week screaming for Rosa from his jail cell while Wally continued his unsuccessful search. Wally traveled to the church, hoping to find her grandparents' last name. However, a visiting priest refused to disclose personal information, despite pleading and begging. The first week of May 1952, Private Kepler was placed on a transport to Korea and was sent directly to the front line.

Being in-country for six weeks, Eddy missed the lingering Korean winter and late spring thaw. He was thrust directly into hot temperatures and high humidity that rendered the men uncomfortably sopping-wet—no cooling Adriatic Sea breeze in sight. The stench of body sweat was a dead give-away to their position.

Mail caught up with him several weeks after his arrival. Although his mother continued to write faithfully, chastising him for his silence, Harriett's correspondence dwindled in frequency to once a month. Wally wrote once, reporting unsuccessful search results. Rosa and Joey had vanished.

After such an easy assignment in Trieste, Eddy hated Korea. He hated the heat, his soaking wet skivvies, eating

K-rations, and living in trenches. He hated not finding Rosa; he hated that he was drafted despite marrying Harriett to avoid it. His life consisted of digging holes, fighting fiercely, eating slop, sleeping on the ground, then repeating.

Fighting was heavy the past several weeks. His company was on an endless quest for one hill, gaining real estate only to lose it the next day.

The morning began with heavy shelling from both sides in the distance. Eddy's company was dug into the side of a rocky hill, with minimal vegetation for shade or cover. Although early, the sun scorched the ground, raising a misty fog. The air was dense with water and the smell of artillery smoke clung to the humidity. Command predicted slow fighting today, with the main push several miles away. Taking advantage of the forecast, most of the men wandered out of their fox holes to eat breakfast and to try to catch an infrequent fleeting breeze.

Eddy happily fed his hungry belly, having just finished a four-hour watch. He pulled out the latest letter from Harriett and reread it.

"Shit," Eddy announced.

His hole mate, Sam Santino, straightened up. "Now what's your beef, Kepler? All you do is complain."

"Shut up, asshole. My wife wants a divorce." Eddy crumpled the letter and shoved it into his pocket.

"I don't blame her one bit." Santino sunk back into the hole.

"Well, keep your trap shut. I need some sleep." Eddy's arguing was interrupted with a cry from down the line. Senses dulled and tired, he reacted too late to the warning call and the sound of gunfire. A sniper's bullet entered Eddy's shin from the front, clipped the tibia, and exited the back of the calf.

The bone cracked, the leg collapsed. Eddy winced, then fainted.

"Medic!" screamed Santino. "Kepler's hit!"

∞ ∞ ∞

Eddy awoke to a floating sensation and the *whop-whop* of aircraft. Metal reflected a flash of sunlight. He closed his eyes to block the glare, then prayed in disbelief for an immediate demise.

His next recollection was on a ground stretcher, with men hurriedly stepping over him and dozens of other wounded soldiers surrounding him. His ringing ears deciphered triage saying, as they loosened then retightened the tourniquet on his leg, "This one can wait. The bleeding is stopped. Not too far down the list—he's still in danger of losing that leg."

Eddy fainted as the nurse tagged him yellow.

He regained consciousness in a hospital bed. Groggy and in pain, he tried to roll onto his side. Only one leg moved; the other caught and pulled. Fire shot through his leg that was suspended in traction.

He yelled out in agony, "Help me!"

A busy orderly scurried to his bed. "What ya need Mac? Pretty busy here, so if it's not an emergency, don't interrupt. I got dying men to tend to."

"I'm in pain. Do I still have both my legs?" Eddy gagged; the stench of burning skin, blood, and hot metal overpowered the odor of men wedged tightly into the cramped tent. Thrashing, he screamed, "Where the fuck am I?"

His blood pressure increased; sweat dripped from his forehead as he swooned.

"Okay, buddy. Shut up." The orderly called for a nurse. "This one's in shock and needs morphine."

A calm voice ordered, "Settle down. You have both legs."

Eddy felt the needle prick then drifted into hallucinating sleep. Fitfully, he dreamed of Rosa and Harriett together in battle, fighting over Joey, then fighting with him. Eddy lost both battles.

The fourth time Eddy awoke, bright spotlights blazed from above. He squinted. Men and women buzzed around him with less urgency than in the last room.

"Good evening, Private," a masked doctor said as a nurse placed a plastic covering over Eddy's mouth." I'm going to have a look at that leg of yours. Close your eyes. Nite-nite."

Eddy waited but never got groggy. "Doc?"

"Shit," replied the surgeon. "I thought the gas would make it. Sorry son, we're going to have to do this the old-fashioned way. Too many surgeries today, not enough supplies. Morphine's already gone." The doctor turned to a nurse. "Find some leather."

Eddy's eyes widened in horror. The nurse stroked his head and placed a leather strap into his mouth. "Settle down, son, and bite hard on this. It's going to hurt, but it will be over quickly."

"Bite hard!" the doctor said as he manipulated the bone into place with a snap.

The pain radiated through Eddy's body. He understood the phrase *seeing stars*. Head spinning and ears ringing, he collapsed into unconsciousness yet again, thinking, *God, help me through this never-ending day.*

∞ ∞ ∞

A petite blonde nurse sponged his head as Eddy finally opened his eyes. "Who are you?"

She smiled and continued his bath. "Nurse Dillard, but you may call me Cindy. Welcome back. I'm surprised you slept through the night."

Eddy looked around the tent as he slowly remembered the previous day. "Where am I?"

"You're at the 8076 M.A.S.H. You were hit in the leg." Cindy moved to his leg, removed the bandage, and cleaned the wound. "Looks great. You'll be up and about in no time."

Eddy reached forward, trying to sit up. "Do I still have two legs?"

"Yes, you do." Cindy redressed the break. Before moving on to the next patient, she added, "You are one lucky guy, Private. The bullet only clipped the bone—clean break. The doctor will cast you today." She walked away.

"Wait! Don't go yet," he said as he reached for the back of her apron. "I need pain meds; my leg is on fire."

"None left, only aspirin, but I'll give you two." She dumped them into Eddy's hand. "These will help, some."

Eddy swallowed the two white tablets. "Wait, stay and talk to me."

"No can do, Private. Other pretty boys need my help this morning."

Eddy watched eagerly as Nurse Cindy Dillard tended to her other wards. *It's been too long since I've seen such a pretty girl,* he thought. He lay on his cot, trying to force sleep when the doctor entered.

"Private Kepler. I'm going to check your leg. If it looks to be healing, then I'll apply a walking cast. You'll be mobile tomorrow."

"Tomorrow?" Eddy thought for a moment. "Anyone else from my unit in here?"

The doctor checked his chart for his company information. Seeing Bravo company, he frowned.

"Sorry, son. You were luckier than the other guy. We lost a sergeant from Bravo."

Applied pressure above and below the break caused Eddy to wince. "Easy, Doc. How about some pain meds?"

"None to give. Echo and Delta companies were not as lucky as Bravo. Casualties were high, and supplies are low. I'm out of morphine and blood." As an afterthought, he added, "What I'd do for some O negative blood right now."

"I'm O negative, Doc. Need some blood?" Eddy held out his arm.

The doctor's eyes widened. "Let's get you cast first before I go poking your arm. But, I'll be back this afternoon to drain you, Private! On that, you may bet."

The doctor instructed an orderly who arrived with plaster of Paris and fabric strips. He applied the first layer of gauze, starting with open toes, then worked his way over the break and up to the knee.

"Holy hell. How big is this thing?"

"Sorry, son," the doctor applied a coat of plaster of Paris. "Your whole leg needs to remain immobile, including the ankle and knee. This will be hot and itchy, especially in this weather. I wouldn't do it if it weren't necessary. Orderly, take over."

Layer after layer was applied until the leg, and before long, foot to knee was encased. The orderly smoothed the sole for easy walking and added a rubber heel pad. Next, he rounded the top edges near the knee, ensuring no sharp, jagged edges. The final thin coat was leveled to a velvety finish.

"Keep still, buddy. This will take a couple of hours to dry properly. If you need to move your bowels, call for a bedpan." The orderly hung a urinal next to his bed. "Enjoy the rest of today, Private. You move out of the high-rent district tomorrow."

Eddy grunted. Reaching into his pocket, he retrieved Harriett's letter. The tears streamed down his face as he read. *You're a fuck-up, Kepler. You've lost both of them.* Muffled sobs lulled him into a dreamless fitful sleep.

The orderly nudged his arm. "Wake up, Private. Time to feed your friends."

"What?" Eddy rubbed his eyes, still moist from before. "I'm starving. Is it time to eat?"

"You haven't eaten today?" He checked his list.

Eddy's stomach obliged by growling. "Not that I remember. Sounds like my belly doesn't remember either."

"Okay, let's feed you first. I don't want you fainting. You did enough of that yesterday." The orderly laughed. "Big burly man like you dropped like a girl."

"Hey, that wasn't nice."

"The truth sometimes hurts, Private."

The orderly returned with a tray of greenish-gray, semi-solid slop. Eddy gagged. Reaching for his mouth, he muttered, "That's disgusting."

"Wait till you taste it! Dig in."

After he ate some, the orderly tapped Eddy's arm. "Got any good veins? Aah. There's one."

The needle slipped into his arm. Three bags later, Nurse Dillard came to collect Eddy's donation.

Eddy, lightheaded and hungry, forced a smile. "Cindy, was it? Glad to see you. Can you stop draining me now?"

She clamped the IV and pulled the fourth pint. "We're keeping the needle in, Private Vampire. We need more blood from you." She reached into her pocket and dropped an apple and a wrapped sandwich onto his lap. "Here, I'll sneak you some more food from the officer's mess tonight. You need your strength. The bloodletting continues while you're in camp."

"Thanks." The infamous Kepler grin crossed his face for the first time in five months.

PRIVATE VAMPIRE

AUGUST 1952, KOREA

*E*ddy strolled through camp, jumping puddles and dodging raindrops on his way to the medical tent for his daily appointment. He, along with the entire camp, remained in a constant state of *drenched*. Daily deluge over the past thirty days dampened clothing and spirits alike. The open toes of his cast leg were shriveled, while the rest of his cast itched and smelled like wet dog.

He poked his head into the door. "Doc, I'm here. Left arm today, okay? When am I getting out of this godforsaken swamp? I want this off!"

His call was met with a grunt from the company clerk, not the usual doctor or nurse that drew his blood. "Oh, Kepler. Hey, the doctor's not here right now." Corporal Dennis Foust paced around the room, rubbing his head. "Where the hell am I going to get seven pairs of alligator forceps, a generator, penicillin, and thirty pairs of dry socks?"

Eddy's ears perked up. Another supply issue to solve. "What's that you need, Sergeant?"

"Not now, Kepler, I have a problem."

"Yep. I hear you mumbling. Maybe I can help?" Eddy pushed his way into the tent and took a seat.

Corporal Foust glared at the GI. "You're one bold SOB, boy."

Eddy grinned. "Yeah, I know. Now, what kind of generator do you need, and what was the other thing...an alligator what? The socks and penicillin are a piece of cake."

Corporal Foust stopped pacing and faced Eddy. "Private, if you can provide dry socks, I'll pull some strings to get you in the officer's mess."

Eddy tugged on his sagging trousers. "You got a deal. Can you make a couple of phone calls for me?"

"Base to base?"

"Yep. Call the supply Sarge in Trieste. He'll get Wally Stuart, my ah...partner. We'll get you whatever you need."

∞ ∞ ∞

Four days later, the camp commander summoned his company clerk. "Congratulations, Corporal Foust. I don't know how you worked that miracle, especially after I tried to pull strings myself."

Colonel Bowers motioned to a stack of boxes filled with vials of penicillin, ampoules of morphine, multiple sizes and shapes of clamps and forceps, and precious, dry socks. Case after case of dry socks.

Foust blushed. "Thank you, sir. I wish I could take credit for this, but it was Private Kepler. He's the one with connections."

Bowers glanced over his camp roster. "I don't see a Private Kepler listed. Is he new?"

"Nah. He's a recovering patient. The vampire. The guy in the cast that smells like a dead skunk." Foust laughed at his own cleverness. "Stupid idiot walks daily in this rain. The cast never dries out. But he sure is connected."

"You're telling me our O negative source provides more than blood?" Colonel Bowers straightened the papers on his desk. "Foust, get me the private's file, *stat*."

Three days later, Eddy made his daily wet trek to the medical tent. Colonel Bowers was waiting for him.

"Private Kepler?" asked Bowers.

Eddy saluted the commander. "Yes, sir."

"I understand you're the one responsible for getting my supplies." Bowers motioned for Eddy to have a seat.

Standing, Eddy said, "Yes, Sir."

"How the hell did you pull that off? *I* even tried but was denied. Sit." His hand went to the chair. "What pull do you have that I don't?"

"Well, I have a couple of contacts in Trieste, sir."

Bowers smiled and sat. Eddy followed suit. "Yes, Private, I read your file. It looks like you had glowing reviews before you got mixed up with some girl. You were a good supply man until that silly business of going AWOL."

Eddy pursed his lips in response.

Bowers continued. "Stripped rank. Looks to me like you should be in Leavenworth, not Korea. Any of this business illegal?"

"No, not illegal. Creative, but with the law, mostly. We cut corners, avoid red tape, move things along faster."

"Hmm. Ongoing enterprise?" Bowers scratched his chin. "Tell me about the girl."

"Sir, I'd rather not." Eddy clenched his teeth.

"Son, if you want any chance of avoiding the frontline, I suggest you change your mind."

Eddy leaned back, sighed, and began talking, starting with Harriett, then Rosa, and ending with Joey, while Colonel Bowers listened quietly.

∞ ∞ ∞

Bowers discussed his proposal with his second in command, who called the base in Trieste. The men met two days later.

Bowers reviewed his notes. "Looks like this man Hill has a beef with Kepler."

"Yes. But I got the dirty from Kepler's old supply sergeant. Hill has the hots for the girl Kepler impregnated, so it's personal. Other than going AWOL, the kid is a decent soldier—arrogant, but resourceful. Physically strong, just not the brightest. Thinks with the wrong head."

"Considering his connections and being a private blood bank, am I making a mistake bringing him on?"

"He's a pretty boy. Thinks highly of himself. But if we can keep him away from the nurses, I'd say go for it."

Bowers evened his stack of papers. "Call Kepler in. I'll talk to the boy."

∞ ∞ ∞

"Kepler, have a seat." Eddy sat immediately. "I'm sure you're aware of why you're here."

"Yes, Sir." Eddy dried his palms on his pants.

Bowers sniffed. "Wow, when is that smelly thing coming off your leg?"

"I barely notice it anymore. I think next week." Eddy relaxed slightly.

Bowers blew his nose. "I spoke with your commanding officers in Trieste and at the front. I am working on the paperwork for a transfer, but it depends on your attitude. If I bring you over, do I have your word you'll be on your best behavior?"

Eddy cleared his throat. "Are you asking me to be celibate, sir?"

"No, Private." Bowers laughed. "But, I expect you to use birth control to prevent any additional pregnancies. If you need education on that, our doctors will provide it. No thoughts of AWOL. You're here until the end of your tour. Understood?" Bowers stood.

Eddy left his chair. "Sir, I'd be crazy not to accept your offer. I'm still in Korea, but this is better than the front line soaking wet. At least here, I sleep in a tent."

"Welcome to M.A.S.H. 8076, private Kepler. You'll bunk with Corporal Foust from now on."

∞ ∞ ∞

Two days later, the rain began to lessen. Humidity off the charts, late-summer heat conquered daily showers. Eddy returned to the medic's tent for his scheduled blood draw. Each soldier he passed stopped to speak. Some welcomed him to the 8076th; others gave him cigarettes. One nurse kissed him on the cheek.

The door to the tent was open, so Eddy walked in. "Hey, Doc. I'm here for my daily drain. Can I get this cast off yet?" Eddy scratched his raw leg.

"Kepler, good to see you!" The doctor shook Eddy's hand. "Thanks, buddy!"

"Why is everyone so nice to me?" Eddy flicked mud from his exposed toes.

"The socks. The entire camp was issued a new pair of dry socks. Foust gave you credit." The doctor extended Eddy's booted leg. "And the penicillin. I don't want to know how you arranged it, but I'm thankful you did. You just saved a bunch of youngsters."

"Glad to help." Eddy sat and raised his pant leg. "Can I be rid of this?"

The doctor stiffened at the stench of the cast. "Yikes. We better get that off you before it rots your leg." Smiling, he lifted a small saw from the shelf.

Eddy scowled. "Careful there, Doc. I want my blood let from my arm, not my leg."

36

GHOSTS IN THE ATTIC

SEPTEMBER 1952, CAMPBELLSVILLE

*H*arriett changed into her nightgown and bounced onto the bed, sandwich and milk in hand. Madison College offered many postgraduate evening and weekend classes for working students. Today was the first day back after the summer break. She took a bite and opened her steno pad to review her schedule and curriculum requirements. With any luck, she'd be awarded her master's degree in three years.

As she read and ate, she thought she heard a noise. She stopped chewing to listen. Sure enough, a clawing sound came from above. *Geez, Louise, what is that?* She shuddered as she reviewed a mental list of potential culprits. The crash of something toppling over caused her to bolt upright.

She dialed the phone. "Earl, it's Harriett. I hate to bother you so late, but there's something in my attic. Can you come over?"

"Right now?" Earl rubbed the sleep from his eyes.

"If it's not too much trouble. It's too big for a mouse. Something fell."

"Okay."

Her fingers twitched as she replaced the receiver in the cradle. She threw on a fuzzy pink robe, but decided it was inappropriate.

Fifteen minutes later, Earl rang the bell. "Are you okay?" he asked as Harriett, wearing trousers and a blouse, ushered him inside.

"Yes. It's scratching and knocking things over. Several things came thundering to the floor." She bit her lower lip. "I'm sorry to be such a wimp. I was afraid to go upstairs without backup. I'd call Papa, but he doesn't have a phone."

Earl laughed. "No problem. Wow, this place looks great!" He glanced into both side rooms as he approached the front staircase. "You've spent some money!"

Harriett blushed. "I hate to admit just how much. But it is looking more like a home, isn't it?"

"Yes—but furniture doesn't make a home; people do."

The color drained from Harriett's face.

"Oh, Harriett..." Earl grabbed her arm. "I'm so sorry. I didn't mean...my brother's an idiot."

"Shall we discuss Edgar Jr. after we catch my intruder?" Harriett picked up a laundry basket and followed Earl up the steps.

"Ouch! 'Edgar Jr.!'" They both grinned.

"Snare now, scandal later."

Harriett handed him a shiny new key. Earl opened the door to the attic and shone his flashlight. Scampering paws and more tumbling boxes came from the far-left corner. His light followed the sound.

"You have a ceiling light?" Earl asked at the same time Harriett flipped the switch. Two bare bulbs illuminated, casting long thin shadows across the massive expanse.

"Geez, Louise. What did Songers leave up here?" Harriett peeked around Earl at stacks of boxes and hanging items.

"From the looks of it, they left behind everything they

didn't want to deal with." Earl skirted a pile as he moved forward. "Have you ever been up here?"

"No. I know that sounds terrible. I needed a key. I've just had enough to handle, with the first two floors and the basement. Not to mention the gardens." Harriett sighed. "Papa has been such a saint helping me. I couldn't have done it without him."

The attic was finished, ceiling, walls, and floor. Even at six feet tall, Earl walked upright with ease.

"Over there." He pointed to four shining eyes. "Give me the basket and go get a broom. I think you have two pet raccoons."

Harriett heaved a sigh of relief. "Racoons I can handle. Rats, ghosts, not so much." She giggled. "Be right back with the broom. Want a shotgun?"

"Good God, Harriett. I didn't take you for Annie Oakley."

"I roamed the woods with Papa my entire childhood. Of course, I can shoot. I don't really want buckshot in my wall, but I also do not want raccoons in my roof."

"A broom will do." Earl closed in on the mammals. Harriett returned to find two chubby raccoons hissing and baring their teeth.

"They're not happy fellows, but they'd make a nice coat!" She handed Earl the broom.

He whacked the first over the head—one unconscious raccoon. The second snarled, showing its claws. Earl raised the broom; the animal jumped straight toward him. Harriett swung a second broom, connecting midair. The raccoon fell beside its mate.

Earl looked at his tiny sister-in-law. "Good arm. Thanks. I forgot they attack."

"They do, especially when they have rabies. Careful sweeping them into the basket. Let's send them on their way before they regain consciousness." Harriett viewed the animals, then searched the attic and found a discarded blanket. "He doesn't look rabid. Wrap the basket in this."

"You're very resourceful, for calling yourself a wimp!" Earl carried the basket down the back stairs, through the kitchen, and outside to the forest's edge. He dumped the still mammals into a heap and whispered, "If I were you, I'd skedaddle before she gets a chance to shoot you in the morning."

Inside the house, Harriett flicked the lights on one by one, illuminating the entire property. She then poured boiling water into a teapot and placed cups and saucers on the table.

"Well, now that we're both wide awake, how about something to eat?" She pushed a plate of cinnamon rolls toward Earl.

"Did you bake these?" Earl hungrily took a bite. "Wow! Yummy."

"Yes. It's so funny. I can bake cakes, bread, cookies, but I can't *cook* to save my soul. I just don't get it. I can read, I'm bright enough, but I am a lousy cook."

Earl reached for her hand. "Any man would be happy to have you as a wife, cooking abilities or not."

Harriett hesitated before pulling away. She sat, head down, eyes lowered, silent.

"I'm sorry, Harriett. That was uncalled for." Earl pushed back his chair and stood. "I should be leaving. May I take one of these rolls home for Mother?"

Without looking at him, Harriett packaged two cinnamon buns in waxed paper. Instead of handing it directly, she lay the parcel on the table.

"There you go," she said, motioning. "One for each of you. Thank you for helping me tonight. I'm sorry to disturb your sleep."

"Harriett." Earl reached for her again.

"No, Earl, please don't." She took a step backward.

"I just want to say I'll be back to patch their entrance point. After tonight, I don't think they'll be back tomorrow. But they may be dumb enough to try it later."

"Hmm. Yep, animals try-try again. Thank you."

She ushered Earl out, watching as he descended the steps. When he was halfway down, he turned, glancing back. She waved, then, spinning around, she closed and locked the door. She aimlessly wandered through the house to extinguish the lights; it was forty-five minutes before she changed and jumped back into her bed.

Sleep evaded her for hours.

37

CHUTES AND LADDERS

OCTOBER 1952, CAMPBELLSVILLE

*O*n a Friday night in mid-October, Olive paced the kitchen waiting for Tabs to return from Harriett's work. The door opened just after six-thirty.

Olive glared at her husband. "Where have you been? I held supper for you!" She spit the words at Tabs as she wrung her handkerchief.

Ignoring her, Tabs hung his jacket on the back of the door.

"I asked you a question." Olive reached for his arm; Tabs pulled away.

"I get home every day at the same time. What's your problem today?" Strolling to the sink, he washed his hands and face, then sat down at the table.

"*That* is the problem!" Olive hissed.

"What are you talking about, woman?" Thirty years of marriage had eroded the gentle, kindly man to tolerance, with only strained love remaining.

"You're gone every day, all day. Working for your precious Janie. Well, I have chores for you also."

Both his hands brushed through his hair, stopping to cover his face. "Fine. What do you want me to do?"

The pale blue color was barely visible through the slits of her eyes. "You need to stay home tomorrow." She flung a piece of paper at him. "Here's my list! I expect it to be completed before you go back to Harriett's." She spun on her heel and clomped out of the kitchen.

The paper clipped Tabs' cheek. He scanned the seven items: gutters, coal bin, windows, pantry, china closet, floors, and walls. *She wants me to clean the entire house!*

Calling after Olive, he asked, "Where's supper?"

"Feed yourself!"

∞ ∞ ∞

On Saturday, Harriett drove to Madison for one early morning class. Fog settled low in the valleys as the earth released its last stored heat into the chilled autumn air. The sun was directly overhead when she returned to Campbellsville. Tabs was not to be found. Harriett grabbed a rake and began piling leaves in the backyard. It was edged with mostly pines, but one large maple tree had shed its canopy of summer shade. Within an hour, the grass beyond the patio was once again green.

Good time for a bathroom break, she thought. Her grumbling stomach reminded her that she had not eaten lunch. She removed her work boots at the kitchen door; heading inside, she constructed a ham and cheese sandwich, then sliced the last of Tabs' tomatoes as a special treat.

One bite into her lunch, the phone rang. Harriett ran to the office. "Hello, Harriett Bailey Kepler speaking." To herself, she thought, *I probably need to install a phone in the kitchen. This house is too big for only one receiver.*

The caller was silent for a moment. "Mrs. Kepler. This is Arlie Burke, Doctor Paulson's nurse." Arlie hesitated. "Can you come down to the doctor's office? Your mother is here."

Harriett gasped. "What's happened to Mother? Is she okay?"

"Mrs. Kepler, there's been an accident. Your mother is fine. We need you to come immediately."

"Of course. I'll be there in five minutes...please tell me what is wrong." Harriett insisted.

"Not over the phone Mrs. Kepler. Thank you. Mrs. Bailey specifically requested you." The phone clicked dead.

Harriett threw her uncovered sandwich into the refrigerator and grabbed her handbag. She fumbled, searching for her keys.

"Come on," she said, pulling them from the bottom.

Minutes later, she parked the car. The harsh, bright light and antiseptic smell caused her body to quiver as she sprinted into the office.

"Hello. Where is Olive Bailey?" Harriett asked the empty lobby. "Hello, anyone here?" she said, waiting for the sound of footsteps.

Nurse Arlie Burke opened a side door. "Mrs. Kepler, thank you for coming so quickly. Your mother is in here." She motioned into a secondary waiting room furnished with only chairs.

Olive sat, head in her lap, hands covering her face. She looked to be crying. Harriett rushed to her side to embrace her. "Mother, I'm here. What is wrong? Are you sick?"

Harriett withdrew when she met Olive's gaze, puffy red eyes wet with tears. "It was an accident, I swear it. I didn't mean to..."

Unaccustomed to raw emotions other than rage, Harriett grabbed her wrists. "You didn't mean to what, Mother? What are you talking about?"

Olive gasped, bursting into violent sobs. "I only meant to jiggle, a joke."

"You're not making any sense." Harriett stood and turned to Arlie. "What is she talking about?"

"In here, Mrs. Kepler." Arlie ushered Harriett into a different room, starker than the last. A body covered with a sheet lay on the examination table.

A chill went through her, heart palpitating with anticipation, she began sweating. "Who is that?" she asked, voice quivering.

Arlie slid back the covering. Tobias Bailey lay motionless on the metal gurney. His pale skin was already turning cold but absent rigor. Closed eyes and a slight smile gave the impression of sleep. The only indication of concern was an unnatural bend of his neck.

Harriett screamed. "Papa! Oh my God! What happened to Papa?" Air refused to flow through her lungs. Her legs wobbled; a bottle crashed to the floor as she reached out to steady herself. "No, Papa, you can't leave me!"

Arlie's firm grip prevented Harriett from melting onto the floor. "Please sit, Mrs. Kepler. I know this is a shock. There was an accident." The nurse snapped an ampoule and waved the pungent, ammonia, smelling-salts under Harriett's nose.

Harriett jerked her head then slouched into a chair, burying her face in her hands. "Is he gone?"

"I'm afraid so. He fell off a ladder and broke his neck."

"A ladder? When did this happen?" Harriett fumbled for her handbag, searching for a handkerchief.

The empathetic nurse handed her a tissue then rubbed her back. "About forty minutes before I called you. Your mother's neighbor called the ambulance that brought them in. Olive asked specifically for you."

"What is she talking about, 'a little jiggle?'" Harriett inhaled, blew her nose, then straightened her back. Her body shook, but her mind regained composure.

"I truly don't know. She's been incoherent since she

arrived. Doc gave her a sedative before he left." Arlie swept the shattered glass into her dustpan.

"The doctor's not here? Where did he go?" Harriett's breath steadied and slowed.

The nurse handed her a glass of water. "After he pronounced your father, he went to inspect the scene of the accident. He'll have extra paperwork to file, considering the circumstances. You know—rule out foul play." She paused. "The county sheriff is with him."

Harriett took several deep breaths before speaking. "Please call my sister, Alice. It's Saturday, so she'll be at the pharmacy helping Teddy. I want her here before we do anything." She searched the room as if looking for an escape route but found none. "What do we do next?"

"Truthfully, I'm not sure. Doc may want to perform an autopsy; the county coroner may initiate an inquiry. The best thing to do right now is to take your mother back to your house. She can't go home just yet until the investigation is complete."

Harriett stood and smoothed her blouse. She stroked Tabs' face. "Papa, dear Papa. How will I ever survive without you?" Kissing his forehead in a final goodbye, she whispered, "I love you so much. Be at peace. You're the best father ever to walk this wretched earth."

She lingered a moment before turning to Arlie. "Thank you, Nurse. No need to call Alice. I'll do that from home, and I'll inform the rest of my family."

Arlie led Harriett back to a sleeping Olive. Her head flopped to the side, and she was snoring loudly.

Harriett shook her shoulder briskly. "Mother, for God's sake, wake up, you…" She stopped herself from belittling Olive in front of Arlie. "Mother, we're going up the hill, like it or not. Now get up, and for once in your life, cooperate."

Slowly, Olive stood as Harriett tugged on her arm, pulling her out of the office.

Arlie called after them. "I'll be in touch, Mrs. Kepler, to tell you what's next."

∞ ∞ ∞

Harriett rubbed her numb head. Olive was sound asleep in her guest bedroom. Alice, Albert, June, and Esther sat around the kitchen table. The sisters' husbands were in charge of the children.

"Now what?" asked Albert. "What do we do with Mother?"

Harriett sullenly moved her head back and forth. "I still can't believe it. It's a bad dream." She refreshed their glasses with iced tea.

Alice massaged her aching back. "I'm in a fog. Do you really think she pushed him on purpose?"

"She's more than capable of it!" Albert balled his hands into fists. "The woman is a pathetic bitch."

Harriett nodded. "I'm sorry, guys, but I will not care for her. I'll contribute money if it's necessary. But she's not living here, and I'll not stop in to visit her." Harriett ran her hands through her hair. "I just can't, after she's treated me so callously. I consider her dead, too!"

Esther and June glanced at each other. June sighed. "I've been terrified of her my entire life."

Esther agreed. "Why do you think I allowed myself to get pregnant?"

Alice laughed. "Allowed yourself? As a ready-to-pop mother, do you 'allow yourself?'"

Esther ticked her tongue. "You know what I mean. I knew premarital sex was taboo, but Darrell and I were in love." She giggled. "Still in love. It was my escape."

June crumpled a napkin, throwing it at Esther. "Yeah, you abandoned me. Threw me to the wolf!"

Harriett interrupted. "We can discuss our feelings another time. Right now, we need to decide her fate."

Alice rubbed her bulging belly. "Do you think we can convince the guys to take turns looking in on her? She's still mobile, more than capable of daily activity. It's house maintenance and such that we need to see to."

Esther nodded in agreement. "Right, and she probably doesn't want us around. She never had time for us while we were growing up, always locked herself in her private parlor," she said, crunching a cookie. "She'll not want company now. She'll probably celebrate seclusion."

Harriett considered the suggestion. "Alice, that's a good idea. If Teddy, Darrell, Dave, and Albert look in weekly, alternating months, it's only twelve individual visits a year. Creative wives should be able to compensate somehow!"

Esther and Alice both scoffed. "If we have to be that 'creative,'" Esther said, "we'll end up pregnant! Again!"

"Listen to sweet, innocent Harriett. You sound like a woman of the world!" Albert guffawed. "What are they teaching you in college?"

∞ ∞ ∞

Harriett muddled through the next day in a haze. The rawness of grief engulfed her in agony as if her body were being tortured with thousands of needles on fire. She anguished; her heart shattered as she watched her mother's near jubilant mood.

Fortunately for Harriett, Dugan and Co.'s bereavement policy prevented Olive from a triumphant snooping expedition. Olive attempted to sneak up the backstairs on more than one occasion, only to be thwarted by Harriett.

"Mother, stop now! Don't you dare creep away." Harriett shouted from her office when she heard the door leading to the back stairs open.

"I'm going to take a nap. Harriett, what has you so tense?" Olive stomped down the hallway, barging into the den. "Nice room. Makes my old office at the homestead look like a dump."

Harriett glanced up from her work. "You had your own office?"

"Of course, I did. I was the accountant for Westchester Farms, back in its heyday." Olive fingered the spine of several books as she read their titles. "Not a bad collection. You know, I own several first editions of what are now considered classics. Behave yourself, and I'll bequeath them to you."

"Mother, we never engage in conversation. Why so talkative today? Please, I have work to do."

"Keep that attitude, and you'll get nothing from me, Missy!" Olive sneered.

Harriett slammed her hand on the desktop. "I want nothing from you. I am capable of supporting myself."

"*I'm capable of supporting myself!*" Olive mimicked. "What exactly is your job now? Tabs said you were promoted, but wouldn't tell me details."

Harriett's lips curled slightly. *Good for you, Papa*, she thought. "Mother, if you must know, I am vice president and chief financial officer at Dugan and Co. A corporate officer."

Olive held her breath. Closing her eyes, she rebuked her youngest child. "You work with numbers? Can you not do anything without copying my lifelong dreams?" She spit the question. "My education, my house, my husband; what's left that I can call my own?"

Harriett clutched Olive's shoulders. "Mother, I tolerate you because you gave birth to me. There is no love between us. I capitalize on my talents. *My* talents, not yours." She twisted Olive around. "I suggest you take that nap now."

"You're no different than me, Missy," Olive smirked. "Same mean streak too!" Harriett covered her ears to block the clomping up the steps.

"I am nothing like you, and I never shall be. You have no love in your heart, no forgiveness. The sooner you are gone, the better." Immediately regretting her outburst, Harriett groaned. "Argh, Mother! You bring out the worst in people."

She was answered by Olive's cackle. "The future will test your powers of forgiveness, Missy!"

∞ ∞ ∞

A gusty autumn wind blew, chilling all of Campbellsville who gathered at the old Westchester family cemetery for the funeral of Tobias Bailey. Harriett snuggled close to Alice and Albert. Earl stood directly behind her, on the ready. June and Esther clutched each other. Olive stood alone beside a stand of birch trees garbed in a new black dress, shoes, hat, purse, and coat as the minister pronounced a benediction.

Esther muttered to Darrel, "That's where I was conceived. Mother seduced him," she said, pointing to the trees.

His eyes popped. "How do you know that?"

She wiped the tears from her eyes. "Papa confessed the day I announced I was pregnant. He was so understanding. So kind."

"That he was." Darrell squeezed his wife as he gathered Heddy and Violet into his embrace. Lloly and Toby stood holding each other's hands, pretending to be stoic little men.

Harriett studied the gravestones, including the tall, stately obelisk of her grandparents, Polly and Henderson Westchester. Beside it was the curved stone topped with a carved eagle of her infamous uncle Fred, adorned with a fresh bouquet of flowers, as well as the addition of several newer graves, that of her Aunt Ginny and Uncle Ben. It was Harriett's first visit to the once majestic—now dilapidated—farm.

From the top of the knoll, acres of dying daisies and sunflowers crowded uncultivated fields that used to grow corn and wheat. The porch roof of the Georgian house swayed like the back of an old nag. The exterior walls of the left wing teemed with tangled vines, the tentacles crumbling chimneys and window casings.

She whispered to Alice. "I bet this place was once spectacular."

"I was only three or four my last visit, so I don't remember. That was when Grandfather died."

Harriett glanced at her Uncle Benny and Aunt Ingrid. "Who is living in the house, now that Ben is gone? Benny's still in town. Whoever it is, I hope we're permitted to visit the cemetery."

Albert answered, "Aunt Bessie resides in the cottage. The house was left empty when Grandfather died in 1929."

"No wonder it's run down. It would take a small fortune to restore. Too bad. I bet it was glorious."

Alice blew her nose then anxiously tugged on Harriett's arm. "Harriett, I can't bear the thought of Papa being gone. I need a distraction. Think we could go exploring?"

"Geez, Louise Alice. Now is not the time or the place. You're ready to burst at the seams, and you want to go exploring." Their whispering was interrupted.

"Alice, no baby yet?" asked Tildy Jamison, Olive's sister.

"Hi, Aunt Tildy. No. I'm four days overdue, but considering this, I'm glad it waited." Alice nodded at Harriett. "Do you remember my sister?"

"Yes, a pleasure to see you again, Harriett. How are you holding up? I understand you and your father were extremely close."

Harriett sniffled but refused to cry. "I'll manage, Aunt Tildy. Thank you for asking."

"Come visit us, all of you. We're only over there." Tildy pointed to the adjoining property. "I'd love to have company." Tildy motioned to an assembly of women. "I arranged for our DAR chapter to attend. It is only proper. Esther, June, and Alice are members."

Alice added, "That was kind of you."

Tildy glanced at Olive. "How's she doing? Despite appearances, I think she loved him."

Harriett recoiled. "If she did, she had a queer way of showing it. She made his life miserable."

"Harriett dear, she made *everyone's* life miserable."

Conversation ceased as a color guard marched up the slope. "Present arms! Fire!"

All five Bailey children flinched as the sound of rifles ricocheted off the surrounding hills. The command was repeated two more times, each round piercing Harriett's heart. The ceremony ended with two coronets echoing Taps. The beloved father and World War One veteran, receiving full military honors, was lowered into the ground.

The pastor announced, "Tobias's family and the local chapter of the DAR invite you to join them for lunch at the Campbellsville Social Hall."

Not a dry eye could be found as the multitude of friends and family, coworkers, and veterans trudged off the hill to their waiting cars. Olive turned her back on Tabs, lingering at Fred's grave before leaving. Without Eddy by her side, Harriett leaned against Earl for support. Her sisters relied on their husbands while Albert and Laurie walked arm in arm.

"This is worse than losing Lupi." Alice sobbed to Teddy on the drive back to town. "I'm devastated."

Teddy twitched at the mention of Alice's first husband.

"I'm sorry, darling. Your family will get through this together."

"I'm worried about Harriett. She's been so strong. This is more than she needs, what with Eddy incommunicado. She and Papa were so close, I'm afraid she has a breakdown." Sharp pain prohibited her from speech. She grabbed her belly. "Teddy, darling, head to Madison. I think this baby is on its way!"

HOW DO YOU PLEAD?

OCTOBER 1952, CAMPBELLSVILLE

*O*live, anxious to return home after her three-day confinement with Harriett, rode in the hearse and headed directly to Maple Street after the funeral services.

Teddy phoned the Social Hall to announce the birth of their second daughter, Maggie. Emotions peaked, celebrating the birth of a child while grieving the death of their father. One by one, the mourners extended condolences and departed. The county sheriff waited for the Bailey reception line to dissipate before approaching.

"Mrs. Kepler," Sheriff said. "I would like to speak with you first, then add your siblings. Is now a good time?"

Harriett sighed, exhausted. "Now is fine. What's on your mind?"

"Please, shall we sit someplace private?" He motioned to the opposite end of the room. Harriett discarded her trash and followed. "Mrs. Kepler, you were the first to arrive at Dr. Paulson's, is that correct?"

"Yes. Arlie Burke called me because Mother asked for me. But the ambulance dropped both off at the doctor's. Why?" Harriett tilted her head questioningly.

"Did your mother say anything strange to you?"

Harriett exhaled and paused. "Mother said it was an accident, she only meant to *jiggle*. I have no idea what she was talking about."

"I see. I interviewed her privately, but she offered nothing except contempt." He glanced at his notepad. "I think there's more to this story, but I don't have actual physical proof." Exhaling, he added, "I spoke with the neighbor. He had nothing to add but a hysterical Olive begging him to call the ambulance. I believe it's time to call in your brother and sisters."

Tabs' children sat in a circle, waiting for the sheriff to enlighten them.

"Thank you all. I know this is a difficult time. Your father was a pillar of the community. I can't think of a more widely respected man. His loss will be felt for years to come." The sheriff hesitated before continuing. "As you are aware, Dr. Paulson performed an autopsy, and we investigated the scene of the accident immediately after it occurred."

Albert interrupted. "Yes, Sheriff. Poor Harriett housed Mother for three days. Can we get to the point?"

The sheriff drummed his fingers on the table. "Well, considering the circumstances, I believe you have grounds to press charges of criminal negligence against your mother. She may be indirectly, even directly involved with the ladder falling."

"What?" June began sobbing. Esther's face drained of all color.

Albert's fist pounded the tabletop. He stood then kicked over a chair. "That wicked bitch."

Harriett rubbed her eyes, then spoke in a calm, low voice. "There is nothing we can do to bring him back. If we press charges, what happens?"

"Worst case, she's charged with second-degree involuntary manslaughter. She could spend five to ten years in prison. Best case..." He paused. "Well, she's acquitted, you rack up attorney fees, and nothing happens."

"Will you arrest her if we don't press charges?"

"No. I don't have enough evidence to move forward on my own. But if you charge her, I'll be forced to continue the investigation." He wrung his hands. "I wish it were simpler, but it's not. As it is, the investigation is closed."

"What did the autopsy show?"

"Nothing, Mrs. Kepler. No drugs or alcohol. Cause of death was a broken spinal cord, fractured at the neck due to the fall."

The bright autumn sunlight was fading into long afternoon shadows. A month past the equinox, days grew shorter as winter loomed. Darkness spread over the room, matching their mood.

"I see. So we charge her, or we forever hold our peace. Well, what do you guys think? Albert? Esther?" Harriett searched each of their faces.

Esther's eye twitched. "She's our mother. I can't do that to her."

"Well, I say let the bitch rot in hell." Albert pranced around, unable to remain still.

"June?"

June gulped deep breaths of air. "I wish Alice were here, too. He was the best father in the world, but...I'm with Esther. I can't put her away."

Harriett stood. "Please give me a moment to think," she said before walking away. Several minutes later, she returned. "Is this majority rule?"

"Yes, Mrs. Kepler. I'll consider your collective decision." Sheriff continued his finger drumming.

"We shall not press charges. Even if Alice sides with Albert, which I don't think she will, it's three votes to two.

Olive Bailey has already lived her life in prison. She isolated herself from anyone that loved her. Being in a physical prison will make no difference to her." Harriett, gazing into the eyes of her siblings, was met with disgust from Albert and relief from June and Esther. "The sentence she serves will be complete ostracization from her children. None of us want anything to do with her. Our husbands have agreed to take turns checking in on her once a week." Harriett extended her hand to the sheriff. "Thank you, sir. We appreciate your diligence."

"Quite welcome, Mrs. Kepler. Good day, Albert, Mrs. Cline, Mrs. Ralston. Please accept the condolences of my staff and me." He left the Bailey kids huddled together, June and Esther hugging and crying, Albert stomping, and stoic Harriett standing dry-eyed.

∞ ∞ ∞

It was after seven in the evening when Harriett slumped into her office chair to open the past week's mail. Sorted and stacked, she tossed the trash and filed the bills. Instinctively she opened her desk drawer and removed her stationary.

> Oh, Eddy, I desperately need your strength and support right now. I have just lived through the worst week of my life. I never imagined a heart could break into so many pieces. I am devastated that you have abandoned me, but those feelings are nothing compared to the pain and agony I feel today.
>
> Papa is dead.

Harriett dropped her pen. The tears streamed down her face, blotching the ink. Every cell in her ached. She pulled on her hair, hoping physical pain would interrupt her emotional anguish; it didn't. She was so engulfed with grief that she didn't hear the doorbell ring. Pounding on the door triggered a jump.

"Earl!" She dried her eyes then blew her nose. "What are you doing here?"

"May I come in?" Earl grinned self-consciously before moving forward. "Here, these are for you." He pulled a bouquet of sunflowers from behind his back. "You need a little sunshine."

Harriett stared perplexed at her brother-in-law, eyes puffy and red. "Thanks," was all she could manage.

She stood inside the second set of doors without moving, head downcast, fidgeting with a button. Finally, Earl touched her shoulder. "Harriett, is it okay if we sit down?"

Harriett jumped at his touch then rubbed her neck before answering. "I'm sorry, Earl, where are my manners? It's been a difficult day. Please come in." Forcing her feet to move, she dragged her way to the living room.

Before she could ask, Earl said, "Harriett, why don't I make you some coffee. Which cupboard?"

Grief flooded over her like a wave crashing onto a rock. She collapsed onto the sofa and began sobbing uncontrollably. Earl cringed at the sound of her weeping. Opting for boiling water for tea, he quickly returned to Harriett.

"Oh, you dear sweet girl." Earl sat on the couch, his arm around her shoulder. "I'm so sorry. I know you loved him so much."

She felt the warmth of his breathing on her neck. She gasped for air. "The worst of it is, it was a senseless accident." Hearing the words out loud sent a shudder through her body. "Oh God, Earl!" The sound was more like a wail. Harriett flung herself at him, burying her face into his chest. He gently enfolded her in his arms, allowing her to cry, purging the pain.

"There, there. No need to be strong, just cry it out." Earl

squeezed her tightly, unsure of what to do next. Her scent was intoxicating, but her grief was raw. She needed strength, which he happily supplied.

Fifteen minutes later, she straightened her back. "Please forgive my lack of control. I didn't mean to put you in such an awkward situation."

Her usually sparkling eyes, now moist, red, and dark, pleading for relief, looked like the sad orbs of an abused dog. Earl held both her hands, his thumbs rubbing the tops.

"No one should have to bear such grief alone. I'll always be here for you, Harriett. I promise." He moved closer.

She slid to the edge of the couch, eyes widened, and scoffed. "Another Kepler promise to be broken."

Earl pulled away. "That was cruel! I am not my brother. If I make a promise, I keep it." He ran his hands through his wavy hair, the same Kepler waves as Eddy.

"Cruel?" Her brow puckered. "Cruel is not having my husband here for strength when I need him the most. Cruel is losing the man I love more deeply than my own life, at the hands of my mother!"

Earl stood towering over her. "I am not my brother." The words were steady and succinct. "I keep my promises, and I assure you that I shall always be here for you. I…"

Harriett turned away. "I'm sorry. I wasn't being fair, accusing you of Eddy's crimes." She gulped for air like a fish on a line.

"No, you weren't, but it's understandable." Earl's brow softened. His gaze was interrupted by a sound from the kitchen. "You stay, compose yourself. I hear the kettle whistling."

Harriett managed a grin. "The pot is probably dry."

"Then I'll boil more. When I return, I want to talk about Olive. You mentioned foul play?"

"Not today, Earl. Let's talk, but not about her. She's no

longer part of my life." Harriett followed Earl into the kitchen. "Earl, I know I'm being mercurial, but I think you better go. I'm exhausted, depressed, and too vulnerable. Thank you for the flowers, and thank you for caring."

Earl stepped in front of her, blocking the path. "Harriett." He leaned in and kissed her forehead. "I'm here for you, now and forever. Please remember that."

Earl turned and looked back at the end of the long hallway, hesitating a moment before letting himself out. Harriett extinguished the gas burner, then returned to her desk. She reread her letter to Eddy, crinkled it into a ball, and tossed it into the trash. She lay her head on the desk.

Eddy Kepler, why can't you be more like your brother?

39

BYE-BYE EDDY

MARCH 1953, KOREA

*E*ddy adjusted quickly to his life in a M.A.S.H. unit. The amiable provisioner befriended both men and women. Nurse conquests were no challenge; his weapon of choice, a pair of silk pajamas or some perfume, ensured a harem of willing dates. The heat of summer gave way to freezing snowy winter. M.A.S.H. 8076 hunkered down for its third winter in country. Low morality was lifted slightly when Private Kepler supplemented their storeroom with extra blankets and a much-needed heater for the operating tent.

The camp commander, Colonel Bowers, valued Eddy's creative procurement skills. When orders came in for Eddy to rotate home, Bowers called him into his office.

Bowers was sitting behind his desk when Eddy knocked on the door. "Private Kepler, come in, have a seat. I have a proposition for you."

Eddy saluted his superior then took a chair. "What's on your mind, sir?"

Bowers handed Eddy his discharge order. "You've fulfilled your obligation to Uncle Sam, son. It's time to go home."

The color drained from Eddy's face.

Bowers continued. "I know about that little girl in Trieste. I managed to pull some strings, make special arrangements as a thank you. We may not have survived this hell hole without your ingenuity."

"What are you talking about, sir?"

"If you like, you can rotate home via Italy, so you can look for the girl and child."

Eddy regained color. A smile crossed his face. "You can make those kinds of arrangements?"

Bowers laughed. "Son, look at what you managed to pull off. Yes! Is three or four weeks enough time to look for her before you ship out?"

Lowering his head, Eddy fumbled with his belt buckle. "Sir, if I find them, I'm not going back to the states."

Bowers clasped his hands together on the desktop. "And what if you don't?"

Eddy was silent.

"Allow me to do this. You'll go back to Trieste, stay on base as a civilian, have a couple of weeks to search. I'll schedule you on a boat home the first week of May. You miss the boat, then you stay or find your own way." Bowers met Eddy's gaze. "If you decide to go back home, you better be on that boat."

"When do I go?"

"In two days. You can take a chopper out to Seoul and go from there." Bowers stood. "That's all, Private."

Eddy saluted again. "Thank you, sir."

"Thank you, Private Edgar 'Vampire' Kepler."

∞ ∞ ∞

The mess tent was packed with soldiers enjoying the heat generated by the ovens and stoves. Eddy sat with Corporal Foust, company clerk, and head nurse, Cindy Dillard.

Cindy sipped her coffee. "So, Private Vampire, you're going home. Lucky you." She smiled. "I'll miss our rendezvous, but...I do have a husband to consider."

Foust chortled. "And Kepler has *two* wives!"

"What do you mean, two wives? All this time together and you never told me?" Cindy stopped eating and folded her hands on the table. "This should be good!"

Eddy kicked Foust. "That's enough...keep it to yourself."

"I think otherwise. No one besides the Colonel and Major knows your history."

"What did he do?"

By the time Foust finished telling the story, most of the camp was gathered around listening to his tale of Eddy's adventures.

One of the nurses, dreamy-eyed, purred, "That's so romantic! Going AWOL for your love."

Cindy questioned, "Romantic for whom? I feel sorry for the poor wife at home." She slapped Eddy on the shoulder.

"Hey, that hurt!" Eddy rubbed the spot.

"Good. That should hurt." Cindy punched him again.

"Hey! You knew I was married, and it didn't bother you."

"I always assumed that you were going back to your wife in the states, just like I'm going back to my husband. You're a real louse to abandon her, Eddy. Not cool at all!" Cindy slammed her tray on top of the pile waiting to be washed. "Don't bother coming over tonight, Eddy. Good-bye."

"But Cindy! It's my last night in camp."

"Find someone else to keep you warm." Cindy stormed out.

40

HIDE AND SEEK

APRIL 1953, TRIESTE, ITALY

*E*ddy arrived back in Trieste the first week in April to find Wally and Sergeant Hill gone. Many of the men he once befriended had left—Sully, Sarge—having served their time or transferred to another post.

Eddy's bunk was with Alpha company. Private Edgar Kepler Jr. was now known as Eddy, the lucky guy on a layover waiting for a boat home. Eddy found himself down at the motor pool, looking for a set of wheels.

"So, where's Corporal Stuart?" he asked the GI behind the desk.

"Stuart? You mean Wally?"

"Yeah, Wally Stuart. When did he leave?"

The private opened a file drawer and scanned some paperwork. "Looks like he was out of here in January. I never met the guy, only heard talk of him."

Eddy frowned. "Well, he was a good fellow, the best of friends. So what was the dirt on him?"

"I heard he was best friends with the legendary Go-to Guy; that cat could find just about anything you needed."

Eddy grinned. "Yeah, and what else?"

The private shook his head. "I don't know. Something about a girl, baby, sergeant Hill, AWOL. Wally helped them out." The private closed the file. "Just happy to see Sergeant Hill go. That guy was one grumpy dude."

"I see. You got a home address for Wally?"

"Yep, but you're not getting it. That's private information. If you're such a good friend, then Wally would have told you already."

"Sure, you're right." Eddy conceded without filling in any other details. "How can I get access to a vehicle?"

"Well, let me see your papers."

Eddy handed them over.

"Says here you're to have access to whatever you need. Take the first jeep in line, Buddy. How the hell did you rate that?"

Eddy grabbed the keys. "It's Private Go-to Guy, to you."

"Holy shit!"

∞ ∞ ∞

Eddy drove along the coast toward Santa Croce, searching for Isabella and Giuseppe—last name: unknown. He pulled into the church's parking lot where Joey was baptized and entered the sanctuary, interrupting daily mass. Eddy took a seat in a back pew and waited.

At the end of the service, he intercepted the priest. "Father, I need some information. Do you speak English?"

The priest looked at Eddy with vague recollection. "Yes, son, how may I help you?"

"My son was baptized here last December. Good God, no, it was December of 1951." He grunted in disbelief. "He's going to be two. I was hoping you could tell me the last name of his grandparents and maybe their address."

"What is your boy's name? His mother's name?"

"My son is Joseph Edgar Kepler; my wife is Rosa. The grandparents are Isabella and Giuseppe, but I don't know their last name."

The priest flushed, recalling a request for secrecy. "I'm afraid I can't share that with you, son."

"What? You know, but you won't tell me? What kind of holy man are you that keeps a father away from his own son?" Eddy squinted, his hand closing and opening into a fist.

"Calm yourself. I am the kind of man who provides the confidentiality of the confessional. I was entrusted with keeping their whereabouts to myself. I can tell you this much; they no longer reside in Santa Croce."

Eddy kicked a pew, sending shock waves ricocheting through the empty building. He stepped forward; the priest stepped back.

"Please leave, son. Their secret is safe with me."

"But—"

The priest held up his hand. "Stop. Go before I call the authorities."

Eddy paused. *The last thing I need is a civilian record*, he thought. "Fine, I'll go, but you are making a mistake, old man."

"Then I shall answer for it in heaven."

∞ ∞ ∞

Eddy found the nearest phone booth, closed the door, and opened the phone book, searching for entries with the first name of Giuseppe or Joseph. It only took a minute to realize that one in every three men was named Giuseppe. A hand rapped on the door. Eddy looked up, mouthed profanity, then exited, slamming the door shut before the waiting caller could enter. He stormed down the street, flicking several crude finger gestures.

On his way back to base, he detoured to Castle Miramare. The gardens were in full spring bloom. Eddy listlessly roamed through trimmed hedges, rose bushes, blossoming trees and flowers. The breeze from the Adriatic carried floral scents. Growing despondent, Eddy plummeted onto the gravel walkway, close to where he and Rosa first hid in the shadows. The tears gushed from his eyes. Lost in his thoughts, it was several hours before he found his way back to Trieste.

The jeep seemed to be on autopilot, heading to the Piazza Grande. He stopped short of the square and observed several groups gathered on various corners. *Please be here*, he thought. A group of girls parted. Eddy held his breath as he spotted the back of a petite black-haired girl dressed in silk. A gust of wind blew her hair away from her neck, revealing a strand of pearls.

"Rosa!" He yelled as he ran across the quadrangle. "Rosa, it's me!"

The girl turned around; terror spread across her face at the sight of a charging man. Eddy stopped dead in his tracks. It was not Rosa.

Dragging his feet, he returned to the jeep.

"I'll confront Romano," he said aloud.

The winding road led up to a gated villa overlooking the harbor. Beautiful blooming bougainvillea cascaded over the iron, giving the appearance of a living fence. Two guards stood at the entrance. Lights shone in the distance, illuminating an expansive garden filled with lemon and olive trees. Flowers dripped over the sides of concrete urns that flanked the gate to a palace.

Eddy called from the open window. "Buddy, come here."

The guard's finger touched his chest. "You want me?"

"Yes. I have a question." A pack of Lucky Strike cigarettes popped through the window in Eddy's outstretched arm. "I'll trade American cigs for some information."

The guard snatched the pack out of his hand. "What do you want? You a GI?"

"Not a GI now. Does Magistrate Romano live here?" Eddy pointed to the enclosed villa.

"*Si*. I get a pack for that?" The guard smiled at his good fortune.

"That, and information about his daughter."

"His daughter?"

"Yes, Rosa."

The guard shrugged his shoulders and looked at his companion. "You know anything about a Rosa?" he asked.

The other guard went pale. "We don't speak of her. She left years ago, Magistrato disowned her, forbade us to ever speak of her."

"Do you know where she lives?" Eddy offered another pack of Lucky's. "Come on, fellow. This is serious. I need to know."

"Damn right, it's serious. I'll lose my job, so I don't speak." He softened slightly when he saw the pleading in Eddy's eyes. "But, in all honesty, I don't know where she is."

Eddy crumbled the cigarettes in his hand, dropped the pack, and drove off, leaving the guards cursing at the waste of delicious American smokes.

Every day in April, Eddy repeated his quest, visiting the priest first and the guards second, in hopes one party would buckle from the pressure. No one did.

41

PRODIGAL HUSBAND

MAY 1953, CAMPBELLSVILLE

*T*he Christmas holiday was dismal and depressing. The family gathered at Esther's; however, only the children celebrated. Olive requested a dinner invitation but was turned away and sent home with a plate of food.

Teddy and Albert convinced Olive to spend money on a new gas furnace. The middle-aged woman eagerly agreed, not wanting to descend into the bowels of the basement to stoke a coal fire every morning. The wood-burning cookstove was replaced with a gas range, compliments of Teddy, Albert, Dave, and Harriett. Had the siblings known of Olive's money stash, she would have footed the bill herself. Regardless, Olive's lifelong quest for independence was now complete— minus her degree and title.

Spring finally arrived, but the pain of losing her father remained raw for Harriett, more so than for her sisters and brother. Alice and Teddy were busy with baby Maggie, already six months old. Esther's oldest son Toby, Tabs' namesake, completed his junior year in high school. The family planned his future, skimping and saving money for college. June and

David busily packed their belongings to move to Atlanta in July. With transcontinental air travel on the rise, larger airports needed to expand. Dave got a job as a pilot with Delta Airlines at the Atlanta municipal airport, Candler Field. Meanwhile, wedding bells were in the air for Albert and Laurena Williams. Tabs' only son had proposed shortly after the funeral, and Laurie eagerly accepted. The wedding was scheduled in July, one week before June and Dave's move south.

The Bailey husbands and Albert made good on their promise of caring for Olive. They collectively decided to take a month at a time, three months each year of once-weekly visits. Albert, the meteorologist, opted for the summer months, which consisted of grass cutting, window washing, and gardening. Kindhearted Darrell chose snow shoveling. Toby volunteered to replace his Uncle Dave in the lineup until he graduated.

Twenty-two-year-old Harriett Bailey Kepler, the youngest and only female executive in the history of Dugan and Co., propelled herself to legendary status. Competent and confident, Harriett burst onto the local corporate scene, twelve credits into her master's program.

Harriett donned a sweater to enjoy the spring night. She rocked back and forth on an aluminum glider located on the stone terrace in the back of the house. She sipped a late evening glass of wine. Red and orange azalea bushes partitioned the patio from the back grassy croquet court and woods beyond. Birds busily chirped their goodnights as the light faded into dusk.

Bats circled through the trees to a hooting owl. Harriett, reluctantly accepting nightfall, headed inside to open the mail waiting on her desk. The first three envelopes were invoices. She placed them in her pending bills file. She picked up an envelope with an airmail stamp, overseas postmark.

Curiously, she ripped open and removed a letter. She immediately recognized the handwriting.

> Harriett,
> I've been discharged. Pick me up at Indian Town Gap on
> May 24th at eleven am.
> Thanks,
> Eddy

Her wine glass crashed to the floor and shattered. She
swooned in her chair, pulse rapid with sweat dripping from
her neck and forehead. Did she imagine the letter? She
reread. Eddy was due home on her twenty-third birthday.

"Papa!" she screamed. "Oh Papa, I need you!"

Harriett paced the house, up and down the stairs several
trips before making up her mind. She returned to her office
and dialed.

"Hello," said the friendly baritone.

She cleared her throat by coughing. "Earl, may I bother
you to come over?"

"Harriett? Is everything all right?" His voice contracted.

"No, it's not." She plunged to her knees with a thud.
"Earl!" she pleaded, then dropped the phone.

∞ ∞ ∞

Earl scaled the front steps, taking them two at a time. He
jiggled the door handle. *Let it be open.* It was. Rushing through
the double set of doors, Earl headed straight for the office
where the phone was connected. He cradled the receiver. He
found Harriett still lying on the floor, awake, and rolled into a
fetal position.

"Harriett?" Sitting on the floor beside her, avoiding the

shards of glass, Earl touched her shoulder. Her entire body trembled. "Harriett, what's wrong?"

She remained curled, her chest pressed close to her knees. One arm reached back, paper in hand.

Earl took the paper and read. He slumped forward before muttering, "That son-of-a bitch has some nerve."

Several moments passed before Harriett mustered enough strength to sit upright. At eye level, sitting beside her, their eyes met. "Earl, I can't go. I just can't."

Earl reached for her hand. "I'll pick him up."

She jerked away from his grip. "I'm at a loss. None of this makes any sense. How can he expect to just waltz back into my life?"

He lifted her to a standing position, hands under her arms. She shivered at his touch. He gently encircled her waist and led her to the kitchen. "Harriett, sit down, please."

She complied. Earl flipped the light switch. The harsh, bright fluorescent light revealed three years of wounds etched on her face. Earl recoiled in recognition of the damage carved by Eddy. He made coffee before speaking.

With the pot percolating, Earl sat across from Harriett, her face drained of color. "Harriett, Eddy was always coddled. When Bill died in the thirty-six flood, Mom was devastated." He rubbed his eyes. "Eddy was only seven or eight, so Mom channeled her grief into spoiling Eddy."

Harriett shook her head. "Don't defend him. He's imma-ture, uncaring, and despicable! He hasn't written in over three years, and he expects me to drive all that distance to pick him up. Does he expect to move in, too?"

Earl sighed. "I'm not defending him, only trying to explain." Standing, he moved to the stove to extinguish the burner and pour coffee. "Trust me; I wish he'd have stayed missing!"

Harriett caught her breath. "Maybe I have the same

wish." She reread the one-line letter. "Once upon a time, I was so in love with him."

Earl managed to caress her arm as he handed her a cup. "And now? Are you still in love?"

She looked down. "Earl, that question is unfair."

"How so, Harriett. It seems straightforward to me."

She stuttered. "I—I have feelings, but…"

"Enough said."

"Earl."

"No, Harriett, it's okay. You're his wife. I said I'd get him, and I will." His shoulders slumped. He looked past her into the darkness outside. "Do you want him back? In this house?"

"Earl." She shook her head. "Never…at least, not yet."

"I'll have Mother prepare his room. He can stay with us… until you work things out."

Harriett peered into Earl's eyes. "You are always so kind to me. You come whenever I need you, and now that Papa's gone, that's more frequently." She sighed. "Oh Earl, another place, another time…perhaps."

Earl stroked her hair, her body tingled. "Harriett, I shall always be your rock, with or without Eddy." Kissing her cheek, he drew her close and let her weep tears of regret.

42

HONEY, I'M HOME!

MAY 1953, CAMPBELLSVILLE

*T*he bus pulled into the parking lot outside of Fort Indiantown Gap. Eager soldiers bounced down the steps to anxious loved ones, waiting with open arms. Eddy slung his duffel over his shoulder, searching for his beloved coupe. Nothing in sight. Deciding Harriett may have sold the car without his consent, he frowned, then looked instead for a petite brunette. Nothing.

The parking lot emptied; the bus drove away. Eddy sat on a bench, alone, wondering if Harriett even got his letter. *I think I remembered the new address. Hell, it's Campbellsville. They'll deliver to her even if it's wrong,* he thought. About fifteen minutes passed before a Chevy Bel Air convertible parked in front of him.

Earl wound down the window. "What are you waiting for? An engraved invitation? Get in."

Eddy sighed. "Hi Earl, nice wheels. Where's Harriett?" He strolled to the passenger side, traced the chrome trim with his finger, and sat down, tossing his luggage in the back seat. "Why are you here, and not my wife?"

Earl pursed his lips tightly. "You have some nerve asking

that. What? Was it three years in between letters? And you actually expect her to drive here to get you?"

Eddy scratched his head as Earl took down the top and headed west. "Well, she is my wife."

"How many wives do you have, little brother? How many times did you break your wedding vows?" Earl slammed the dashboard. "Because *she* remained faithful to you!"

"Why are you getting so hot and bothered?" Eddy flushed. "Well, yeah, I do have another wife."

Earl slammed on the break, stopping on the berm. The men lurched forward; Eddy's bag rolled to the floor. Earl punched Eddy's arm. "I knew you couldn't keep a promise."

"Ouch. That wasn't necessary." Eddy rubbed his shoulder. "Did you expect me never to have sex? Seriously?" He looked up and down the road for traffic. "You want to be a jerk? I'll hitch home."

Earl grabbed Eddy's head, jerking it to face him. "Be my guest, but I don't see tons of options here. Sex is *one* subject. Calling another woman your wife is an altogether different one."

"Can I at least explain myself?" The Kepler grin was ineffective on Earl.

"You don't need to tell me anything. It's that beautiful girl you married who deserves the truth. She still loves you, you asshole!"

"That's good to hear!" Eddy grinned. "Then she'll let me into my house."

"*Your* house? Why would you call it yours?"

"Because we're married. I hear it's quite the abode!"

Earl nearly choked. "Did you contribute any money toward the purchase?"

"No."

"Then it's not your *abode*; it's hers. And if she's smart, she'll kick your sorry ass out for good."

Eddy grabbed Earl's shoulders. "What the fuck, Earl? Did you tell her to do that?"

"No, Eddy. If I had, I wouldn't be here to take you home." Earl looked ahead, out the windshield. "Let's go, Eddy. We have several hours of driving; you have plenty of time to share your sad excuses."

He pulled forward. Eddy retold his life with Rosa and Joey, and how it all ended with a trip to Korea.

∞ ∞ ∞

The car parked in front of his mother's house, to Eddy's dismay. Earl turned off the ignition and removed the keys. "Are you coming?"

Bewilderment covered Eddy's face. "Why are we here?"

Earl laughed. "After what you just told me, you have to ask? You're more stupid than I remember."

Eddy grabbed his duffel and reluctantly opened the door. "Mom, I'm home!"

Abigail Kepler appeared out of nowhere. She raised her hand and lashed Eddy across the face with one smack. Earl chuckled at the echoing sound.

Eddy rubbed his cheek as he stared at his mother. "Mom! Why'd you do that?"

"You no-good louse. You're just like your father. I should have clocked him a good one years ago." Eddy caught her raised hand before she could strike again. "Your father died, and you didn't even send a silly card. Three years Eddy, and you don't write your mother or your wife. I thought I taught you better."

Eddy smirked. "I think Dad taught me more than you did, Mom."

Abigail's rage turned somber. She sat at the dining room table sobbing, face in her hands. "I worried about you the entire time. I lost Billy and your dad; I couldn't bear to lose you also. The *not knowing* was the worst, Eddy." She met his gaze. "Can't you understand what you put me through? What you put Harriett through?"

Eddy's face reddened. He paced the room as he pondered his mother's words. Her pain over his neglect was no different than his pain over Rosa's disappearance. *Maybe I am a louse*, he thought.

Several moments passed in silence. "I do understand." Eddy snuggled close to Abigail. "Mom, I'm sorry. Really I am. Forgive me?"

"I'll forgive you, but I'm your mother. Don't expect the same from your wife!" She blew her nose, then tucked her head into his chest as she cried.

∞ ∞ ∞

Harriett refused to celebrate her birthday on Sunday, May 24, 1953, despite Alice baking her favorite chocolate cake and inviting her to dinner. Word of Eddy's return quickly spread throughout the family. Toby came to his aunt's rescue, vowing to "hit the bum with a baseball bat if he tried anything funny." Albert and Teddy activated a spy ring to track his whereabouts. Darrell warned his bosses that the ne'er-do-well was back in town.

Instead of a party, Harriett worked in the garden. The stack of discarded weeds grew as the afternoon passed by. Heddy, Lloly, and Susie remained at Harriett's side all day, helping with her chores. To Toby's dismay, he had a ball game and couldn't help as much as he would have liked.

Harriett couldn't help but reject her melancholy as her attentive nieces and nephew loyally mothered her. The four sat drinking iced tea when the front doorbell rang.

All heads snapped to attention. Eleven-year-old Lloly

jumped to his feet. "I got it, Aunt Harriett. You sit still." The boy scampered inside, down the hallway to the door. He opened it to find a tall, handsome, wavy-haired man in his mid-twenties.

"Who are you?" asked the visitor, who tried to push his way inside.

Lloly blocked his entrance. "Who are you? And what do you want?"

Eddy brushed the boy aside. "I live here. Get out of my way."

Lloly stumbled but regained his balance. He caught the man by the sleeve and tugged. "This is my aunt's house. Stop, or I'll—"

"Lloly, honey, you can let go of him." Harriett stood in the hallway watching. She scrutinized the tanned face and arms of her husband. His face remained chiseled and dashing, however, he no longer possessed a raw animal magnetism, the kind that once sent shock waves through her body. She moved close enough to smell the fresh scent of soap. Her knees wobbled. He seemed shorter; his once broad powerful shoulders were now slightly slumped forward.

"Eddy, you're not welcome. Please leave." Her hands trembled; she went pale.

Two heads peered out from the kitchen at the exchange. Heddy motioned for Lloly. "Come on, Lloly," Heddy urged. "We can go out the back door and get Uncle Teddy."

"You two go. Run fast. I'll stay here with Aunt Harriett. I don't like him!" Lloly, hands on his hips, stormed back into the hallway. "Mister, you better do as my aunt asks. The cops are on the way!"

Harriett wrapped her arm around Lloly's waist. "Thank you, sweetie." She kissed the top of his head.

Laughter bellowed from deep inside Eddy's frame. "Look at you, little man. Protecting your aunt."

"Eddy, don't be such a bully." Harriett pulled the boy closer.

Lloly wrenched free and threw out his chest. "I'll not ask you again; you better leave."

"Leave, or you'll do what?" Eddy scowled at the boy. The sound of multiple shotguns being primed halted the conversation. Eddy turned around to find Teddy, Albert, Darrell, and Dave standing behind him, all holding guns at the ready.

Harriett broke into nervous laughter as she wiped her sweating palms on her trousers. "What's this? The posse? How did you get here so fast?"

Albert tapped Eddy's arm with the barrel of his Browning twelve gauge. "I think I heard this gentleman ask you to leave. Get a move on."

Harriett exhaled as she glanced at Albert.

Lloly moved behind his father, Darrell, who patted him on the head. "I'm proud of you, son. You're a brave young man standing up to a bully, defending your aunt."

"This is between me and my wife!" Eddy shouted and swatted at Albert's shotgun—only to find Teddy's Cooey 84 replacing it.

"Eddy, I don't want trouble. You are not welcome here." Harriett's voice faltered.

"Eddy, she's our sister. We've watched this poor woman suffer at your hand for three years. The two of you need to work things out—or not. But today is not the day. She's seen you; she knows you're back, and she doesn't want you here." Albert clenched his teeth as he ordered, "Turn around and go home."

Harriett sucked in her cheeks. She gathered all her strength. "Enough, Eddy! Do as I ask. Get out!"

Eddy pounded the door frame. Both Harriett and Lloly jumped. "This isn't over by a longshot."

Harriett bit her lip then took a deep breath. "Guys, thank

you. Please lower the guns." She nodded to Albert and Teddy. Moving to Eddy, she stood directly in front of him, chest out, head up, staring straight into his eyes. "As for you, Mr. Kepler, *leave*. If you ever want to reconcile with me, you'll reign in that attitude of yours!" She exhaled. "I am not the same little girl you left behind three years ago, as you drove off, never looking back. You're the one that created the change in my life, but by God, I'm the one who determines which direction it takes. Do you understand?" She waited for an answer. Hearing none, she asked again. "Do you understand? Now leave. It's my birthday, not that you'd remember. I'm not dealing with you today. You made me wait three years; you can wait a couple of days on me."

Albert and Teddy moved to Harriett's side as she continued: "Today, I'm eating cake!"

Reluctantly, Eddy turned to leave. This time, he deliberately looked back at this new force of nature that he called his wife.

43

SECRET, SECRET, WHO'S GOT A SECRET

MAY 1953, CAMPBELLSVILLE

*H*arriett drove to work the next day, arriving hours before the rest of the office. She wanted quiet time to think without background chatter from bus passengers.

Solitude would not be possible during business hours. At eight, quiet time ended. She peeked her head out of her door. The lights in the still, dark hallway illuminated as a maintenance man went room to room, flipping switches. Kimberly Coil unlocked and stowed her purse in her desk drawer.

"Miss Coil, thank you for coming in early. This will be our busiest week of the year, our first fiscal year-end together. Are you ready?"

"Absolutely, Mrs. Kepler. Your first meeting today is at nine-fifteen with Jim LaMantia. And I have preliminary recaps of each department ready for your approval." Kimberly laid her hand on top of a stack of papers two feet high.

"Splendid. You're a great support, Kimberly. My door is open if you need me."

Around nine, a shadow passed Harriett's door. She called to the familiar silhouette. "Kathryn, have a minute?"

"Sure, Harriett. How was your birthday? Did you like your gift?" Kathryn dropped a tote bag on the floor before retracing her steps.

Harriett smiled, twisting the ties of a pink and yellow neck scarf to face forward. She smoothed the lapels of her pink suit jacket. "Yes, I love it. Boy, do I have some news."

Kathryn checked her watch before commenting. "I have ten minutes before I need to be at my desk. How did it go yesterday?" Kathryn unlatched her handbag, removed her gloves, and placed them inside.

Harriett motioned her inside the office. "Eddy's home!" she said as she sat down. "Close the door."

"Oh my goodness! What happened?"

"He tried to barge into the house, claiming it was his home. Can you believe it?" She peered across her desk at her friend.

Kathryn's eyes grew wide. "I can. Did you stop him?"

"It was so cute—little Lloly championed me. He physically blocked Eddy's entry. Heddy and Susie were there also, keeping me company. They ran over to Alice's to get Teddy."

Kathryn gasped, hands on each side of her face. "Did you need help?"

Harriett chuckled. "It seems my entire family was staged at the Jensons' just waiting, shotguns in hand."

"Guns! You needed guns?"

Harriett nodded. "They definitely gave me the advantage. Eddy declared he was staying until Albert and Teddy shoved double barrels in his face. I know this is just the beginning."

"How do you feel after seeing him again? Did you have any old feelings?"

"I wish I didn't." She sighed. "I'm in love with him, but I don't like him very much. He is such an arrogant jerk. Does that make any sense?" Harriett shuffled her feet. "I don't know what I'll end up doing. For now, I'm worried about year-end at Dugan and Co."

The clock on the shelf chimed nine times. "Gosh, I gotta run. You better fill me in at lunch."

Harriett shook her head. "Lunch is at my desk. Too much work." Harriett opened a drawer to reveal a paper bag. "Kathryn, keep this to yourself, please."

"Sure, sweetie. Have a good day."

∞ ∞ ∞

Promptly at nine-fifteen, Kimberly announced Jim LaMantia, Harriett's operations manager replacement. Another stack of files was deposited on top of Harriett's desk.

"Mrs. Kepler," LaMantia said. "Using the system you created, these numbers came directly from each department head. I matched them against my tally." He handed her two typed pages. "Here are the discrepancies."

Two hours later, LaMantia left with a list of follow-up items. Based on this meeting, LaMantia generated a compendium of names for Glen Vincent to review, reward, reprimand, and potentially terminate.

Harriett extended her hand. "Thanks, Mr. LaMantia. Good work."

"I believe I owe you a word of thanks. I only recently discovered that you were the one who recommended me for the position. I appreciate your faith in me."

"You've just proven your worth, Jim."

∞ ∞ ∞

The afternoon flew by as Harriett plodded through the stack of reports in preparation for final executive approval.

Mr. Roland knocked for his three o'clock meeting. Kimberly Coil sat at the ready, steno book in hand to record.

One by one, Harriett recapped her findings, and one by one, Mr. Roland endorsed her work, concluding sound fiscal standing for Dugan and Co.

"Harriett," Roland said. "The Dugan family will be pleased to know that the business is in good hands." He scanned the room's new furniture arrangement of the smallest corner office that used to be his own. Harriett's desk faced the window instead of being in front of it. Blue-and-white striped padded seat covers were added to the wooden chairs in front of her desk. Roland's oversized leather club chairs, sized for his six-and-a-half feet, now resided in his office—they were replaced with two smaller, stuffed, green-and-blue floral pieces, separated by a side table and lamp. The floor of the conversation area was defined with a plaid, green, blue, and yellow rug. Sophisticated femininity had replaced the classic, old-boys'-club style.

"Thank you, Mr. Roland." Harriett motioned to Kimberly. "Miss Coil, you're excused. Thank you."

Roland hung back, waiting for the door to close before speaking. "Harriett, don't you think it's about time you call me Tom? You've been an executive for a full year. I'm sure Glen Vincent feels the same. The executive team needs to be on a first-name basis." He motioned to a floral chair, sat, and spilled over the edges.

Harriett puckered her brow as she joined him. "If you say so, Mr. Roland—I mean, Tom." They both laughed. "I'll at least try. You may have to remind me a couple more times if I slip."

"Fair enough." He tried to turn to face her directly but was too wedged in the chair to do so. "Now, I sense you have something else on your mind besides year-end reports."

Harriett crossed her legs. The full, gathered skirt of her suit fell discreetly, covering her knees.

"I'm sorry, do I seem distracted?" she said, the ankle of her top leg twitching back and forth.

"No—call it a fatherly intuition. Living with so many women, you begin to read their moods." He placed his hands palms-down on the top of his knees. "So, tell me what's on your mind, Harriett."

She stood and walked toward her desk. "Personal stuff; nothing to do with work." Harriett faced the window.

Roland pushed his body out of the chair to join her. "I figured as much. Does it have anything to do with the handsome soldier husband of yours? The one who has been missing in action for three years?"

She turned, her tiny body a shadow in his large frame. "Does everyone know my business?" The question sounded more like a demand.

Roland stammered. "No, but I was personnel manager, remember? It was my place to know what's going on in key employees' lives."

She crossed her arms in front of her. "Well, since you ask, he is no longer missing. He crashed my birthday party yesterday."

"I see." Roland's face flushed. "Harriett, may I give you some fatherly advice? Don't let him ruin all you've worked so hard to achieve. I've seen it happen too many times when focus is an issue. Things you love dearly are risked; your education, lifestyle, and eventually your job."

Harriett met Roland's gaze. "Am I that distracted today? Mr. Roland—Tom, why are you asking me these questions? I am focused." She tapped the stack of reports on her desk.

"You are. I want to be sure you stay that way." Roland's face color intensified. "Kathryn had mentioned that your husband was back."

The hair on the back of her neck stood on edge, Harriett sucked air through her teeth. With slowly accented syllables, she quipped, "I requested confidentiality. Thank you, Tom. Feel free to comment if my performance suffers. Otherwise, I prefer to keep my personal life just that. Personal!"

"Understood." Roland reached for Harriett's shoulder. "I'm here, as a father, if you need me."

She jerked away. "*My father* is irreplaceable. Good afternoon, Tom."

∞ ∞ ∞

The next morning, Harriett delivered employee copies of the general report to Kathryn's desk. "Miss White, please see that each member of the Dugan team receives a copy.

"Hey, what's with 'Miss White?'" Kathryn looked up from her typing to scratch her head.

Harriett dropped the paperwork onto her desk. "We shall keep our relationship on a professional level until you learn to keep my confidence."

Kathryn cringed. "Did Mr. Roland say something?"

"Yes." Harriett's eyes narrowed.

"I asked him to keep it to himself." Kathryn frowned. "I can't believe he didn't!" She hurried to embrace her friend in reconciliation.

An outstretched arm halted Kathryn's advance. "Oh, like how I asked you not to mention Eddy to anyone? It seems Tom isn't the only one who can't keep his mouth shut."

"'Tom?' You're on a first-name basis, now?"

"Yes, Miss White, as an executive team member. We're Tom, Glen, and Harriett." She glanced toward Vincent's office. "Did you tell Carolyn at lunch?"

Kathryn lowered her head, shoulders slumped. "But I asked her not to repeat."

"I see. Thank you, Miss White." Perfect posture, Harriett walked calmly, her heels rhythmically clipping the wooden floor. Once inside her office, she closed the door, covered her face, and cried.

44

ROOM SERVICE

*A*bigail stirred a pot of vegetable soup. She waited for Earl to return home from work.

"Mom, when's supper? I'm hungry," Eddy called from above. He lay on his bed all day, doing nothing except bouncing a ball off the wall. *Thud, bump, thud bump,* repeatedly reverberated through the house.

"Eddy, why don't you come downstairs?" Abigail hollered as she set the bread on the table. "And can you stop that noise? You're driving me crazy. Earl will be home soon."

Pouting to himself, he replied. "Don't feel like it. Bring me up some food, okay?"

Juggling a bowl full of soup and a glass of iced tea on a tray, Abigail wobbled, climbing the flight of steps to serve her son. At his door, she almost spilled it, trying to shield her eyes.

"Edgar, put on some clothing!"

"Nothing you haven't seen. Put it there." Eddy pointed to his dresser. "I'll get it in a minute."

Abigail harrumphed and closed the door after her, carefully grasping the banister as she descended the staircase.

291

The table was set when Earl entered the Kepler house to the smell of warm brown-and-serve rolls. He put his lunchbox in the kitchen, washed his face, then kissed his mother's cheek before sitting down.

He looked at the two place settings. "Where's Eddy?"

Abigail sighed as she ladled soup into bowls. "In his room."

Earl unfolded the evening newspaper. Turning to the "help wanted" section, he asked, "Did he go job hunting today?"

"No."

"What did he do then?" He lay the paper down and buttered a bun.

"Nothing. He stayed in his room. Making a clatter, banging a ball." She rolled her tongue over her front teeth then smacked her lips. "I don't know what to do with him. He expected me to deliver his food."

Earl slurped liquid from his spoon. "Did you?"

"Yes. He said he was starving."

Earl stopped eating. He gripped his mother's hands. "Then you're enabling him. He'll join us if he's hungry enough. Mom, he's a grown man. Stop babying him."

"Earl, will you talk to him? Set him on the straight and narrow?" she asked nervously, as she bit her fingernails.

"Eddy is not a 'straight arrow' kind of guy. The only one who stands a chance of influencing him is Harriett. But, for you, Mom, I'll talk to him."

∞ ∞ ∞

Earl helped his mother wash and dry the dishes before knocking on Eddy's door. Abigail retired to the living room with her stitching, trying to overhear.

"Eddy, it's Earl. We need to talk."

Eddy tossed the ball so that it struck the door. "What's up? I'm busy."

Earl opened the door and barged in on a half-naked man lying on his bed, clad only in boxers, with a glove in one hand and a baseball in the other. Empty beer cans and girly magazines were scattered on the floor.

"Good God, are you drunk? Look, Eddy." Earl swiped a can off the seat of the corner wooden chair and sat. "You can't be demanding Mom hike up and down the steps, hands full, waiting on you hand and foot. The woman is sixty-seven years old."

Eddy rolled onto his side so his back faced Earl. "I didn't 'demand' anything. I asked; she delivered."

"Look, just because Harriett, like any sensible woman, has shunned you, doesn't mean you can sit around and mope all day. Go find work." Earl threw the newspaper in Eddy's face. "The mill is hiring. Maybe you can get your old job back?"

"I don't want my old job back. I'm used to being important." Eddy blew out a loud rumbling gas bubble that smelled of stale beer to accentuate his answer.

"You're a real piece of work! I told Mom you were hopeless."

Earl waved his hand to dissipate the stench. He was already on the top landing when Eddy called after him. He returned to see Eddy sitting upright, fly gapping, legs dangling over the side of the bed.

"Hey Earl...tell me about Harriett. What's she been doing?"

Earl rolled his eyes. "Showing your dick won't prove your manhood to me! As for Harriett, your wife is an incredible, amazing woman. She has her degree now. I'm sure she wrote to tell you if you bothered to read her letters."

"Yeah, I got tired of hearing how special she was. She did

this; then she did that! Blah, blah, blah." His fingers mimicked a mouth opening and shutting.

"Wow. Eddy. Jealousy does not become you. She has accomplished so much for being so young. She's working on her master's right now, even with being CFO. Not yet twenty-five, and she's a corporate CFO."

"Like I said, blah, blah, blah." Eddy tossed a can at Earl. "What about that house? Have you seen it?"

A quick reflex easily deflected a direct hit. "Of course. It's beautiful. She's still working on the décor; her taste is impeccable."

"Listen to you, big fancy words! *Décor. Impeccable.* Putting on airs, Earl?" This time, Eddy threw the ball at Earl's nose. "Catch! Hey, can you take me up the hill so I can pick up my car? I need my wheels."

Earl's laughter echoed through the Kepler house. "Oh, you want your car, do you? I'm afraid you have a problem. Harriett sold that piece of rust and bought herself a real executive vehicle."

"She did what? How dare she..."

"Eddy, think a minute. No one heard a word from you in three years. For all we knew, for all *she* knew," he shrugged his shoulder, "you were never coming back. As your wife, do you expect her to hold on to something that reeked of sex and booze?"

Eddy began pummeling his mattress with his fists. "That bitch!"

Enraged, Earl balled his hand to deliver a jab to the jaw. It popped. "Don't you ever speak about Harriett like that!"

Eddy nimbly sprang to his feet. Clenched fists raised and ready, legs apart and balanced, he challenged. "Just try that again, asshole."

"I'm not fighting you, Eddy. That was a warning. You'll

have hell to pay if you badmouth Harriett." Earl shoved Eddy backward. He bounced as he hit the bed.

Eddy sneered. "If I didn't know better, I'd say you had a thing for her!"

"My 'thing,' as you call it, is *respect* for a brilliant woman who happens to be my sister-in-law. That's my 'thing!'" Earl slammed the door angrily, finally admitting to himself his true feelings for Harriett. Halfway down the steps, he called back, "You need transportation? Use your two legs."

∞ ∞ ∞

He'd been home for two days without a bath when Eddy decided it was time to shower and make the rounds. He had friends to visit, gossip to hear. Hair slicked back with Brylcreem, he opened his closet and reached in. To his surprise, it was empty. Plan B: search his duffel for his least-wrinkled trousers. Dressed in a pair of Levi's, cuffed and pegged, white T-shirt, white socks, and loafers, with his tanned biceps exposed, he looked like a James Dean or Marlon Brando stunt double.

Sauntering down Pine Street, Eddy scanned for signs of his old high school gang. A late spring breeze carried the scent of freshly cut grass. Folks doing regular daily business bustled up and down sidewalks that were void of kids, with school in session for another week.

The bell above the door tinkled as he entered Jenson's pharmacy. Two women sitting at the counter sipping drinks, backs to the door, turned to see who had arrived.

"Oh my goodness. Eddy Kepler!" Jumping off her stool, a slightly plump brunette flung her arms around his neck. "Welcome home, Eddy!"

"Thanks. Good to be back." He pushed her away. Scrutinizing her up and down, Eddy asked, "Do I know you?"

The woman gasped, then slapped his face.

"What the hell was that for?" asked Eddy as he rubbed his cheek.

"You don't remember me? Really?" Her hands went to her rounded hips. "I'm Lynette! You knew me well enough in high school."

Her companion giggled. "Eddy knew *everyone* in high school. Do you remember me? Karen Garland."

The blood rushed to Eddy's face. "Lynette, sorry, I didn't recognize you." He stuttered. "Three years is a long time away. Oh, hi Karen. You were both in the class ahead of me, weren't you?"

Karen answered while Lynette regained composure. "Yep, we graduated with Harriett. Boy, you know how to pick 'em. I hear she's some bigwig in Madison. Living in that big house on the hill."

"Yeah, looks like plain Jane is a cool corporate cat. College degree and all," added Lynette.

Eddy sat at the counter, ordered a Coke, and slurped through a straw as he listened.

"So Eddy, when'd you get in?" A coquettish grin crossed Lynette's face.

"Sunday. Tell me, have you seen my car around?"

Both women giggled. "Harriett sold it to some kid. Drives around like it's a shrine to the infamous Eddy Kepler, the star on the football field and in the back seat."

"Think he'd sell it back to me?"

Karen cocked her head to the side. "Why would you want it? Buy something grown-up."

Lynette put a dollar on the counter. "I got these," she called to the eavesdropping clerk, on alert and ready to report to Teddy. "Eddy, welcome back. Oh, did I mention? Bobby Renner and I are married and expecting our first baby." She rubbed her rounded body. "He got back from Korea five months ago. Hey, maybe you and Harriett can come over for dinner some night? It would be good for Bobby's career to be in tight with someone like your wife."

Eddy stared past Lynette. "I'll ask her and let you know. If you see any of the old gang, tell them I'm back."

"See you around, Eddy." The bell tinkled again; the women waved goodbye as they walked down the street, chatting loudly to each other.

45

OUTSIDE LOOKING IN

*E*ddy restlessly roamed the streets of Campbellsville, tossing and catching a ball as he walked. He hoped to reconnect with his glory days and rekindle old friendships. He was weary of Abigail's company, despite her catering to every whim. To his dismay, none of his teammates appeared during the day. The concept that men in their twenties had jobs with families and wives to support evaded the realm of his world.

Dinner was served each night when Earl returned home from work, at approximately six. Each night as they ate, Eddy listened to Earl harp on the subject of employment. And each night, Eddy stormed out of the house, slamming the door as he left for his nightly late-night trek past Harriett's home.

The house on Hill Street glowed a warm shade of light periwinkle, a reflection from the foyer's blue crystals. Eddy sat on the ground, leaning against a tree, waiting to glimpse his wife scurrying past the window. If he positioned himself farther down the street, he had a clearer view of her office, the room where she spent most of her time. Her silhouette, head slightly bent forward, sat in shadow every evening in the same spot. Despite the late hour, Eddy assumed she was at her desk.

On Tuesday night, a Chevy Bel Air parked on the street in front of the house. The hair on the back of Eddy's neck stood on end as he watched Earl close the door and walk up the stone staircase. Eddy carelessly stood, risking his hiding place, as Harriett opened the door and greeted Earl with a kiss on the cheek.

"That son of a bitch!" Eddy pounded his fist on the tree trunk. "He's seeing my wife!"

∞ ∞ ∞

Earl pulled on the second set of double doors, ensuring they were closed and locked before speaking. "Harriett, so sorry to bother you this late."

"Don't worry about it. I'm still at my desk. Would you care for a drink?" Harriett walked back to her office, opened the ice bucket, and plunked cubes into two crystal glasses.

"Since when did you start keeping a bar next to your desk?" Earl chuckled as Harriett reached for a bottle of whiskey.

"Ahh, let's see. Sunday!" She smiled at her brother-in-law. "I'm not a big drinker, and I don't like it straight, but a seven and seven is fine, or with sours." She flipped off the cap from a Seven-Up bottle. "Want yours straight, on the rocks?"

"Perfect."

Earl scrutinized the monogrammed, cut-crystal tumbler. "I don't think I've ever had whiskey in such an expensive vessel. Hmm. 'EKH.' Would have been more appropriate to exclude Eddy."

Harriett clinked in a toast. "A gift. I have a set of eight. What can I say? It's still a man's world."

"Speaking of men, has my brother been bothering you?"

Earl relaxed into the leather chair, then crossed his legs. "He's been gone every night. The boys at the club say he leaves around ten, but he doesn't come home until long past midnight. Can't have him harassing you!"

"He's not been here. God only knows what he's doing. Earl, you are the sweetest man." Harriett blushed. Earl blushed in return. "I appreciate your kindness. You are good to me!"

"Harriett, I care about you more than I should." As soon as he spoke, he regretted his words.

Harriett sipped her drink. "Earl." A deep sigh escaped her mouth. "Earl, I am overwhelmed right now. It's my first year-end as CFO. Eddy appeared out of nowhere." She shook her head. "It's too much. I don't know how I feel, but one thing is sure: I am still a married woman."

Harriett's proclamation was interrupted with a rap on the door. The couple looked at each other.

"I'm not expecting anyone," Harriett said, "especially not this late."

"I'll get it. You stay in here." Earl opened the first set of doors. As he unclasped the lock, an outline that looked like Eddy retreated down the steps. "Eddy? What do you want?"

His question was met with the flash of a middle finger.

"Earl, who's there?" Harriett peeked around her office door. "Is everything okay?"

"Yes, Harriett. All is well." Earl gulped his remaining whiskey in one swallow. "I think it was Eddy, but he just walked away. It was bizarre." He shook his head. "I don't want him hanging around here uninvited. You call me, any day, any time. Do you understand? I'll come immediately."

"Thanks, Earl, but I'll be fine. Now, I really must call it a night. I have at least another hour of work before sleep." She collected his empty glass. "Good night, Earl. Thank you for everything." She awkwardly hugged his neck, then tried to imperceptibly kiss his cheek.

Earl waited outside at the door until he heard both sets shut and lock. He then drove his Chevy up and down the street, unsuccessfully looking for his wayward brother.

46

FORGIVEN

*W*ith Tuesday and Wednesday's twelve-hour workdays complete, Harriett sat at her desk preparing for her Thursday year-end meeting with the Dugan family. Dugan and Co. remained privately owned, but offered options to the executive team. This was her first year to qualify for a potential bonus plus a company stock option. The light outside her window faded into darkness as she stacked the last of her reports to be distributed early in the morning.

Kathryn knocked on her door. "Harriett, may I come in? Please?" Sweater and hat donned, ready for a cool evening, she waited to be invited in.

Harriett exhaled. The week's workload had helped her avoid Kathryn, although she knew she needed to resolve their issues. "Come in, Kathryn."

Kathryn sighed. "Oh, thank goodness I'm once again 'Kathryn.' The 'Miss White' thing went on too long. Look, Harriett, I'm sorry I broke your trust."

She pulled a small bag out of her tote. The aroma of freshly roasted cashews filled the room.

"You didn't!" Harriett reached for the bag. "My favorite."

Kathryn easily held it above her head. "For you—but only if you promise to forgive me."

Harriett smiled, then jumped, grabbing the sack. "I promise, you're forgiven. How can I stay mad at my best friend?" She opened the bag. "Want one?"

"Yes! Carolyn and I shopped over lunch, and I had to smell them all afternoon. Almost killed me not to eat them!" She offered her arm to Harriett. "So, tell me, how are you holding up?"

Harriett completed her preparation, flicked off her office light, and took Kathryn's arm. "I'll tell you all about it, but let's get out of here. Supper? My treat." The women walked the dark hallway to the elevator.

"You're riding instead of walking five flights?" Kathryn felt Harriett's forehead for fever. Harriett always walked the stairs for exercise.

"Tonight, I'm riding. Too exhausted."

The attendant opened the door. "Good evening, Mrs. Kepler. Miss White, you're working late today."

"Year-end reports, George." They rode in silence, waiting. The elevator door closed.

Kathryn burst out, "So, have you seen Eddy this week?"

"Luckily, only on Sunday. I think he showed up last night, but Earl turned him away. I'll fill you in over dinner."

Kathryn raised her eyebrows. "Earl was there?"

"Yes. He was just checking up on me, that's all." Harriett frowned, hesitated, then hugged her friend. "I'm sorry I was so hard on you."

Kathryn returned the embrace. "I've learned my lesson. *Confidence* means to keep your mouth shut!"

The women laughed, arm in arm, as they walked to Harriett's car.

47

MEMORIAL DAY

MAY 1953, CAMPBELLSVILLE

*T*he people of Campbellsville, bedecked in red, white, and blue, lined the streets in preparation for the Memorial Day parade. Like every other patriotic holiday in the valley, Saturday, May thirtieth generated national pride. Flags flew from every porch and lined the sidewalks. Local dignitaries bloviated to throngs of families gathered at the high school campus.

Harriett sat with Alice on her front porch, waiting for the marching band to pass by.

"I can hear the drums. They're getting close," Alice said to two-year-old Polly. The blonde, curly-haired toddler danced as she waved a flag.

Harriett bounced seven-month-old Maggie on her knee. "Polly looks more like you every day."

"I know," Alice said, "it's scary. And like Mother, too!"

Harriett scowled. "Alice, we agreed not to mention her."

"I know, Harriett, but it's tough when I see her likeness in Polly. Aunt Tildy gave me an old oil painting of Grandmother Polly. She said it used to hang in their dining room." Alice shook her head. "It's uncanny how much this little one looks like her namesake." Alice lifted her daughter to her lap.

"Okay, I'll allow you to skip a generation. Talk about Grandmother Polly, if it makes you happy, but avoid Mother!"

The band climbed the side street to the cadence of drums. Turning onto Hill Street, the drum major twirled his baton. Whistles sounded three times, and the band began playing a Sousa march. Up and down the avenue, spectators clapped and cheered as the Campbellsville High School marching band high-stepped *eight to five* down the street.

"That was enjoyable!" Harriett said as she lay Maggie in the stroller. "Are we ready?"

Polly grabbed Alice's hand, her little legs struggling to keep pace with the adults as they walked the three blocks toward the center of town. Two camping stools were hooked over the buggy handle for easy carrying.

"Are you going to the carnival tonight? Teddy is picking us up at seven after he closes the store. We'll eat hotdogs and French fries for supper. I don't have to cook."

"No, it was a long week with the end of the fiscal year. I'm staying home and resting. Although, carnival French fries sound good."

The sisters wheeled the children into the community activity area of the high school campus. The smell of fresh popcorn drifted through the air.

Two refurbished tennis courts, the obstacle course designed by Tabs, a baseball field, and the parade grounds with picnic tables and benches provided a charming gathering area for Campbellsville. During the summer months, most children, young and old, spent entire days playing there.

Alice and Harriett parked in front of the grandstand, waiting for the speakers to begin. Harriett unfolded her camp stool and scanned the crowd, hoping to avoid two people. To Harriett's dismay, Olive sat in the row in front, three slots over. She was dressed in a striking navy suit, matching heels, hat, and gloves, and waving a flag. The curls of her newly permed, gray hair coiled into a short bob.

Harriett poked Alice and whispered, "Good grief, she's right there. She looks good, better than she did for Papa. Have you talked with her since his death?"

Uneasy, Alice said, "Yes, I have, Harriett. She wanted to meet Maggie." She clasped her hands together and tilted her head. "I can't keep her from her grandchildren."

Harriett leaned in toward Alice. "Why not? She never wanted her own kids." Harriett looked away. "I'll save this conversation for a later date, but I have not seen her and don't intend to either!"

"Harriett, don't be angry. She wanted to join us over the holidays and was refused. The family is keeping its pact." Alice looked skyward, hoping for intervention from the fluffy white clouds.

It came as the microphone crackled. Someone said, "Testing, one-two."

Five men in suits and hats took seats on the grandstand as the master of ceremonies addressed the crowd. "Good afternoon, ladies and gentlemen of Campbellsville. What a glorious day it is. Today, I have the pleasure of introducing your mayor, our own World War II hero, Mr. Harry Boring."

Alice grinned at Harriett; both women remembered the day Harry banned her from playing ball. "I bet he'd invite you to play today on a town committee!" Alice whispered to her sister.

"That was funny. You got to play because the boys liked watching you jiggle when you ran. My skill got me kicked out!"

The afternoon sun beat down on the spectators. Maggie began whimpering. Alice adjusted the buggy's bonnet to shade her from the sun as she rocked it to and fro. The infant fell asleep to the humdrum monotony of two more speakers. Forth to the microphone was the local American Legion Commander.

After touting community service accomplishments, the commander continued, "And I want to recognize our latest soldiers to return home safely. Please stand when I call your name: Corporal Bobby Renner...Sergeant Keith Boring, brother of our mayor...and, returning just last week, Private Eddy Kepler."

Harriett's stomach flipped, and her skin went cold despite the warm afternoon sun as she eyed the crowd. He was two rows forward, directly in front of her.

Alice inhaled. "Harriett, I must admit, he's as handsome as ever."

"Shush! You always favored a fetching face. Too bad his personality doesn't match." Harriett bounced Polly on her lap as Eddy turned and spotted her. His face lit up. He smiled the infamous Kepler grin as he waved.

"As soon as this is over, I'm sneaking out of here," Harriett said. "Can you manage with both girls?"

Alice shrugged her shoulders. "Do it every day. If I put the hood down, Polly can sit in the stroller with Maggie."

Harriett folded her camp stool, then made a quick exit at the conclusion. She escaped to the edge of the sidewalk before Eddy intercepted her.

Grabbing her arm from behind, he spun her around to face him. "There you are, my wife. I have a question." Scooping her around the waist, he targeted her mouth.

Pulling back, she eluded his advance. "And what question do you have for me?"

Eddy smiled broadly. "It's been a week. You've made your point. Can I come home tonight?"

Harriett sucked in the sides of her cheeks. "Home? Where would that be?" May felt like a stagnant August afternoon as the blood surged through her body.

"You know, home. Your house on the hill." Eddy linked his arm through hers to drag her back to the parade grounds.

She stuck out her butt to wiggle free. "Eddy, you just clarified your fallacy. It's *my* house, not *our* house."

"Come on, Harriett. I don't have any clothes at Mom's. Earl said he moved them over for you."

"If that's your only issue, then I'll gladly box up your things. You may pick them up later tonight. I'll place them outside the garage door."

Eddy nuzzled her neck. "Remember these kisses, Harriett? If I recall correctly, your neck was a sweet spot." His tongue licked behind her ear.

Harriett swatted his face. "Stop it, Eddy." She spun and shoved. He stumbled backward as Keith and Harry Boring approached.

Anxious to rekindle old friendships, Eddy yelled, "Hey fellows, so glad you found me. I've been looking for you all week. How is life?"

Harry tipped his hat, answering first. "Oh, hi Eddy, good to see you. I'm here to ask a favor of Harriett." Harry took her arm and led her away from Eddy and Keith.

"What's with our industrious mayor?" Eddy asked Keith. "He used to be excited to see me show up at the ball field."

Keith chuckled. "Eddy, that was at least twelve years ago. Time marches on. Boys become men. You are one lucky guy, by the way; your wife is quite the catch. How did you predict that she'd blossom into such a beautiful, successful, career woman?"

They watched Harry enlist Harriett's help concerning town finances.

Eddy stared at Keith. "All this talk about Harriett. What about me? Care to know how I managed in Korea? I was nearly killed."

Keith, stammering at a loss for words, was rescued when a woman called from across the field, interrupting their conversation. "Gotta run Kepler. Keep that woman happy, and you'll have it made."

Shoulders dropped, Eddy sulked back to the grandstand, walking within earshot of Earl, who joined Harriett and Harry's conversation. The trio was laughing. Earl leaned over; kissing Harriett on the forehead, he wished her goodbye.

"Earl!" Eddy called to his brother. "Wait up."

Eddy trotted across the freshly mowed grounds, kicking up grass clumps as he went.

"Sure." Earl smiled as he waited for Eddy and watched Harriett walk down the street.

"What's with the kiss?"

"Are you jealous?"

"She won't let me kiss her. Why do *you* get that privilege?"

"Since when do women prefer me over you?" Earl chortled. "Anyway, that's a stupid question, Brother."

Eddy pulled on Earl's shoulder. "No, it's not. I want to know what's going on. She's *my* wife! I saw you the other night at her house. Why so late a visit?"

Earl pushed back. "Nothing is going on."

"Well, it's been a week, and she won't let me in the house yet."

"Do you think one week is penance enough for three years? Be on your best behavior. Come clean about the Italian girl and baby. Get it all out in the open, then give her time to digest, accept, and hopefully forgive. In the meantime, use every means possible—flowers, candy, jewelry, although she's not into material things."

"And how the hell am I supposed to do that? I'm broke."

"Start with getting a job, idiot." Earl scowled.

"I'm out of here. Enough of the 'job' shit! See you at home." Eddy jogged across the field, searching for his old high school clique, girls or boys. His breath was labored and his chest tight by the time he reached the far side. He sat down, panting, and pounding his fists on the ground, wondering why he felt so out of shape. He grabbed the top of his head and buried his face in his hands. *How did my life get so fucked up?*

∞ ∞ ∞

Harriett climbed the steps to her house. She surveyed the school property, bustling with patriotic revelers from the front door. With a clear view of the entire valley, she watched the carnival crew erecting colorful tents and booths in the Legion parking lot. She thought back to a previous date, where she and Eddy had tossed softballs to win a stuffed animal. The giant toy, once treasured, now sat in the corner of an unfurnished bedroom, collecting dust.

Why did you quit on me, Eddy?

She sat rocking, watching, and thinking until the street-light cast shadows on the sidewalk as dark as those in her heart. Aimlessly, she walked to the kitchen, opened the refrigerator, and numbly stared inside. After a moment, with glazed-over eyes, Harriett crumbled to the floor. Sitting with her head on her knees and her back against the closed door, she wept.

Papa, I need you now more than ever!

The clock in her office chiming ten roused her from her trance. When she was halfway up to her bedroom, the doorbell rang, followed by a fist pounding loudly on the door. She tensed. None of her family would show up late without calling first. Was it Earl again? He wouldn't strike the door.

Sneaking quietly down the steps, she wondered if the carnival attracted a transient criminal. Perhaps it was only a delinquent youngster, playing a prank. Maybe one of her sisters needed her. She opened the inside doors and slid against the wall with the lights out. Her nose touched the pane as she peered, unseen, through the sidelight. A fist pounded again. She jumped and squealed at the silhouette of a man. Besides the moon and one light, the street was dark and empty.

Deciding her visitor most likely heard her, she flicked on the overhead porch light, grabbed an umbrella for protection, then opened the door.

Sighing in relief, she said, "Eddy. What in the name of heaven are you doing here so late? You scared me."

"Expecting rain?" Eddy motioned to her hand then thrust a bouquet of wildflowers in her face. "For you." He slurred his words, then reached out to steady his legs.

She sneezed. "Have you been drinking?" Harriett brushed his hand away. The flowers tumbled to the porch.

"Who, me? Only a little." His lips parted into a boyish grin. "I'm home!"

He pushed forward into the outer entry before Harriett could block him.

With legs parted for stability, Harriett extended her arms, planting her hand firmly on his chest. "Stop, Eddy. I don't know why you think you live here. This is my house. Please go."

"Ahh, come on, sweetie, you know I love you!" He crooned his neck. "Give me a little kiss."

"Eddy, back off. I'm serious." She waved the umbrella in front of his head.

"But I've been home a full week, already. I need some womanly attention." He tried to tickle her.

"A week is all you can go without sex? How did you manage the past three years?" Her eyes widened in realization. "Wait, don't say a word. I don't really want to know." She pointed the tip of the umbrella at his nose. "Go home, Eddy. You've been drinking."

"I am home. You're my wife." He yanked the umbrella out of her hand, throwing it on top of the flowers.

"On paper only."

Harriett looked in desperation for a different weapon but found none. Eddy tried to lift her to carry her inside but stumbled, inebriated. Quick to react, Harriett shoved him; his momentum took him down. She sprinted through the inner doors, then closed and locked them before he regained balance. Harriett flipped on every light in the house, hoping to attract the attention of a passerby.

The charming "Kepler smile" disappeared when he realized he was outsmarted. Curling his hands into balls, he hammered the glass windows of the inner doors. Harriett looked on in horror, thinking he might break through the beveled panes.

"Eddy, stop. Just stop!" she screamed. "If you think you're winning me over with this behavior, you're wrong!"

"Let me in, Harriett. I deserve to live here," he said, face plastered tightly on the door window.

Flabbergasted, Harriett laughed. "'Deserve?!' You're not only drunk, but you're also delusional!"

"I want my car back, Harriett. I need wheels. What did you do with my car?"

"It's long gone, Eddy. For goodness' sake. Go home and sober up."

"Then I want to be paid for my car. I *demand* that you give me money for it. You had no right to sell it!" Eddy pummeled the glass.

The word "demand" enraged the tiny woman. Grabbing a fireplace poker from the office, she opened the doors. Brandishing the rod in Eddy's face, she drove him backward.

"You 'demand?!' You want my money? You're not getting any. Get out of my house, you no good creep. So help me, I'll have you arrested for trespassing."

"You can't. I'm your husband."

"This property is deeded in my name alone. So I can, and I will!" She swung the poker like a whip. Eddy ducked his head to dodge her blow and tumbled backward, rolling down several steps. Harriett ran back into the house and locked both sets of doors. She spent the subsequent hour closing and locking all the windows on every floor, not wanting to risk a ladder intrusion.

At eleven, she dialed the Kepler residence. Earl answered.

"Earl, is Eddy home yet?" She drummed her fingers on her desk nervously.

"No, why?"

"He's drunk. He tried to force himself into the house. Demanded I pay him for his car."

Earl blew air through his puffed cheeks. "Do you need me to come over?"

"No, the place is secure. I lunged after him with a fireplace poker."

Earl chuckled. "I'd have paid good money to see that. Did he leave?"

"Only after he fell down the steps." Adrenaline dissipating, Harriett giggled. "I guess it was sort of funny, in hindsight, watching him roll head over heels, with me waving an

313

iron rod in his face." She paused. "I only called to warn you and to...well, check up on him."

"You shouldn't have to deal with his antics." Earl paused. "I hear a car door. I gotta go. He won't bother you again."

"Earl?" Harriett called before he hung up. "Will you pick up his clothes tomorrow?"

48

THE PRICE OF A SECOND CHANCE

*T*he smell of coffee and burnt toast turned his stomach. Eddy Kepler moaned, then crawled out of his bed, holding his head on both sides.

"Stop the noise," he whispered to no one. The clang of pots and pans rattling intensified. Eddy stumbled into the kitchen. "Mom, keep it down."

To his surprise, he saw Earl beating an iron skillet with a ladle high above his head.

Eddy cringed. "Earl, what the…?"

"Good morning, my delinquent brother," Earl said, striking more vigorously. "What's wrong? Headache?" He chuckled as the noon sun shining through the window caused Eddy to squint.

Eddy covered his eyes with one hand. "You asshole. Quit it. I'm hungover."

"I know you are." Earl tossed the skillet into the sink with a clatter. He snatched Eddy's T-shirt with both hands, jamming him against the wall.

Eddy tried to move freely, but Earl pinned his arms to his sides. "Let go of me, Earl!"

315

Eddy squirmed. Earl held fast, his nose pressed against Eddy's, his breath hot on his neck.

"Eddy, listen up. You ever threaten Harriett again, I swear I'll kill you." Earl gritted his teeth together in a snarl.

"What are you talking about? And why are you defending *my* wife?"

Earl flinched at the stench of alcohol on his breath.

Earl pressed his forehead against Eddy's, moving his head back. "She called me after your visit last night, when you tried to move in."

"Why's she calling you?"

"Someone needed to look after her while you were gone." Earl thrust his arms upwards, lifting Eddy off the floor.

"Put me down."

"I'll put you down, but you listen to me, Brother. She's been through an awful lot these past years; no thanks to you. Her father dying was almost too much for her to bear."

"What did you say? Tabs Bailey is dead?"

"Last fall. Did you even read her letters?"

"I told you the other day. I read some of them." Earl's grip loosened, and Eddy wiggled free. "Geez, Earl, cut a guy a break! Lighten up."

"You start treating that woman with respect. I mean it, I'll kill you if you hurt her. And so will her brother, and brothers-in-law." Earl shoved a cup of coffee at Eddy. "Sober up. We are going over this afternoon for you to apologize and to pick up your clothes."

Eddy sneered. "I'll go back, but without you."

"No way in hell I'm letting you go alone after last night's stunt."

∞ ∞ ∞

With refreshments strategically placed on the living room

coffee table, Harriett waited in her office. Earl had phoned two hours earlier, warning that he and Eddy were visiting. A large cardboard box filled with Eddy's clothing sat in the outer entranceway.

Interrupted by the doorbell, she placed her pen on the desk, then, folding a list of about ten items, tucked it into her pocket.

"Earl, Eddy, please come in. Coffee and cookies are in the living room." Harriett motioned toward the left archway as Eddy gawked, taking in the glory of the hill house in daylight.

"Are these his clothes?" Earl asked, kicking the box.

"Hey, careful!" Eddy warned. "You might break something."

Harriett shook her head. "Don't worry. Your trophies are safely wrapped inside of clothing."

Pouting, Eddy followed Harriett. Taking a seat on the couch, his leg jiggled up and down.

Earl spoke first. "Harriett, thanks for seeing us on such short notice. We'll gather his property and be gone quickly. We both appreciate your time." He poked Eddy's side. "Don't we, Eddy?"

"Yes."

Harriett's eyes connected with Earl's as she handed him a cup of coffee. "Eddy, would you care for a cup?" she asked without looking at her husband.

"Sure." He hesitated, then grabbed her arm; she turned to face him before he continued. "Harriett, I'm sorry I was such a jerk last night. I had too much to drink."

She glanced back at Earl questioningly, focusing on him as she spoke. "Yes, you were drunk. You were too aggressive for my liking."

Eddy grinned. "I seem to remember you swinging a mean fireplace poker. Defended yourself rather well." Turning to his brother, he broke their stare. "Earl, I'd like to have a conversation with my wife. Do you mind giving us some privacy?"

Earl looked at Harriett. "Only if Harriett says okay. If not, I stay."

"I want to speak with Eddy, also. Earl, do you mind waiting in the kitchen?"

"Not at all. But yell if you need me! I'm within earshot." Earl grabbed a shortbread cookie before leaving.

After waiting for the sound of footsteps to fade, Eddy met her gaze. "Harriett, I'm sorry. About last night, about not writing, about all of it." He hung his head. "I do love you."

"I don't understand your motives. Three years of silence was torture, unnecessary cruelty, Eddy. Why?"

"I was a fool." Getting down on one knee, he kneeled before her, closing his hands in prayer. "Please, Harriett, give me another chance. Will you take me back?"

Her eyes narrowed as she held her breath. Minutes passed before she answered. To Eddy, it seemed like hours.

With a deep sigh, she finally spoke. "If I even consider this, I have conditions. Do you understand?"

Springing to his feet, Eddy grabbed both her hands. "Yes, Harriett, I understand."

She inhaled. "I'm not sure you do. I'm not just letting you waltz back into my life. I've changed, Eddy. I'm not the naïve, innocent girl you married."

She pulled her hands out of his and unfolded her list.

"All conditions," she said, "and I mean *all*, must be met before I even consider taking you back. First and foremost, I want to know the truth. Why didn't you write? What happened in Italy? Tell me all of it. I refuse to live a lie." She was interrupted by a cough coming from the kitchen. "Secondly, you must have a job. I'm not supporting a man."

Eddy nodded his head in agreement.

"Third. You are required to contribute toward our

household expenses and mortgage." Before he could speak, she continued. "I realize that I'll probably make more money than you; I'll be fair. We can work on a percentage basis. Let's just say you pay one-third, and I'll pick up the rest. This is roughly based on your previous salary in the mill."

"That's fair enough. I'm happy—"

"I'm not finished. I've established a savings account specifically for household repairs and improvements. I require you to contribute five percent of your monthly salary to that savings."

"Ah—Harriett, who pays for clothing?"

"Anything you want for clothing, entertainment, alcohol, you pay for yourself." Harriett glanced at her note, then continued. "I'll pay for my schooling, as well as anything needed for business expenses."

Eddy bit his lip. "You sold my car, Harriett. What am I supposed to do for transportation?"

"I'm prepared to pay you two hundred dollars for it, which is more than I sold it for. But I want to be fair." She offered him a check.

Eddy reached to embrace her. "Harriett, this is more than I hoped for." He leaned down for a kiss. Harriett turned her head to the side. She heard feet shuffling in the kitchen.

"Eddy, I'm not done. Please sit down and allow me to finish." She gently pushed him away. "You may not be happy with my next contingencies, but…" she sighed again. "I am adamant. You are my husband in name only. Once criteria are met and I permit you to move in, you'll sleep in a different room until you completely prove your worth. That is, *if* you're capable of redeeming yourself."

"Harriett!" His brow creased as he shuffled from side to side.

"I expect you to remain faithful to me." She smiled at

him. "Eddy, if you can't fulfill my demands, you are welcome to file for divorce."

"Fine. I agree. But this is torture."

"Oh, I'm not done yet." The corners of her lips spread upwards. "Currently, Albert and my brothers-in-law look in weekly. I expect you to relieve them of *all* duties—and the family shall hold you accountable."

"I don't understand. What are you talking about?"

"If you expect to step foot into this house, then you—and you *alone*—are responsible for taking care of Mother."

Eddy choked, spitting coffee across the room. "You want me to look after Olive? Are you out of your mind?"

Laughter came from the kitchen.

"Oh no, Eddy. I am quite sane. She's independent enough, but is aging and can't manage heavy chores with Papa gone. Once a week, you'll need to stop in to cut her grass, tend to her garden, shovel the snow, and so on."

"I can't stand that woman. I don't think I can do this."

"Well, now you know exactly how I feel. Right now, I don't like you one bit. But you are my legal husband, and I made a vow. I'll give you *one* more chance, but only if you meet my conditions. Regardless, take your box of possessions. You stay with Earl and Abigail until I say otherwise."

Eddy balled his fingers into fists; his face turned scarlet red. The veins in his neck pulsed.

Harriett paused before recapping. "So, I want the whole truth, upfront. You must work and share costs, sleep in a separate bedroom, and…" she burst into a giggle. "The care of my despicable mother is all yours."

Her only response was the sound of Eddy grunting and Earl in the distance giggling.

"If you want me, Eddy, you get Olive! You choose. Take it or leave it."

EPILOGUE

---

*E*xcerpt from *Between Two Dreams*, book 4 of The Women of Campbell County saga.

∞ ∞ ∞

The hand on his shoulder startled Eddy Kepler back to reality. His fingers ran through his thinning grey hair before reaching for the crystal tumbler. He sipped the diluted bourbon. The term *on-ice* no longer applied.

"Dad," Shelby repeated. "Dad, are you listening? I said I know the story of Rosa and Joey."

Eddy's sweaty palms tingled. "How could you possibly know?" He paused for several moments. "Is she alive?"

Shelby opened her briefcase and pulled out an envelope stamped *airmail* with an Italian return address. "This is going to be a long night. Let us eat something before I begin."

Turning to the other occupant of the room, she asked, "Wally, will you help me in the kitchen?"

∞ ∞ ∞

S. LEE FISHER

Want more from Campbellsville? Join Eddy, Harriett, Olive, Rosa, Joey, Shelby, and their friends and family in the final installment of The Women of Campbell County series, *Between Two Dreams*, coming late fall 2022.

AUTHOR'S NOTES

- This is a work of fiction. Any use of names that coincide with those living or otherwise is by request and with the written permission of those persons.
- A dispute between Italy and Tito's Yugoslavia over Trieste, Italy prompted the United Nations to send Canadian and American troops to suppress a communist takeover.
- Austrian archduke Ferdinand Maximilian built Castle Miramare between 1856 to 1860.
- "DAR" refers to the National Society of the Daughters of the American Revolution. All members must prove a direct lineage to an ancestor who fought in the revolution. The author is a member in good standing of the Myakka chapter, Florida, and is an associate member of the Jacob Ferree chapter, Pennsylvania.
- "Eight to five" refers to taking eight steps in five yards. This term is used by marching units.

ALSO BY S. LEE FISHER

A Mystery of Grace Newman

(Newman Spring Publishing, October 2019)

The Women of Campbell County: Series

Becoming Olive W. Book 1 (RNS Publishing, March 2021)

Westchester Farm, novella 1.5 (RNS Publishing, January 2022)

Under the Grapevine Book 2 (RNS Publishing, January 2022)

Hill House Divided, book 3 (RNS Publishing, February 2022)

Between Two Dreams Book 4 (RNS Publishing, scheduled for
publication late 2022)

Use this link to subscribe to my newsletter to download your FREE
copy of the novella, *Westchester Farm*, the story of Olive's and Tabs'
wedding.

https://dl.bookfunnel.com/dp5tcj7pkt

Thank you for leaving a review on Amazon.

S. Lee Fisher

ABOUT THE AUTHOR

Pharmacy to Fiction.
Award-winning writing as a second career.

S. Lee Fisher, aka Dr. "P.," a clinical pharmacist, was born and raised in "small town" Pennsylvania. After moving to Pittsburgh, she enjoyed a successful corporate career managing retrospective clinical programs for the PBM side of a Fortune 20 company.

Fisher began writing fiction as a means of channeling the pain and grief of her father's passing. In the process, she discovered that she enjoys the creativity of telling stories.

Now a full-time novelist, Fisher lives on Florida's gulf coast with her husband of 38 years, Ralph. When she's not writing or dodging hurricanes, she enjoys painting watercolors, ballroom dancing, and swimming.

Becoming Olive W., Book 1 in the Women of Campbell County Series, won four awards in 2021 and is awaiting outcomes on several other nominations.

www.sleefisher.com

Facebook: @SherriLeeFisherProgar
Twitter: @ProgarSherri
Amazon: @author/sleefisher

Made in the USA
Middletown, DE
14 January 2024

47863972R00186